The MESSIAH

ALSO BY LEE HAYES
Passion Marks
A Deeper Blue: Passion Marks II

ZANE PRESENTS

The MESSIAH

LEE HAYES

SBI

STREBOR BOOKS

NEW YORK LONDON TORONTO SYDNEY

Strebor Books
P.O. Box 6505
Largo, MD 20792
http://www.streborbooks.com

© 2007 by Lee Hayes

ISBN-13 978-1-59309-136-1
ISBN-10   1-59309-136-2
LCCN 2007923507

First Strebor Books trade paperback edition July 2007

Cover design: www.mariondesigns.com

10 9 8 7 6 5 4 3 2 1

Manufactured in the United States of America

For information regarding special discounts for bulk purchases, please contact Simon & Schuster Special Sales at 1-800-456-6798 or business@simonandschuster.com

Special Thanks to Erica Kennedy, Author and Friend

Special acknowledgments to: Marco L. Brooks, Cheryl M. Brown
and Mark'us Young for your tireless and unselfish efforts to
help me realize a dream. It shall come to pass...

To my D.C. family and friends: Adrian, you know
how much I love you. To Demond Finney, Derrick Franklin,
Alfonce Reese-Franklin, all I can say is thank you
for being your authentic selves and allowing
me to share your world.
The best is yet to come...

Just like the triumph of a warrior's journey
Just like the love and strength that I have given
Just like the rewards of a bee's honey
I now have victory, because I have risen.
—DON FLOYD

PROLOGUE
IN THE BEGINNING...

Jazz McKinney

The buzzing sound of flies will resonate in his ears *forever*. That annoying, dissonant sound caused by the rapid vibrations of tiny wings that had stolen the peace from countless languid summer evenings was the only thing he could focus on, as he lay battered and bloodied in a field of orange, yellow, and blue. Stunning summer hues dotted the landscape on the grassy knoll as his world morphed from living colors to a gray and mangled mesh of madness. Jazz McKinney struggled to keep his eyes open, but he knew the uncontrolled swelling would soon blot out his vision and his view of the world would darken. *Maybe forever*.

Yet, given that grim reality, that buzzing sound kept him holding on to life.

That ceaseless buzzing—a sound that rang louder than his own listless voice—numbed the pain of the million ant bites, which stung his limp body. Each time he opened his mouth to scream for help, the sound rang hollow; not even a decibel and barely a whisper. So, he sent his silent prayers to the heavens and hoped that God was listening.

He remembered trying to scream, but there was no sound. He remembered trying to move, but the only movement was the involuntary shooting pains that kept him immobile.

Though he often thought it cliché, his life did indeed flash before his eyes. Sadly, all he could see was the nameless faces from a thousand midnight encounters. He had taken residence in a world created by fantasies and actions without consequence; a reckless world where instant gratification was like sweet nectar and remorse simply didn't exist.

He mentally erased their faces at the conclusion of a lustful rendezvous, often never knowing their names. Now, those same strangers who had been his one constant in life, were poised to be his one constant in his death. Oddly, a death he invited in part to a late-night "craving."

He didn't imagine his body would survive very long in its present condition—broken and battered. *And isolated.* In his moment of ultimate desperation, when all seemed lost, something more meaningful should have filled his head. He should have been focused on life after death and his final resting place in eternity, yet he could not free his mind of their faces. And that buzzing. That damned buzzing tormented him.

As he lay there, blood oozing from his busted body, the hollow faces spiraled around his head in a choreographed ritual of torture. *Go away*, he thought, but the reflections of his misdeeds were permanent fixtures in his mind. The images were so real to him in those fevered moments that he wanted to reach out and touch their ethereal silhouettes, but he didn't have the strength.

The nasty flies were drawn to his rotting flesh, which would soon sizzle in the intense summer heat when the sun took its rightful place in the sky. Jazz feared they would devour him and leave no remains to be claimed; all that would endure after he faded would be naked bones. The moonlit brutality he experienced at the hands of a stranger now gave way to a dazzling daylight despair. His fears of dying in an abandoned field and the intensity of his pain did not fade when the sun majestically rose.

As he lay prostrate in the field, the events that led to his predicament replayed in his head but he didn't want to remember. He didn't want to relive the attack. He wanted to pretend it never happened, but each time he attempted to move, the pain forced him to remember. Each time he looked around at the weeds and flowers and dirt and broken glass that surrounded him, he could not deny the attack.

Jazz vividly remembered what *he* did to him. He could still feel every thrust, every fist, and every kick as his body continued to throb with waves of pain.

He remembered *his* deranged laughter, which ricocheted in the night.

He remembered crying out, only to be answered by a kick to the face.

He could still see and feel the boot that caused blood to gush from his nose. It was a Timberland.

Jazz remembered the incoherent prayers that escaped from his attacker's twisted mouth while he lay in the field.

Jazz remembered begging *him* to stop and apologizing profusely for his actions, but that only caused laughter to swell and spill from *his* vile mouth.

Naked, dizzied, and pleading for his life, he remembered staring up into the dark sky as his vision blurred, while his attacker's voice shifted between manic states of rage and calm. Even as he lay bound in the field, he remembered. He could not forget. Jazz bore the shame of his lust and tried to imagine being somewhere else. He tried to imagine this was someone else's nightmare instead of his own. But the details of the night's betrayal raced through his fleeting consciousness like strong river currents.

The evening started with such promise but ended in such despair. Pain, visions, voices, and memories splashed on the canvas of his mind. He fought to push them away, but they stood their ground, refusing to leave, scrambling and heightening his anxiety. Scenes of torture traded places with apparitions of bliss; visions of violence exchanged posture with images of pleasure. After all, Jazz was facing his senior year in college— a year of promise and partying; not his death.

His roommate Montre had gone home to California for the summer and left him in Washington, D.C. to fend for himself. He felt partially betrayed since the duo had discussed subletting an apartment for the summer and working at Fashion Centre at Pentagon City to pay the bills. Jazz had envisioned a fun-filled, carefree summer. He wanted to run wild in Chocolate City and let D.C. know it had been graced by his presence.

He wanted his last summer in the city to be seared in a blaze of glory. He wanted to leave the men saddened, wobbly, and shaken, but happy that they had experienced his magic, if only for a small moment in time. So when Montre told him he had to return home to help take care of his ailing mother, Jazz was disappointed, but he understood.

He was thrilled at the thought of graduating and moving to New York

City thereafter to jumpstart his stagnant modeling career. After years of local modeling, he told himself he'd give the Big Apple a two-year try and if it didn't work out, he'd get a job using the degree he was earning in mechanical engineering. *Quite an accomplishment for a disavowed stepson of a preacher*, he thought.

Just as relaxing thoughts of his past began to numb the sting of his current existence, a pain in his chest jolted him back to reality. He began to tremble as he took rapid, ragged breaths; they felt like his last breaths. He gasped for air; fought the feeling of despair that began to swallow him. He could feel his heart racing, beating in his ears, his throat, and his loins. Then everything went black.

††††

As the sun rose and illuminated the morning skies, Jazz squinted against its burning rays. His blood-caked body was now noticeably bruised and swollen. A single tear crawled down his left cheek and found a home in the corner of his mouth. He stuck out his tongue to taste its salty residue. It was enough to remind him that he was indeed still alive—but for how much longer, he didn't know. How could a night destined for pleasure culminate into an evening of so much despair? Dark memories crept in as Jazz recounted those events that would now change his life forever…

It was a quarter to midnight when he had stepped out of his car, locked the door, and kept his keys splayed between his fingers in case he needed to defend himself from some brute lurking in the shadows. An unusual vibe, which permeated the night air, unnerved him, but he dismissed his intuition as simple paranoia and pressed on.

A quick lightning flash moved across the sky, followed by a low rumble of thunder. He took a moment to scan the area and when he was satisfied that no one was around, he walked with speed toward the structure. Trepidation was his traveling partner as he moved briskly forward. During these midnight meetings, a sense of fear stimulated his desire. He walked with due speed, continuing to look around for other people, including the police, who often cruised the area on the fringes of the city. He couldn't imagine having to explain to the police why he was lurking near the abandoned church at such a late hour.

As he neared his destination, a decrepit, gnarled wooden sign pointed toward the church like old crooked fingers guiding him to the path of salvation. When Jazz was close enough, he paused for an instant and looked up at the structure. From his distance, he could read the letters above the doors: "Olive Branch Baptist Church. All are Welcome."

As he moved closer to the chained fence, which protected the deserted edifice, the warning in his heart grew, but he would not yield to that feeling. An ominous presence rode the stiff night air, as if some unseen force skulked around from all sides. Partially excited *and* terrified, Jazz pressed deeper into the night. The fear of being caught while meeting a stranger to do whatever deeds men who meet in the dark of night did is what Jazz was counting on to multiply the force of his orgasm threefold.

As he scurried across the vacant parking lot, he heard a slight rumbling behind him, which sent a cold shiver up his spine, in spite of the evening's balmy temperature. He stopped, spun on his heels, and exhaled in relief as he saw an old soda can rolling across the lot in the gentle breeze. He resumed his march toward ecstasy.

When he reached the fence surrounding the church, he prayed it would be unlocked so he could walk through it instead of going around it, but when he yanked on the chain, it barely moved. *Damn.* He looked up at the barbed wire that sat like a crown of thorns atop the fence and decided that he was not skillful enough to climb the fence without seriously injuring his body. He had to find another way in. With his hands in his pockets, he turned and quickly walked around the behemoth structure, wondering why he had agreed to meet *him* at such a place.

When he got around the corner, he found that the side gate was locked and chained, but he remained undeterred. Quickly, he looked around the perimeter and found a place in the fence in which he could pass without injury and, with surprising prowess, he scaled the fence. Nothing was going to stand between him and what *he* had to offer. He landed flatly on his feet and paused a moment to scan the area before moving toward the back of the church.

The closer he got to the rear of the small white structure, the quicker his heart raced. These mysterious encounters that he had grown accustomed to made sex wildly exciting. He had grown out of missionary sex when he was seventeen and moved quickly into things there were more titillating and dangerous.

For Jazz, sex was freedom; sex was power. Thoughts of his next encounter and taking his escapades to the next level occupied much of his daily thoughts. Pushing the envelope and stretching sexual boundaries was his drug—his driving force. He wasn't a sex addict, but he loved sex. He loved doing the unspeakable and scandalous. He loved gobbling and rubbing and pulling and yanking and plowing and breathing and using fingers and tongues and holes and toys and ropes and candles and wax and anything else he could incorporate into his romps to intensify the experience. He loved meeting people who, like him, weren't afraid to explore the universe and be used as willing vessels to help him reach that ultimate orgasm. That's all that mattered to him.

He leaned against the back of the church for only a few minutes, blowing nicotine smoke circles into the air to calm his nerves. Standing in the darkness, with no signs of life, those minutes felt like hours. He listened for any sound of movement, for the slightest disturbance, for anything that would announce *his* arrival. Jazz took a long drag from the Benson & Hedges he pursed tightly between his lips and rolled an empty beer bottle underneath his foot to take the edge off the night.

Then, he heard a faint sound coming from the other end of the structure. He didn't move. Instead, he waited for confirmation. It sounded like dry grass being crushed underneath heavy feet. Then, he heard it again. The crunching sound that dried leaves and grass made underneath a foot was unmistakable in the dead of night.

He peered around the corner toward the other end of the building. He did not see anything, but all his senses were acute. Curiosity got the best of him and he stepped out and walked toward the noise. He took a few steps forward and then stopped. Something didn't feel right. The moonlight cast a shadow on the ground—the shadow of a man.

"Hello?" Jazz called out. The hairs on the back of his neck stood on end, but he pressed on, hoping his feeling would give way to sexual pleasure.

"Hello?" he called out again, sounding a bit desperate. "What's going on?" he mumbled to himself as he let the cigarette dangling from his lips hit the ground. He stomped it out with his foot. "Wassup, man? Don't be shy. Come to Daddy," he said, trying to sound playful. As the words left his mouth, *he* jumped out from around the corner and struck Jazz across the face with what felt like the strength of a hundred men. Jazz hit the ground with an incredible thud.

"What the fuck?" he screamed. The only response he received was fists that rained down on him in torrents. Jazz threw wild blows into the twisted face of his attacker, but to no avail. The punishing barrage of heavy fists continued to pound into Jazz's body like mortar. Jazz's terrified screams echoed in the night, but ultimately went unanswered. He knew he was alone and that if he were to survive, it would be all up to him.

He covered his face with one hand while the other desperately searched for something on the ground he could use to defend himself. He grabbed at anything and everything he could, but cupped fistfuls of dried grass instead. Spit dropped onto his face from the salivating mouth of his attacker. Then, Jazz grabbed a small rock from the ground and swung wildly, the blow landing right above his attacker's left eye. *He* fell backward, covering *his* face with *his* hands.

Jazz, trying to seize the opportunity to flee, forced himself to stand. He tried to run, but he was unsteady and shaky. When he got his balance, he heard the breaking of the bottle before he actually felt the impact on the back of his skull. In the flicker of the second that it took for him to realize what had happened, he felt the presence of evil looming on the edge of night, dancing a wicked jig in the dark and laughing at his misery. Jazz fell to the ground on his back and looked up to see the menacing figure above him again.

Jazz felt his vision blur and the coming darkness ready to devour him whole, but the boot that smashed into his ribcage brought him back to consciousness with piercing pain. Jazz lay on the ground, an agonizing throbbing covering his body. He tried to scream but his voice wouldn't carry.

The stranger moved away and fell to his knees.

Even through the blistering pain, Jazz heard a voice emanating from *him* that sounded as if the night itself was speaking words which were not meant to be deciphered. *His* raspy voice rose to slightly above a whisper as *he* spoke with rapid speed. It almost sounded as if *he* was speaking in tongues.

"The Lord is my shepherd; I shall not want. He maketh me to lie down in green pastures: He leadeth me beside still waters. He restoreth my soul: He leadeth me in paths of righteousness for His name's sake."

Jazz cried out.

"Yea, though I walk through the valley of the shadow of death, I will fear no evil; for Thou art with me; Thy rod and Thy staff they comfort me. Thou preparest a table before me in the presence of mine enemies: Thou anointest my head with oil; my cup runneth over. Surely goodness and mercy shall follow me all the days of my life: and I will dwell in the house of the Lord forever."

When *he* finished, lightning lit up the sky and Jazz heard the thunder roll. He felt death was nearby.

The stranger sprang to *his* feet like a panther. Suddenly, panic gripped Jazz like an immovable force around his neck. He knew that more was coming. He struggled to make sense of what had happened. *His* face morphed into something unrecognizable and unreal. The spindly hairs of *his* moustache came to life and reached toward Jazz like hissing serpents poised to strike. *His* face resembled burnt flesh that was scorched by hatred and disgust. *His* eyes changed into bottomless black pits that showed nothing but contempt. What little light the moon provided was sucked into *his* hateful eyes, making the dark night its darkest ever. *His* full mouth stretched into slivers of tightly drawn flesh and Jazz closed his eyes and prepared for his painful demise.

He turned his back to Jazz and recanted the prayer again. Jazz writhed in pain and tried to scoot away from his antagonist, but he was quickly met by another kick to the ribs.

"My son, you have brought my wrath upon you because of your sins and unclean acts. You are an abomination," *he* said in a gritty, throaty whisper that felt like jagged fingernails scraping the skin off Jazz's back; even still, *his* gruff voice carried enough force for Jazz to feel it. Jazz tried not to show panic or fear, even though fear had engulfed him. "But, fear not, my child. I am your redeemer. I have come to save your immortal soul from eternal damnation." *He* snapped *his* head back and looked to the heavens as *he* extended *his* arms as if surrendering to a higher power. A wild and delightful smile covered *his* face as *he* looked up and started to recant another prayer. *His* body swayed from side-to-side and an unsettling smile shone on his face.

"A-ma-zing grace, how sweet the sound, that saved a wretch like me," he bellowed out in an uncanny yet angelic voice. Jazz tried to move along the ground, but could not free himself from that voice. At the same time he was bewildered by pain and bewitched by the spirited song that filled the night air at the same time. He tried to regroup but was startled when he looked up. The stranger's extended arms looked like large black wings that spread the span of *his* reach. When the wings spread out a powerful odor filled Jazz's nostrils and almost made him choke. The stench was so strong and so foul that it lodged in his lungs and made him dry cough.

The sound continued to mesmerize and enchant Jazz—even in this moment—until he forced himself out of the daze. Jazz closed his eyes and shook his head. When he opened them, the stranger peered down on him. The wings were no more. He didn't know if he'd really seen them or if his mind was playing tricks on him.

As Jazz lay on the ground, trying to come to terms with the pain in his head, he could feel *his* greasy hands yanking at his body and then his clothes. Jazz tried to kick him away but to no avail. Jazz's feeble attempt at resistance angered *him*, and *he* pulled Jazz up by his shirt and sent a strong backhand across his face, which sent him reeling back to the ground.

Jazz felt as if his jaw had exploded. *He* repeated the prayer, this time in a more coherent voice while *he* continued to disrobe him until Jazz lay naked—his brown flesh exposed to the world.

"W-w-wait, stop—please," Jazz managed to utter, but his broken words landed on uncaring ears. "Why are you doing this to me? Who—who are you?" Jazz asked as he spit blood from his mouth.

He paused. "I am Alpha and Omega; the first and the last; the beginning and the end," *he* said in matter-of-fact tone. "You will lay naked before the throne of God and repent your sins. You will renounce your wicked ways," *he* said in a voice that boomed across the sky. *He* seemed to be in some kind of trance, walking back and forth and back and forth and uttering prayer. *He'd* walk away from Jazz only to return with a kick or a punch. *He* ordered Jazz on his knees and shocked him by punching him in the eye so hard Jazz thought he had been blinded. Jazz had never known pain so profoundly.

When *he* was satisfied that Jazz was weak enough, *he* dragged his limp body across the coarse grass to the tattered fence at the very edge of the property that separated the back of the church from the woods. Jazz felt sharp rocks and shards of broken glass cutting across his skin as he grabbed at mounds of grass in an attempt to anchor his body.

When *he* got to the end of the field, *he* loosened his grip on Jazz and let him go. *He* walked through the hole in the fence and opened the door to a black van that was parked on a dirt trail. Jazz lifted his head to ascertain what was going on, but dizziness forced him back to the ground.

Then, *he* stepped from the van with handcuffs and proceeded to fasten Jazz to the fence before Jazz realized what was going on. Blood oozed from his weakened mouth when he coughed. Then *he* spoke in a hell-inspired voice as a foul stench permeated the air all around them.

"The reason you are alive is because it is the will of God. You have a job to do. You will be my apostle. The world will take little note of what I say here, but it will remember what you tell them. You will tell them all to repent. You will tell them of the coming apocalypse. You will tell them I am watching. I am *always* watching. You will do this in our covenant or

I will visit you again. Jazz McKinney, you are my sacrifice to righteousness! Do you understand the task appointed to you?"

Pain sealed Jazz's lips, but his will to survive broke through and he mustered enough strength to mumble the word *yes*. Jazz wanted to see the face of this maniac, but his ragged body would not move.

"Mark this day as a return to righteousness. Walk by my side and you will dwell with me forever. You are to undergo circumcision, and it will be the sign of the covenant between me and you."

Circumcision?

Jazz tried to shake himself free from his bondage, but he barely had strength to dangle the fence. *He* moved closer to Jazz whose wild eyes grew at the sight of the sharp stone held in *his* hand.

"Do not fear, my child. I will protect you in our covenant."

Jazz kicked and wiggled his body to fend off the predator, but a powerful fist to Jazz's face ended his resistance.

He reached down and grabbed the wad of skin atop of Jazz's penis. Jazz closed his eyes. Then, as if studying it, *he* looked curiously at the hull that hid the head of Jazz's organ. Suddenly, *he* took the sharp stone that *he* held and started cutting away the superfluous skin. Jazz screamed as loud as he could as the unbearable sensation rapidly inflamed every cell in his body. A hurt like no other hurt he had ever felt consumed him. Then, he found his voice. The sound that escaped from Jazz's mouth was previously unheard by any human ear; it reached the heavens, circled the distant moon and stars, and came back down landing with a shattering thump.

He stood before Jazz, skin in his hand, and spoke. "Tell them The Messiah has returned. And he is angry."

The weight of his heavy words and the pain Jazz felt sent the night hurling around his head.

"THE LORD is my shepherd; I shall not want," *he* continued. "He maketh me to lie down in green pastures: He leadeth me beside still waters. He restoreth my soul: He leadeth me in paths of righteousness for His name's sake." The Messiah walked slowly through the opening in the fence toward the van, opened the door, and stepped casually into the vehicle.

Still bound to the fence, Jazz heard a rumbling noise from above and the sky grew bright as lightning burned an electric trail.

"For as lightning that comes from the east is visible even in the west, so will be the coming of the Son of Man." His words rung like a church bell in the night.

The Messiah closed the van's door and drove away slowly into the dark. In the final moment before his black van disappeared, the sky opened and rain poured from the heavens in buckets.

It rained for exactly six minutes and sixty-six seconds.

†††

A car winding up the road in front of the church crunched the gravel beneath its tires and pulled Jazz out of his recount of the evening before. Ironically, his hope for rescue would lie in the hands of a stranger, as his demise almost did. He simply closed his eyes and waited, still chained to the fence and unable to move. He knew another judgment would surely come from the "good Samaritan" that was about to find and—hopefully—rescue him. It was a judgment he didn't want to face, yet he knew it would be nothing compared to the one the Messiah had administered on him the night before.

Chapter 1

Dr. Garrett Lord woke up suddenly, gasping for air. He lay in the middle of his king-sized bed in his bedroom, bloodied and naked, aside from the small silver cross, which hung around his neck. He was terrified.

He sat up and looked around his room. All was quiet. He listened to the silence in an attempt to ascertain if he was alone. He heard no sounds, except for his breathing, as the morning sun cut sharp slivers through the blinds, giving way to another brilliant summer day. He could hear the birds chirping in the trees outside his window, but his heart was full of dread.

The stillness of the room alarmed him, much like the calm before a storm.

He looked down at his blood-stained hands as if this was the first time he had seen them. Minus their reddish hue, they looked the same; they were the same size and the same shape, yet, in some sense, they looked entirely unfamiliar. Part of him felt as if he was looking at a stranger's hands, and he wondered what had happened.

Then, he noticed the bloodied sheets. The red stains glared up and mocked him while daring him to discover their origins.

Have I been cut? Stabbed? In an accident?

He suddenly panicked as a thousand unpleasant thoughts buzzed through his head.

His frantic hands raced across his taut frame seeking a wound or a cut, but neither could be found. He leapt out of bed with the spryness of a teenager and tore the eggshell-colored silk sheets off his bed and threw them in a corner.

He had to see his face.

As soon as he entered the room, lights above the long, rectangular mirror, which were operated by sensors, lit up the darkened space.

He gasped when he saw his reflection in the mirror.

Dried blood had congealed around his nose, and a bloodied wound above his left eye was visible and sore to the touch.

Sweet Jesus, keep me near the cross.

Immediately, he pumped a handful of soap out of the dispenser into his large hands and then stuck them underneath the faucet, which was also controlled by sensors, causing a cold blast of water to shoot out. He washed feverishly and furiously, trying to scrub away any sign or trace of blood. As he cleaned his hands, a most unpleasant thought crept across his mind; a thought so vile, it caused him to momentarily stop what he was doing. *What if this isn't my blood?*

He scrubbed furiously trying to wash away the stains—and his thoughts. He scrubbed his hands, his wrists, his forearms, all the way up to his elbows. He didn't even care that the water was becoming hot enough to scald.

He then grabbed the expensive soap he used only on his face and lathered up his hands again. He scrubbed his face furiously, nicking his own self with his fingernails at times, until all of the blood had been removed. A pinkish ring formed in his marble sink where the bloody water had risen taunting him—even daring him—to remember what had happened.

He stared at his reflection in the mirror. Something unfamiliar and sinister lurked behind his usually bright eyes. In part, he didn't recognize his own face. It wasn't as if he didn't look the same. It was as if he stared into a trick mirror, in which his image was slightly distorted. He shook his head forcefully to clear his mind.

He needed to know what had happened. He took a deep and deliberate breath and tried to recall the events that could explain his present state, but when he searched his memory, all he could see was blackness. It was as if his memory had been intentionally erased. The last thing he remembered was being in church, on a Wednesday night for a special meeting, listening to his pastor make a startling confession, when his nose began to bleed.

He couldn't even remember the details of the confession.

He remembered sitting in the pews, with his eyes tightly closed, shaking his head from side-to-side, hoping the pastor's words were a cruel joke and would fade away when he opened his eyes. He remembered feeling nauseous and a bit dizzy and then someone tapped him on the shoulder and pointed to the blood that stained his blue shirt. When Garrett touched his nose and he drew his fingers back, they were stained by his own blood.

He remembered darting out of the sanctuary holding his nose.

Everything after that was a mystery.

Not another blackout.

Garrett had thought the worst was behind him. He hadn't had a blackout in six months, but when his nose started to bleed in church, he panicked because nosebleeds usually preceded his loss of consciousness.

Two years ago, he suffered his first blackout. He remembered waking up in a strange hotel on the outskirts of the city, naked, except for the cross around his neck. He hadn't told anyone about his blackouts, except his doctor, who could not determine a physiological reason. He suggested that Garrett seek the assistance of a psychiatrist, but Garrett balked at the suggestion. *I ain't crazy*, he remembered thinking as he marched out of the doctor's office in a huff.

Garrett dried his face and walked out of his restroom, almost in a daze, his breathing heavy, and looked around his bedroom for the clothing he had worn the night before. He hoped to search the pockets for some clue about what had transpired, but he could not find them. He half-expected to see a balled-up pair of slacks and a blood-stained shirt in a corner somewhere in the room, but aside from a half-empty cup of tea on his nightstand, the room was immaculate.

No pants.

No shirt.

No shoes.

He raced over to the closet, tore open the door and stepped into the bedroom-sized walk-in closet. Everything in the closet was arranged neatly, by color and style, with blazers on the left and slacks on the right, from light to dark. Directly in front of him was a wall full of shoes and every pair was accounted for.

He peeled back the hangers and looked closely at all of his blue shirts. The one he'd had on was not there.

Maybe I took it to the cleaners? He tried to wrap himself in that thought, but it didn't feel right.

He stepped out of the closet and gazed around the room. Everything was in perfect order, but something didn't feel right. Even the colorful floral arrangement, which was centered on a round table near the fireplace, looked undisturbed. Then, he noticed something out of place on the table. A lone half-sheet of white paper was on the table. It looked as if it had been deliberately left for him. He looked at the table again and moved closer. He took small, carefully timed steps as if the paper would lunge at him if he moved too quickly. Once close enough, he looked oddly at the unfamiliar handwriting and the unusual word, which was etched across the paper:

covenant

He raised his eyebrows in confusion and rubbed his hands over his bald head.

What does that mean?

It was not unusual for him to find odd objects after one of his spells. In the past he had found clothing that wasn't his, jewelry that he had never seen and on one occasion, he found a lock of jet-black, silky-smooth hair on the floor next to his car keys. Each time he found something unfamiliar, he'd throw it away. He never tried to figure out where the objects came from.

Something powerful at his core had always told him that he didn't want to know.

However, this time was different. This time he wanted to know; this time, he had to know. He knew that he could no longer ignore that something with him was terribly wrong. He could no longer deny his bizarre disappearances or the strange appearance of mysterious objects or his bruised flesh. The mystery of this blackout was beginning to take its toll on him. He could feel a headache creeping up like a slow-moving fog.

Again, he searched his memory, but he simply could not recall anything after he ran out of the church. He knew that he must have gone to the restroom because he wouldn't have gotten into his car while bleeding, but he couldn't remember.

He rubbed the paper between his index finger and thumb, hoping that it would jar his memory, but it didn't.

He jumped when he heard the ringing of his cell phone. Immediately, he looked toward his nightstand—the phone's usual resting place—but it was not there. He listened more closely, but the sound eluded him. He darted quickly through the room, trying to get closer to the sound, when he finally figured out that the ringing was coming from under his bed. He dropped to his knees, raised the bed skirt and peered under it. He grabbed the phone right before his voice mail picked up.

"Hello?" he said. As soon as the word left his mouth, he realized that he sounded out of breath.

"Baby, what's going on?" the exasperated voice on the other end of the phone inquired. "Are you okay?"

"Yeah, yeah, I'm fine," Garrett said as he got up from the floor and sat his naked ass on the bed. Gabriel's voice on the other end of the phone was full of concern and worry.

"Where are you?"

"I'm at home. Why?"

"Are you okay?"

"I'm fine, why? Wassup?"

"Where have you been?"

"What do you mean?"

"Baby, I've been calling you for hours. You were supposed to pick me up from the airport last night," the voice stated dryly. "I'm at your gate. Buzz me in."

Shit.

Garrett hung up the phone and walked over to the control panel on the wall near the intercom system and hit the "open" button so that the gate would roll back. He searched for something to put on and went over to his chest of drawers and pulled out a pair of warm-ups and a "wife beater." Hurriedly, he raced downstairs, all the while his mind searching for answers that would not come. He wasn't sure what he was going to tell Gabriel and he only had a few seconds to come up with something believable.

Garrett anxiously opened the door as Gabriel was about to knock.

"Hey," Gabriel said as he walked in, his face bent with curiosity. Garrett pushed the door shut and gave him a small hug that was uncharacteristic of their usual embrace.

Gabriel pushed away.

"I've been calling you all night. I was worried as hell about you. I thought you had been in an accident or something. I called the hospitals and even the jail. What's going on? And what happened to your eye?" His voice was strained as if the worry had scarred his throat.

"Oh, some kid in the hospital didn't want a shot so he punched me." Garrett laughed nervously as he rubbed the tender spot. "Baby, I'm sorry. I don't know how I forgot." Garrett rubbed his hand over his head hoping the motion would somehow prod his vacant memory.

"What do you mean, you don't know what happened? I spoke to you before I got on the plane in New York and everything was fine. How could you forget?" Gabriel's worry turned to anger.

"I got busy at the hospital." Garrett could offer no reasonable explanation and his default excuse was always work. "We had a couple of serious emergencies."

"I called the hospital and they told me you weren't there."

Shit.

"Well, I don't know who you spoke to, but I was there most of the night; by the time I left I was so exhausted I came home and passed out."

By the expression on Gabriel's face, Garrett could tell that he was not buying into his lie.

"Let me get this straight, you were so busy at the hospital that you couldn't find thirty seconds to call me and tell me to take a cab? Hell, I waited for you for over an hour."

"You know how wrapped up I get in the emergency room. We had three people seriously injured in a car accident on Connecticut Avenue and a kid who fell off a balcony at George Washington University—it was a crazy night."

"And the kid."

"Huh? What kid?"

"The kid who hit you in the eye."

"Oh yeah, the kid," Garrett said as he laughed nervously and rubbed his eye.

"Okay, something doesn't feel right. What's really going on?"

"Baby, there's nothing going on. I'm sorry. I don't know what else to say." Gabriel looked into Garrett's eyes, but the weight of his stare unnerved him and Garrett turned away. "You want some coffee or tea?" he said as he moved toward the kitchen.

Gabriel followed him into the kitchen as Garrett searched every dark corner of his mind for some detail, or image or word that might provide some clue as to what had happened to him. When he arrived at church the previous day, it was a little after six in the evening. Now, it was after nine in the morning and he couldn't recall anything that had happened to him in the last fifteen hours.

"Baby, I'll make it up to you—I promise. Am I forgiven?" Garrett said with a disarming smile as he pulled his mug from underneath the pot. Garrett sensed that Gabriel was more relieved that nothing dire had happened to Garrett than he was angry so Garrett played on that sentiment. "I'll do anything that you want me to," he said in a sing-song voice.

"You're lucky I don't feel like arguing. I'm simply glad you're okay. So, yes, you're forgiven, but you better start thinking of something very special for stranding me and having me worry my ass all night about you. "

"I will, baby, I promise." Gabriel walked slowly over to Garrett and kissed his lips. Instantly, he felt the heat.

"I left a notepad here the other night. I need it to finish this boring-ass story that's due today," Gabriel said as he pulled away.

"I haven't seen a pad."

"I left it upstairs. I'll get it." Gabriel turned and walked toward the stairs. When he disappeared around the corner a thought flashed across Garrett's mind: *the bloody sheets.* Immediately, he darted around the corner, hoping he could halt Gabriel's forward march. He saw Gabriel midway up the stairs, moving quickly.

"Gabriel!" Garrett called out.

"Yeah, babes?"

"I think your pad is down here."

Gabriel stopped. "Really? Okay. Well, I've got to pee anyway."

Garrett raced up the stairs and when Gabriel walked into the master suite, he immediately noticed the pile of sheets on the floor.

"A little early for cleaning?" he asked with a bit of spice.

"Nah, I wanted to get it done before I went in to work," Garrett said. Gabriel eyed him momentarily and walked into the restroom.

While Gabriel peed, Garrett shifted nervously from one foot to the other, hoping he could get out of this situation unscathed. He guessed that Gabriel's investigative instinct wouldn't let this pass. All of the signs pointed toward something being terribly awry.

When Gabriel stepped out of the restroom, he walked over to the sliding glass door, opened it, stepped onto the balcony and retrieved the pad from the table overlooking the swimming pool. When he retrieved the pad, he shot Garrett a most curious look.

"Well, I've got to get to work. Call me later," Gabriel said as he walked out without making eye contact.

"Alright, baby, I'll call you later this afternoon," Garrett called out as Gabriel exited the room.

Garrett exhaled and tried to compose himself when he heard the front door open and close. He knew exactly what Gabriel was thinking; his disappearance, the sheet-less bed that gave the appearance that he was covering up something—Gabriel must've thought he was having sex with someone else. He'd have his chance to fix things with Gabriel, but right now he had to focus on getting his memory back.

Half a day had gone by and he couldn't explain anything. All he knew was that he had woken up naked, with blood covering his hands and a scar above his eye.

At that moment, an eerie presence seemed to move subtly through the room. He couldn't see it, but it was there, like a bad omen.

Then, he noticed something.

He looked toward the fireplace at the huge gold-jeweled crucifix that hung above it. It usually served as a source of inspiration and when times were particularly rough—like now—he'd kneel before it and pray.

But not this time.

It hung upside-down.

He gasped.

Chapter 2

As Gabriel drove away, he balked at the thought that Garrett was lying to him. Granted, they had only known each other two months, but so far the budding relationship had been smooth and Gabriel knew that he was falling for him. Aside from a few telephone conversations that Gabriel would describe as *odd*, no alarms sounded to warn him of impending danger or insincerity on Garrett's part. Gabriel took great pride in his ability to read people and situations. In fact, he often stated that his journalistic success rested upon that unique ability. His honed sixth sense provided him with so much direction, that at times he felt partially clairvoyant.

He reached down into the pocket on the driver's side door and pulled out a CD he had burned full of smooth grooves. He needed something to relax him and help him shake the nagging feeling that was pulling at him and driving him to distraction.

What was Garrett hiding? What was that all about?

He went against his inquisitive nature and decided to focus on something else instead of letting his mind run wild about Garrett. Sometimes you don't want to know, and this felt like one of those times.

Gabriel entered the freeway at seventy-five miles an hour, amidst honking horns and flashing lights, but managed to merge successfully with the rapid traffic on the Beltway, which circled the Washington, D.C. metropolitan area.

He used the control on his steering-wheel column to turn up the volume, hoping the powerful sounds of Jennifer Hudson singing "Love You I Do" from the *Dreamgirls* soundtrack would nullify the negative thoughts circling in his head. He sang loudly, forcefully and with unchained emotion, yet his mind still pondered.

He remembered the night he had met Garrett. Their first meeting had been far from a storybook encounter and had bordered on bizarre. He thought back over the oddity of that first meeting and was amazed that their relationship had progressed to its current state, considering how they had met. It was indeed a meeting he'd never forget.

†††

Gabriel Kaine listened to the pedantic ticking that emanated from the clock on the wall. Its methodic pulse signaled the passing of time, but Gabriel felt as if his life was suspended in time. He was sprawled across his favorite lounger, flipping aimlessly through the never-ending procession of cable channels. Each clicking of the remote and flashing of the station confirmed that he was, indeed, in a rut.

He looked at the clock. It was half past nine on a Saturday night, and he had already exhausted the possibilities of his evening. Out of frustration, he threw the remote control onto the loveseat and marched down the hall directly into his office. He thought his boredom would possibly yield some great idea for his next column or provide insight into the nature of man so that he could finish writing the novel he started two years ago. Like his career, his debut "masterpiece" was going nowhere fast as well.

He plopped down into the chair behind the oak desk and stared at the computer monitor. He didn't know where to begin or really what to do. He had neither words nor ideas. He had more than a mild case of writer's block. Sometimes he wished he had taken his father's advice and gone to law school. He imagined himself slumped over a desk burning the midnight oil while poring over a complicated legal brief.

Instead of writing, he looked at his awards that hung on the wall. He had received a couple citations for his investigative stories and a most prestigious award by the National Society of Black Journalists for a four-part series that he did on the plight of black men, which was featured on the front page of The Washington Chronicle *each Sunday for a month. He was also proud of the huge black–and-gold plaque he received from the D.C. Writer's Club for a story on gentrification in Washington. He purposely hung the award in the center of the wall so that it would immediately attract the attention of anyone who ventured into the room. And he hung it there so that it could serve as inspiration at times like this.*

That was two years ago. How quickly things change.

Ever since he had been banished to report in the Style section, he felt as if he was drifting through life with no direction. His talent hung rotting on the vine and the stench of the decaying carcass that was his career was enough to choke out what little professional self-respect remained. He should have been doing stories that affected the lives of real people; instead, he had been condemned to report on uppity charity events thrown by Washington's vapid glitterati or book signings and fashion shows and concerts by arrogant hip-hop artists instead. The impressive meteoric rise of his career was matched with an equally impressive descent that ended in a blunt thud against the earth.

Gabriel's eyes diverted to the picture in the oak frame on the shelf to his left. Instantly, he was flooded with bad vibes. It was a picture taken two years ago of him and his lover at the time, Robert. In the picture, they were locked in a loving embrace on a sandy beach in San Juan, Puerto Rico. Robert's white skin had been tanned by the island's sun and his green eyes reflected Gabriel's love for him. When things were good with Robert, they were good; but, when things were bad, they were unspeakable.

Gabriel thought about their passionate lovemaking and romantic walks around the monuments in D.C. He thought about all the time—four years to be exact—they'd spent together building a life. And how in one sordid moment, it had all come crashing to an end when Gabriel caught him in their bed with another man. Gabriel kept the photograph of him and Robert as a reminder of how close he had come to destruction. He needed to be reminded to guard his heart more closely next time—if next time ever came. The pain of Robert's betrayal created a permanent scar on his heart from which he never imagined he'd ever fully recover, and he vowed to never be that close to destruction again.

Gabriel rubbed his hands through his mane as if smoothing his untamed curls would somehow bring him release from the mediocrity of his existence. A week ago, he decided the cornrows he sported were played out and unbraided his hair to flow freely in a Maxwell-inspired design. Since then, he'd received a growing number of compliments and was impressed with his own looks as well. He had come a long way from the short fade he used to sport when he was at the height of his temporary fame.

He leaned back in his chair, locked his hands behind his head, and exhaled. On a night like this not long ago, when the air was dry and the mood was heavy, he would have gone out onto his patio, pulled out a cigarette, and let the smoke carry away his loneliness and his discontent. He would have blown smoke circles and watched the ring lose shape and form in the night air. He missed the exhalation that accompanied smoking. More than that, he missed the peace it provided.

In the midst of phone calls, unreturned emails, and anonymous tips, smoking provided a small sanctuary for him in the center of chaos. It was a refuge amidst the storm. For those few moments when the cigarette burned and the ash-colored smoke churned, nothing else mattered. It was the only time during the day when he made time for himself. And he missed that. He quit six months after his doctor diagnosed him with high blood pressure; still, he longed for the solitude it provided.

As he leaned back reminiscing, the phone rang. It startled him and, reluctantly, he picked it up.

"Wassup, shawty?" the voice on the end of the phone said.

"Shawty? That's not my name. When are you going to stop trying to be hard? You're from Sugarland, Texas. That ain't exactly Compton."

"When are you going to lighten up?"

"When I win the Pulitzer."

"Negro, would you stop obsessing. Everything happens when it's supposed to happen. You know you have mad skills when it comes to putting a story down, but clearly it's not your time yet." Gabriel rolled his eyes and shook his head. If someone told him one more time that it wasn't his time, he was going to go postal. "Is there a reason you called?"

"Uhhh, can you watch your damned tone? You ain't too old to get—"

"Scott, what-do-you-want?" Gabriel asked with heightened irritability.

"Well, since you asked so nicely, I am about fifteen minutes from your house and I'm stopping by to pick you up."

"Pick me up?"

"I know you're sittin' around the house looking silly. So I decided to take you with me to this reception given by the Black Doctors Association. It's free food, free drinks. I know you like free food."

Gabriel paused.

"Are you calling me fat?"

"No, sir, but since you brought it up…"

"Drop it, okay?" Gabriel knew he had put on a few pounds but it was nothing to be too concerned about. Yet, he could see that those late-night pizza deliveries and chicken wings were beginning to take their toll. He looked down and noticed the slight bulge underneath his shirt. He could certainly pinch more than an inch. "Where is this function?"

"At the home of one my colleagues in upper Northwest. You've heard me mention Doctor James, right?"

"I think so. That name sounds familiar," Gabriel said. "I don't think I want to go though."

"You don't have a choice; besides, you ain't doing anything anyway. Now, I'm about twelve minutes away, so get off your ass and get ready."

Gabriel knew there was no point arguing with his best friend once he had set his mind on something. And Gabriel knew that Scott was right. If he didn't go to this party, he'd sit at home staring blankly at the computer screen hoping some divine inspiration would overtake him and compel him to write something brilliant. Or he'd spend the rest of the evening in a witless exploration of mundane television that failed to enlighten or even entertain.

"Yes, sir, Doctor Tiller, sir," he said in a feigned military-sounding tone.

"And leave the front door unlocked and leave a martini on the table." Click.

Gabriel was met with a harsh dial tone before he could adequately respond. As he hung up the phone he smiled at his irreverent friend, and at the thought of escaping the confines of his dingy and dusty townhouse. It was a beautiful starlight summer night, and he suddenly felt the need to be liberated.

A part of him smiled at the thought of going out and being social. A part of him missed those days when he and Scott would go out and dance until dawn in a sweaty club. He missed the electric atmosphere and the magic that the night contained. Those youth-inspired nights felt like eons ago, yet he always carried a piece of those times with him.

He even missed Scott dragging him to one of his "bougie" affairs or some swanky jazz bar tucked away in a hidden alcove in what appeared to be an abandoned part of the city. To this day, Gabriel never understood how Scott managed to have a thriving medical practice and still find time to locate all of the hot spots of the city. One thing was for sure, he knew Scott kept his finger on the pulse of D.C.

Gabriel panicked for a second at the thought of going out and mixing and mingling, but calmed himself. He needed to get out and be amongst the living. His self-imposed exile was draining more of his life force than he had anticipated. It had been some months since he had attended any kind of party or reception that wasn't work-related. At his work events, he usually put on a black suit and didn't think about it any further. Even without Scott constantly throwing it up in his face, he knew that he had put on a few extra pounds, but it wasn't time to call Jenny Craig. Reluctantly, he walked up the stairs and into the master bathroom and grudgingly stepped onto the scale.

This has got to be a joke, *he thought to himself.*

He stepped off and completely undressed, hoping the shorts and T-shirt he wore had caused the scale to be off by at least ten pounds.

Damn.

He had put on fourteen pounds in six months, and he knew that it was beginning to show. He could no longer deny it, as much as he wanted to. He wanted to pick up the scale and throw it across the room out of frustration, but that wouldn't do any good. Instead, he walked slowly into his bedroom with his head held low as if he was a naughty child being sent to his room.

He stood naked before the full-length mirror.

"Shit, I still got it," he said out loud in a less than convincing tone. Sure, there was a small bulge in his midsection, but he could still see faint outlines of his abdominals. Yeah, his love handles were slightly pudgy, but overall he still looked good, he told himself. He hoped his extra poundage wouldn't make his clothes too

tight. He didn't want to look like a two-dollar ho canvassing the street looking for a trick or a treat.

He walked over to the stereo in his room and rotated the dial to Justine Love's and Todd B's Love Talk and Slow Jams on WPGC-FM 95.5. Over the last year, he had grown accustomed to listening to their soothing voices, sound relationship advice, and witty comments. Their selection of music was always on point and exactly what he needed. He turned up the volume as he listened to Beyonce belt out "Dangerously In Love" from her first CD of the same title. He couldn't help but think that it had been years since he had been dangerously in love. And he missed that feeling.

He re-focused his attention on what he was going to wear that evening. As he thumbed through his wardrobe, he realized it was slim pickings. It had been months since he had bought anything new and most of the clothes in his closet were fashionably out of season; and the few things he found didn't fit exactly the way he wanted. He pulled out a simple black button-up shirt and pair of black khakis. With the proper accessories, he could make the ensemble work. He reached up on the top shelf of his closet to pull down his pair of black dress shoes, and when he did, one of his scrapbooks came crashing to the floor bringing with it scraps of paper and newspaper articles scattered across the beige carpet.

"Shit," he said as he bent down to pick up the fragments of his life. He looked at some of the clippings of articles he had written about The Messiah months prior. He had gained notoriety for his in-depth reporting on the beast who kept an entire city on edge for months. In six months, The Messiah had killed six people—all presumably gay—in brutal, ritualistic displays that were reminiscent of Biblical slayings. Then the killer merely vanished—without a trace and without a word.

Gabriel re-read one of his articles that was published on the front page of the newspaper. In big bold letters, the headline read:

THE MESSIAH STRIKES AGAIN: GAY NEIGHBORHOODS TAKE PRECAUTION

It was an intriguing and in-depth account of the sixth murder, which stunned the city and captivated the world. Gabriel had been interviewed by television stations and magazines and even provided clues to authorities. He quickly grew accustomed to the flashing cameras and the spotlight. It was he who had discovered the Biblical connections between the killings, even before The Messiah revealed his identity.

Gabriel reveled in his fifteen minutes of fame, but more importantly, he actually wanted to do his part in catching the monster who had eluded capture for so long.

That was then. This is now.

Gabriel learned that a journalist is only as good as his last story and that the fickle winds of public opinion could change in an instant. One report gone bad and Gabriel found himself journalism's new pariah.

When the killings suddenly stopped, Gabriel was free to focus on other stories. After tasting the forbidden fruit of fame, he longed for its sweetness, but he couldn't do just any story. He had to find the story. He wanted to rock the headlines again. He stumbled onto a bribery scheme involving high-ranking city officials but ended up interfering with a federal investigation that was about to crack the case. Because of Gabriel's zealousness, the city officials and the contractors involved in the scheme were never arrested.

When news of his interference reached his editor's desk, there was hell to pay. Gabriel never forgot the day he walked into the office. He could have sworn he saw smoke seeping from the ears of the middle-aged balding man. He once enjoyed a strong relationship with his editor, but the bonds of that relationship would be tested. Exactly eight months ago today, Gabriel's fast-track career came to a screeching halt.

Since then, his routine had become so predictable. Each morning he would arise at the same time and perform the same tasks in the exact same order: reach over and turn his alarm off at exactly 7:00 a.m.; grab the remote control; click on the television; turn to FX to watch a rousing rerun of Buffy, the Vampire Slayer followed by The Practice; stumble out of bed and into the shower at 9:00 a.m.; have breakfast—a bland meal of a bowl of Quaker Instant Oatmeal and a banana, washed down with a cup of Simply Orange juice—at 9:30 a.m.; and lastly, a long, dreaded walk to his computer where he'd sit and stare to await inspiration that never came. The monotony of his life was palpable.

Gabriel gathered all of the clippings and the scrapbook and threw them on the bed when he heard his front door open and close.

"Gabriel, your ass had better be in the shower!" Scott called out as the door closed. "And where is my martini?"

He didn't bother to respond because Scott knew he wouldn't be in the shower by the time he arrived. He was notorious for being slow when it came to getting ready. Besides Scott knew exactly where Gabriel kept the liquor and could make his own martini.

✝✝✝

Downstairs, Scott meandered through Gabriel's townhouse, reserving his comments until Gabriel emerged from upstairs. He rifled through the stacks of papers and books scattered about the place. Gabriel's once fashionable abode looked more like a repository for discarded literature than it did a townhouse.

Several legal-size yellow pads with scribbled notes were spread out indelicately across the coffee table. Scott picked up one of the pads and attempted to read the indecipherable writing, but tossed it back to the table in frustration. He looked at the matted sky-blue blanket that lay across the tan leather couch and the raggedy slippers that occupied the space below the lounger. He ran his finger across the top of the entertainment center and cracked the thick layer of dust that had long since settled on top. Scott wasn't sure what to think. He knew that Gabriel had gone through a minor depression since he had been demoted, but it was never a cause of concern. Until now.

Scott walked over to the kitchen and opened the cabinet in which Gabriel kept his supply of liquor. Surprisingly enough, the five bottles that were in the cabinet the last time he was over were still there, untouched.

"At least he hasn't turned into an alcoholic," Scott mumbled to himself. He closed the cabinet and grabbed a Corona out of the refrigerator.

Twenty-two minutes later, he heard Gabriel's footsteps on the staircase. He brought the beer up to his thick lips. "My, my, my, you clean up nicely," he said in a gruff voice laced with his thug bravado and looked Gabriel over with envious eyes. In spite of the few extra pounds, his striking features still commanded attention when he walked into a room.

"Don't hate," Gabriel replied playfully.

"It's amazing what a girdle can do," Scott said as he took a sip of his beer. As soon as the liquid hit his throat, he choked and had to set the drink on the table.

"See, that's what you get. God don't like ugly." Gabriel laughed and walked into the kitchen to grab a beer for himself. "And, what do you have on?" he asked as he eyed Scott up and down.

"I told you it was casual." Scott looked down at his Timberlands and baggy jeans. "You got a problem with this?"

"You ain't no thug, so stop fakin'. I don't understand you. You're a doctor. Dress like one," Gabriel replied.

Scott ignored him. He knew he looked good whether in baggy jeans or a Marc Jacobs suit. Although he was every bit of five feet nine inches, he carried himself as if he were twelve feet tall. He was often told he had gorgeous eyes and skin like smooth, dark chocolate, but it had always been a source of contention for him. Growing up in the South, Scott was surrounded by people who placed a high value on light skin. He was the darkest of five siblings and was often teased because of it. In high school, he dated a girl who could not bring him home because her mother told her never to bring anyone home who was darker than a paper bag. Thank God "lightskinned" was still considered "played out" now. He knew he had killer looks and the confidence to match. However, deep down inside, the scars of his childhood taunts remained. He simply chose not to let anyone see them.

"I can dress how I like on my own time so stop hatin'. And, don't worry about what I got on. You need to be worrying about this hovel you're living in. What is going on with this place?" Scott asked as he looked around the room. "I mean, damn, this ain't Section 8 Housing."

"You're such a ghetto snob. You're exactly one generation out the ghetto and wanna talk about somebody," Gabriel said. "Besides, I haven't gotten around to cleaning up."

"Well, you kept this shit up and you'll be living with rats and roaches. This shit is not cute—at all."

"How about you lend me your maid one day and let her come over here and work it out for me?" Gabriel asked jokingly.

"*You know, that ain't a bad idea. I can't have you living like this. Maybe I'll send you my personal trainer, too,*" Scott said with a wink.

"*Fuck you.*"

"*Now, that's plain old rude.*" Scott pressed his hand against his chest as if he had been wounded by Gabriel's words.

"*Can we go now before I change my mind?*" Gabriel asked with noticeable irritation.

"*Somebody's a little pressed about getting to the party. You thinking about finding a man to work you over tonight? I know you must be backed up. For real, when is the last time you've had sex?*"

"*Why are you all up in my business? I'm sure you're having enough sex for both of us.*"

"*Hey—don't hate me 'cause I'm beautiful.*"

"*Whatever, trick, let's just go.*"

"*Well, one good thing those extra pounds have done for you is put some junk in yo trunk,*" he said as he smacked Gabriel on his left ass check.

†††

When they walked into the residence of Dr. James, Gabriel gasped at the breathtaking foyer. The marble floors shone with an unexpected brilliance and two huge pillars stood guard at the entrance into the main room like an old sentry guarding a palace. Gabriel suddenly felt underdressed—in spite of Scott's thugged-out attire. But before he could curse him out for not advising him on how to dress, a distinguished-looking man dressed in all black walked through the double doors with his arms widely extended. Gabriel braced for a hug from this stranger, but breathed a sigh of relief when he grabbed hold of Scott instead. The gentleman was unfazed by their casual dress.

"I'm so glad you could make it," the man said gleefully. His words were perfectly articulated as if he practiced his diction with precision each day.

"I love what you've done to the place," Scott said as he looked around in wonder. "These floors are fabulous."

Gabriel tried to contain his laughter when Scott spoke. Regardless of his dress or how hard he tried to seem ghetto, he managed to slip back into his proper ways easily, which is why Gabriel could not understand why Scott insisted on faking the funk.

"Thank you so much. I recently spent $75,000 redecorating the downstairs area. Next month, I'll do the upstairs. Come here, let me show you something." He took Scott by the hand and led him to a corner where a vase sat on a marble pedestal. "I went to an auction in New York last week, and I had to have this vase. I know I paid way too much for it, but isn't it divine? It used to belong to Elizabeth Taylor," he whispered as if trying to prevent national secrets from falling on the ears of the enemy.

Gabriel looked at the plain-looking blue vase with yellow streaks emanating from its base. You got robbed, he thought to himself.

The man, finally noticing Gabriel, took a step back and put his hand on his chin as if he were deep in thought. His eyes moved from the top of Gabriel's head down to his feet and back up again before settling on Gabriel's face. "I'm Doctor Andrew James. And who might you be?" he asked. The corners of his mouth slipped into a tiny smile.

"I'm Gabriel."

"Do you have a last name, Gabriel? Or are you one of those pop stars who are famous by one appellation?" Gabriel was not at all amused by his feeble attempt at humor. The two minutes he had been in his presence left a lot to be desired. Gabriel's "taste" for pompous homosexuals had already been filled by Scott.

"Yes, I have a last name." Gabriel eyed him and did not speak further. Nor did he smile. The man had already gotten underneath his skin.

"Andrew, this is the guy I was telling you about. The writer—you remember?" Scott interrupted, trying to ease the tension. Gabriel cut his eyes at Scott wondering what he had told the gentleman about him, and then watched as he searched his mind for recognition.

"Ah yes. What a pleasant surprise. I didn't know you were bringing him. And he's even more attractive than you said."

Gabriel forced a weak smile as Andrew took him by the arm and led them into the main area, which was bustling with activity. Gabriel thought about pulling away from the man, but he didn't want to seem rude. Instead, he looked over his shoulder at Scott who winked at him. Gabriel clenched his lips tightly and focused his attention on Andrew, who was talking about himself and the redec-oration, not noticing or caring whether or not he was listening.

When they walked into the room, a noticeable jealousy could be seen on the faces of the men as they turned to look at Andrew with Gabriel on his arm. Gabriel wasn't sure if they were looking at him or Andrew or both of them. He suddenly felt awkward and insecure like he was being judged. Memories of walking into parties thrown by his rich white classmates in high school came to mind. He had a flashback of walking into his best friend's lavish home and seeing heads turn. Although his skin was light, it wasn't "light enough" and he could feel what they were thinking.

"My good man, what would you like to drink?" Andrew asked as he led him to one of two bars that were stationed in the room. Gabriel scanned the room full of professional-looking older men who were engaged in lively and robust conversation. Soft music could be heard underneath the conversation, but Gabriel couldn't recall any tunes in particular.

He felt as if he were in the VIP room of some fancy club and was waiting for the main guest to arrive. Scott had made his way across the room and was hug-ging and smiling a group of guys as if they were childhood chums suddenly reunited. Gabriel watched them walk into the back of the room and disappear.

"Gabriel, we are waiting for your drink order," Andrew said with pompous inflection. "You look a bit flustered. I hope I'm not making you nervous. I tend to have that effect on men."

He was way too cocky for Gabriel's taste and he could feel the blood rushing to his face. "I'll have a white wine," he replied. He didn't really want what he ordered, but chose the first thing that came to his mind in order to get Andrew off of his back.

"Good choice. Make that two," Andrew chimed in.

Upon closer inspection, Gabriel noticed that Andrew was quite attractive and was in—from what he could tell—pretty good shape for a man of his age. Gabriel surmised that Andrew was in his early fifties from his salt-and-pepper hair and graying five-o'clock shadow. He was a man of remarkable presence, taking time to accentuate each movement and each breath like he was entering center stage in an Alvin Ailey show.

"So, you're a writer?" he asked, taking Gabriel by the arm and leading him

through the crowded room. Gabriel was surprised that Andrew remembered anything about him because from the moment they walked into his home, he had
done nothing but rattle on about himself.

"Something like that."

"What do you write?"

"I write for the newspaper." Gabriel looked disinterestedly around the room.
He wished Scott was somewhere close so that he could provide an escape from
Andrew, but Gabriel knew he'd have to rescue himself. "Would you excuse me
for a few moments? I have to use your restroom."

"But of course. Walk through the foyer and take a left. You can't miss it. I can
escort you if you like," Andrew added with a devilish grin.

"I'll be okay, but thanks." Without hesitation, Gabriel pried himself from
Andrew's grasp and walked briskly out of the room. Once he rounded the corner,
he saw Scott down the hall engaged in conversation with a new group of men.
Gabriel cleared his throat loudly to get Scott's attention. Scott noticed the stern
look on his face and excused himself from the conversation.

When Gabriel was close enough to do so, he grabbed Scott by the arm and
pushed him into the restroom.

"Look, I know you want me, but damn!" Scott shouted. "Be careful. This is a
two-hundred-dollar shirt. You know you can't afford to pay for it."

"I know you're not trying to hook me up with that...that man."

Scott took a sip of his drink and smiled. "So, what if I am? I thought you could
use a little attention."

Gabriel exhaled and shook his head. "Is that why you wanted me to come with
you tonight? To hook me up?"

"I may have mentioned to Andrew that I had an attractive, single friend who
I was bringing to the party. If he inferred anything from that, then that's on
him," Scott replied and shrugged his shoulders.

"Knowing you, I'm sure you said more than that. You are a trip," he replied,
not able to contain the smirk that crept across his face.

"Andrew is a nice man. He's rich, attractive, and I can tell that he likes you.
What more can you ask for? It's not like you have men beating down your door
right now."

"I'm doing fine. Thank you for your help, but the next time you try to fix me up with someone, do me a favor and let me know first. You know Andrew is not my type."

"Why, because he ain't white?"

"You can be such an asshole sometimes. Need I remind you that I'm half white?"

"No, you don't need to remind me of anything. I know you're half white. Hell, you tell me every time I see you." Gabriel gritted his teeth.

"I tell you because you always wanna bring race into the equation. Whatever I'm doing is not black enough for you. Not my speech, not my style of dress—"

"Style?"

"Not my hair. Not anything. I don't know why I'm even having this conversation with you."

Scott took another sip of his beer and eyed Gabriel. *"I actually was only referring to your precious Robert."*

"Why do you have to bring Robert into every conversation we have about men? Yes, Robert was white. But before him was Rodney, and he was black. I date all kinds of people. Shit, I don't care about race. Give me a man who loves and respects me."

"Is that what Robert did? Loved and respected you?"

Gabriel was almost out of words for Scott. He knew that his face was beet-red and that Scott was loving the fact that he was getting under his skin.

"I'd like to see you with a brother, that's all." Gabriel looked at Scott and shook his head.

"You know what? I'm over this conversation."

"Good. Now, if you don't like Doctor James, there are quite a few attractive black men out there who I'm sure would like to get to know you. I saw the way they were looking at you when Andrew dragged you in on his arm," Scott replied while trying to contain the slight giggle that began as a tickle in his throat but soon exploded into wild laughter.

"See, you ain't right," Gabriel replied, unable to contain the smile spreading across his face. *"This is why I don't go out with you anymore. You've always got some trick up your sleeve, pun intended."*

"Ouch. That's a bit harsh. I'm concerned about you; that's all. All you do is sit home alone and mope. It's been what—a year—since you and Robert?"

"It's been long enough."

"Damn, that long? If we can put a man on the moon, we can put one on you."

"Whatever."

"I know one thing, you sure are getting sensitive in your old age. Is it the extra weight?" Scott said, trying to inject humor into the situation.

Gabriel squinted his eyes, turned around, and exited the restroom. "Gabriel, wait. You know I'm only playing with you."

Sometimes Gabriel questioned his friendship with Scott, who was difficult and pretentious, at best. This was one of those times. Gabriel marched into the grand room and his senses were overwhelmed by the sound of rowdy conversation and subtle jazz emanating from the stereo. The music and the conversation did little to detract from the gathering storm he felt inside. He finished his glass of wine and placed the empty vessel on a passing server's tray and extracted a full glass of champagne simultaneously. Something told him he'd need a better buzz.

Gabriel brought the glass to his lips and took a sip. Behind him, he could hear Scott's voice, which now sounded like nails on a classroom chalkboard. At this point, he needed a moment alone so that he could process Scott's deprecating and catty comments, which always felt like verbal jabs. He needed to get some air.

He scanned the room for an escape route and saw two glass double doors leading to a terrace. Without pause, he zigzagged down the center of the great room, weaving between clusters of people, hoping to remain unnoticed. He was almost to his destination when he looked up and saw Andrew walking back into the room from the patio with another gentleman. Immediately, Gabriel turned his back and pretended as if he were engaged in conversation with the stranger who stood before him. Gabriel stood still, not even breathing, as if the expanding of his chest cavity would call unwanted attention to him.

"Are you alright?" the stranger asked. Instead of replying, Gabriel listened to Andrew's voice as it became more and more faint, indicating that he had moved past him without incident.

"Finally," Gabriel exhaled.

"Excuse me?" the man replied again.

"Oh, I'm sorry," Gabriel said as he shook off his daze.

"Are you okay?"

The unsolicited concern in the stranger's deep voice caused Gabriel to focus more intently on him. He stared directly into the stranger's piercing black eyes and felt enchanted by his magic. They were like pools of onyx, sparkling and twinkling mysteriously underneath the artificial light. Gabriel felt drawn to him. In ten seconds, Gabriel wanted to know about this man's world, his pains, his gains. He wanted to know him far beyond the usual questions of "what is your name" and "what do you do" and "where do you live" and "what do you do for fun." He wanted to know the man, his essence, and his spirit. He wanted to speak of past lives, future dates, and trips to the moon and back.

In a quick glance that lasted a mere fraction of a second, the oceans of truth contained within the man's eyes untied Gabriel from the shores of his monotonous existence and lifted him to the Promised Land where hope, peace, and love resided. Love. Something Gabriel had long given up on, but something inexplicable in this stranger's presence put Gabriel at ease. In that fleeting moment, Gabriel felt more alive and electrified than he had in months.

"Oh, uh, yeah, I'm fine, thanks for asking." The mystery man towered above Gabriel who imagined climbing up him to reach unknown pleasures. For the first time in many, many, months, Gabriel felt his heart flutter in response to that innate chemical reaction brought on by strong desire and naked attraction. Gabriel smiled nervously and suddenly the room began to dim. He looked around to see if anyone else had noticed, but the darkening room seemed to pose little concern for most of the attendees. As he gazed around, everything and everyone seemed to move in slow motion.

The music in the background grew faint and soon faded out of earshot. He stared at the stranger's lips but they moved as if time itself was slowing down. Gabriel watched this stranger's delicious lips move and contort as he formed words and sounds, but what he said Gabriel couldn't decipher. Gabriel began to panic and his vision blurred.

He couldn't even react to the exploding glass that the waiter dropped in the foyer, but he saw heads slowly turn in the direction of the noise. He was suddenly aware of the tingling in his feet, of the rapid beating of his heart, and his damp palms. All at once he felt confused, dizzy, and dazed, and his feet felt wobbly even though he was standing still. As if the air had suddenly been sucked out of the room, his lungs struggled for breath and he thought he might suffocate.

"Hey—hey, what's wrong?" the stranger asked with caution that had changed to concern. Instinctively, he took the glass out of Gabriel's hand and set it down on a nearby table.

"Help me outside—please. I need some air." Gabriel struggled to get the words out and he wasn't even sure if the stranger heard him, but within seconds, he had placed his arms around Gabriel to steady him and they moved uneasily through the crowd until they reached the patio. He helped Gabriel to a lounge chair to the left of the swimming pool.

"I—can't—breathe," Gabriel uttered. Beads of sweat formed on his forehead and arms.

"Yes, you can. You're doing fine. Now, listen to me. I'm a doctor. I want you to relax and take slow, deep breaths. Can you do that for me?" Gabriel nodded his head in affirmation and held onto the stranger's hand for dear life. All at once, his head started spinning and he felt a pressure on his chest as if some poltergeist was pressing down on him. He felt a strong tingling in his toes, which was usually the first thing he felt when he had a panic attack. He tried to speak again, but speaking took too much attention away from his breathing. He wanted to tell the stranger what was happening to him, but his voice was lost.

"I'll be right back," the stranger said, but Gabriel tightened his grip on the man's hand.

"Does anyone know this man? I need some help!" the stranger called out.

Gabriel thought about all of the people in the room a few feet from where he sat. While he struggled to breathe, they laughed and flirted and played little games with each other. While he resisted losing himself, they frolicked with each other, free from care or concern.

He wanted this attack to end before it completely incapacitated him and subjected him to severe embarrassment. He knew how vicious folks could be and the idea of being the subject of gay party folklore was not something he desired. So he concentrated.

He took slow and deliberate breaths and imagined he was home listening to

India Arie. As he tried to force himself to relax, the stranger kept calling out for assistance. The more he called out, the more anxious Gabriel became. He didn't want anyone to see him in this weakened condition.

"You're going to be okay," he reassured Gabriel, whose wild hair had fallen due to the weight of the sweat that had accumulated atop his head. Gabriel continued to breathe, hoping his efforts would force the anxiety attack to dissipate, but he couldn't focus long enough for his efforts to be effective. He was distracted by the thought of embarrassment.

As he stared blankly into the night sky, the clouds began to rotate and twist violently, as if a great storm had arrived. As much as he tried to ignore the actions of the clouds and focus on breathing and relaxing, they had his full attention. The battle in the sky was accompanied by flashes of lightning, which illuminated the heavens.

As he watched the storm brew, time stretched into malleable strands that seemed to have no end. Then, the largest cloud morphed into what appeared to be a hooded, blackened, faceless figure with long, bony fingers that scratched out from the heavens at him. Gabriel's eyes threatened to bulge out of his head and his breathing quickly accelerated.

"Hey, man, it's going to be okay. I'm here for you. Take deep breaths."

Gabriel looked over at the stranger to divert his attention. He heard some commotion in the room and when his eyes focused, he could see Scott rushing toward him.

"Excuse me, excuse me," Scott said as he muscled his way through the room. "That's my best friend. What's going on?" he asked the stranger in an accusatory tone.

"We were talking and all of a sudden he got dizzy and said he couldn't breathe. I brought him out here to get some air. Does this happen to him often?"

"Gabriel, look at me," Scott said, completely ignoring the stranger's question. Scott squatted down in front of him and stared into his eyes. "Remember your breathing techniques. This'll pass. Just keep breathing."

"Is he having an anxiety attack?" the man asked.

"You're sharp, aren't you?"

Scott's sarcastic comment took the stranger by surprise, and he seemed to catch his breath to hold back the response he really wanted to hurl his way. "I was pretty sure that's what was happening, but I couldn't be absolutely sure. I needed someone he knows to confirm it before I called 9-1-1."

"Well, thank you," Scott said, softening his tone a bit after realizing he had no reason to be rude to the man. The attack lasted less than ten minutes, but it felt like a tortuous lifetime to Gabriel. In those frenzied moments, when nothing mattered—when even breathing was challenging—he felt as if his heart would explode in his chest and he would certainly die. The feeling accompanied by the complete loss of control was an unmistakable and paralyzing fear of death. No other feeling could compare. With each attack, Gabriel felt as if he walked in the shadow of death. He always thought that one day one of his attacks would lead to his demise and that sweet chariot would come to carry him home. He thanked God that day wasn't the day.

✝✝✝

The morning after his embarrassing panic attack, Gabriel sat in front of his television feeling absolutely numb. He didn't want to feel or to remember what had happened out of fear of having another attack. Each passing thought brought flickers of the emotions he felt the night before: anxiety; intense fear; embarrassment.

Gabriel had not suffered a panic attack in eight months. The last time it happened was when he stepped onto a Red Line Metro subway car at Dupont Circle after his editor screamed at him for botching the federal investigation that got him banned to the Style section. Gabriel had been told to take a few days off—which amounted to a one-week suspension without pay—and when he stormed out of the building his emotions were running high. Fueled by anger and professional embarrassment, he raced down the long escalator that extended deep under the earth and pushed his way through the crowded D.C. subway platform.

He felt a bit light-headed, but paid very little attention to it. When he got into the station, an apparent delay stymied his swift getaway. People stacked the platform like sardines in a can, but Gabriel could not wait. He pushed and shoved his way to the front so that he would be sure to get on the train when it arrived.

He had to board the next train so that he could be whisked away from the drama that had just occurred. He was having a Calgon moment. He couldn't believe he had made such an amateurish mistake. In his race for fame and glory, he didn't bother to check his sources or try to verify the information he received. Instead, he took the word of an unreliable source and that blind faith led to disaster.

Gabriel had been secretly investigating the head of the District's Transportation Department after rumors of bribery and corruption raced through the grapevine. One of Gabriel's sources mentioned to him the possible bribery of a high-ranking city official by Meeks Construction Company and Gabriel was determined to break the story. This secret tip led Gabriel to show up at the wrong place and the wrong time. The FBI had been investigating the city official, too, and was poised to have an informant pay him off in a warehouse in Southeast D.C. Due to Gabriel's interference, the handoff never occurred and the investigation was ruined. As was Gabriel's promising career.

When the train finally arrived, he remembered pushing his way into the center of the car and taking the outside seat on the row. All of his thoughts were focused on the demise of his career and if he could recover from the debacle. As soon as the train jetted off through the tunnels, he felt dizzy.

And then he felt the tingling in his toes.

He started to panic.

And sweat.

He tried to control the attack by controlling his breathing, but it didn't work. At the next stop, he had to be pulled off the car and EMS was called, which led to further delays on the Red Line that day. The perfect ending to the perfect day, he thought as he was carried off on a stretcher in front of a crowd of strangers. It was his first attack, but it would prove not to be his last.

✝✝✝

Before Gabriel realized it, he was listening to the "Dreamgirls (Finale)" at the end of the CD and pulling into the underground parking garage at his downtown office. He barely recalled the drive, and the unsure feeling in his gut about Garrett was still there all the while.

Chapter 3

As the sun rose, Jazz lay lost in a world of agony and pain.

Oddly, he wanted to see his attacker's face one last time. He couldn't explain why he felt the need to see it; nonetheless, he *needed* to. Part of Jazz wanted this beast to look at him—to look at his face and into his eyes—so that he could see the poisonous fruit of his hate-filled labor in its totality. Jazz needed him to see the extent of what he had done, and he hoped this man would quiver in disgust at his misguided righteousness.

How could he claim to be of God and inflict this kind of torment? Where was the love? Jazz wondered.

Jazz wanted his attacker to see his tears and his bloody mouth and his swollen eyes and his skinned dick and his ragged body. Jazz needed this beast to see the shattered features of his once proud face. He needed him to see what he had done; he wanted him to see his broken body in all its wretchedness. This wasn't any messiah Jazz knew. He didn't deliver Jazz from darkness into light. He wasn't kind or loving. This messiah was rabidly twisted.

Hours later, the sun continued its rapid ascent and the stifling heat weighed Jazz down even more while he struggled in and out of consciousness. He couldn't let go of his need to see The Messiah's face again. Part of him desperately wanted to see if sorrow or remorse, even in its smallest measure, dwelled within the callous eyes of this devil who left him to die. He wished he could search his face for an ounce of humanity or for something that would yield an explanation as to why he subjected him to such cruelty, but the bitterness of this monster's last words lingered in his ears.

Jazz lay against the metal fence, the handcuffs cutting into his skin, and wondered which breath he took would be his last. He tried to live in memory, far from this place of pain.

He thought about his first concert.

Jazz's mother named him after her favorite trumpeter. He thought about the first time he heard a Miles Davis sonata. He was seven years old and listened with intense scrutiny as the man, who was dubbed the "Picasso of Jazz," blew magic into the brass instrument. The sounds that were released touched something in his young soul and Jazz knew he had to learn to play.

Jazz struggled to remain conscious. He tried to hum a song, but he couldn't play through the pain. He *felt* death. He knew it would be coming for him soon, and he was powerless to prevent it.

So he waited.

In the field, under the hot, summer sun. Under the outstretched branches of the oak tree that did little to cool his battered, bruised, and broken body.

He heard insects buzzing all around him. Their sound stirred up the air as the flies descended en masse and buzzed like an out-of-tune choir. Their elongated note distracted him from his dire circumstances. He listened closely. Maybe they were playing a little jazz or doing a scat with their wings. Maybe they were playing a spiritual, maybe "His Eye Is On The Sparrow."

His ears discerned slight differences in the tone of the buzz emitted by the bugs. Jazz listened closely to their melancholy melody. In lucid moments between fits of pain, rage and despair, he tried to put words to their buzzing, but words escaped him. Then, he realized there were no words with enough force to convey this kind of horror.

He suddenly wished that this God his mother was always referring to would transform him into of one those flies and let him fly off carelessly into the night to become nothing more than an annoyance to star-crossed lovers stealing a moment underneath the summer skies. He wished that he could become weightless and that the breeze would carry him away from the stench of blood and sawed-off flesh.

What if this man who called himself The Messiah had been sent by a higher power to punish and redeem him? What if his mother's depiction of an angry and wrathful God was true? What if he had been chosen, as The Messiah indicated, to spread the word of his return? What would happen if Jazz decided to forsake his mission?

The Messiah had promised to return and inflict punishment if his commandment was forsaken. These thoughts ricocheted around Jazz's head with frenzied and erratic speed, but he dismissed them because the shadow of death was upon him and his opportunity to be a messenger of God would not come to fruition.

He could feel his restless, delicate soul fluttering within his body, struggling to break free of its mortal bonds so that it could join *that* light, that infinite and all encompassing light that has been a part of folklore since the dawning of the first day.

But Jazz wasn't ready to let go of his earthly body.

He listened to the buzz again—it kept him tied to this world, to this mortal place of flesh and bones.

He wished he could scream.

He wished he had told someone where he was going.

He wished he had never agreed to meet this stranger. He didn't want to die alone but as the hours ticked by, that fate was looking more likely.

✝✝✝

When The Messiah reached his destination, he threw the van in park and pounded his fist repeatedly against the steering wheel. The relentless pounding in his head rivaled the ringing in his ears and his blurred vision. He screamed out louder and louder, but the intensity of the haunting noises increased in equal measure and drowned the panic in his voice.

He slid clumsily out of the van onto the hard ground. The voices in his head spoke louder as jarring whispers from the trees and bushes scratched at his ears. He pulled himself up from the ground and raced a jagged and wobbly line through the worn grass and brush toward the dilapidated structure, which was almost completely hidden by greenery.

He leaned against the rickety fencepost to gather his bearings as the shrill voices continued to overtake his thoughts. He inhaled and breathed in the air, but the darkness did not soothe his blackened soul. He took a few steps forward, but stopped midway to the door of the small house and covered his ears with his hands as if that would mute the cries.

He dropped to his knees and looked heavenward, panic and pain etched in his face, and waited for mercy from the skies. Instead of mercy, he heard prayers and fits and last rites from thousands of indistinguishable voices. He heard pleas of forgiveness and voices screaming bloody murder; he heard confessions and condemnations and lies that became truth and truths that altered realities. He wanted it all to stop, but no power he possessed could block out the noise.

Then, as suddenly as the voices began, they stopped.

And he rose.

He pushed open the door of the dank building and walked into the house. The smell of moldy walls and damp floors lodged in his nostrils, but he did not flinch—he had grown accustomed to the smell. He dropped his keys onto the large wooden table that occupied most of the space of the room. He reached down and hit the floor twice with the side of his heavy fist, forcing a lone board to rise up.

He yanked on it until it pointed straight to the sky and then reached down into the hole. He grabbed the cold metal ring in the floor and pulled up a secret door that led to an even more secret chamber. With heavy footsteps, he descended down the narrow staircase into his den.

Once he stepped comfortably into his lair he stopped. Hundreds of crosses were tacked indelicately along all four walls making it almost impossible to see the worn paint underneath. A weathered black Bible set on a small table in the corner opened to the Book of Revelations. Six white candles lined the walls of the cave and provided dim illumination.

He looked at his distorted face in the mirror. He studied it as if it were the first time he had seen it. Somehow, it looked different—unfamiliar—as if the experiences of the evening had transformed him into something entirely new. Slowly, he removed the crown of curls that sat atop his head. Next, he used both hands to remove the hair above his lip and the goatee that outlined a portion of his face. He put his disguise in a cardboard box and closed it tightly. There it would remain—until the next time.

The reflection that stared back at him smiled enticingly. It was time to release. The Messiah slowly and methodically removed all of his clothing as if performing for an unseen voyeur. Then he stood before the mirror naked. He stared at his dangling flesh and his smooth skin. He thought about Jazz and how he had saved his soul. He felt like a redeemer—a healer—who would save the world.

And those thoughts aroused him.

In his disjointed mind, saving souls excited him. He could feel the heat rushing toward the penis and soon, it stood fully erect. The more he thought about his earlier act, the more excited he became. The weakness of the flesh and the pleasures of the body drew his subject to him earlier, and now his flesh quivered. He reached into the pocket of his clothing and pulled out the flap of foreskin he forcibly sliced from his victim's body. He brought it to his nose and inhaled deeply. It reeked of sin. And blood. And he loved it.

As he inhaled the skin, he frantically pleasured himself. His rough hands pulled and yanked relentlessly on his fully erect penis as his frenzy mounted. His crazed thoughts and reflection fueled his fires as sweat ran down his smooth face. His breathing increased and his muscles began to stiffen as he neared that ultimate moment of pleasure. In a fit of ecstasy, his seed shot on the mirror and slid to the ground, and a chilling cry escaped from his mouth.

As he stared as his naked reflection in the cum-stained mirror, he felt ashamed. He dropped to his knees on the cold cement floor and began to pray fanatically. His chant landed with blunt thuds against the unforgiving floor and reverberated off the thick, rocky walls. His deep voice filled every nook in the dilapidated room.

He rocked back and forth with his hands clasped tightly together and pressed against his broad chest. His eyes rolled to the back of his head and foam oozed from his crooked mouth. Then his motion stopped, the muscles in his face stiffened, and he began to speak more clearly.

"Our Father, Who art in heaven, hallowed be Thy name. Thy kingdom come. Thy will be done, on earth, as it is in heaven..."

Chapter 4

Two days later, Jazz still lay immobile and bandaged while unfamiliar voices in the room swirled about his head.

He wasn't dead.

From the conversations going on around him, he knew he was in a hospital. The word "coma" kept being used to describe his state, but he knew he wasn't in one. After all, he could hear them!

At times, faint slivers of light cracked through his swollen eyes. He distinctly remembered seeing a male nurse dressed in white with shaggy blond hair enter and exit the room. He even remembered the nurse carrying a bouquet of flowers that were placed on a nearby table. Jazz wished he could turn his head to view the arrangement, but he couldn't. He'd have to remember them. They were sunflowers—his favorite flower.

Even though he could not yet speak or move, he still could detect light and hear sounds. More than anything, he wanted to stir his body to let them know he was indeed "there" with them. With measured force, he tried to will himself awake. He commanded his eyes to open and his body to move, but nothing happened. Repeatedly, he tried to assert control with the same sad result.

The struggle to speak took its toll on Jazz and he felt himself drifting off to some nether land. Then, right as he felt his mind wandering to that dark place of nothingness, he heard a sweet sound delivered on gossamer wings—his best friend Montre's voice. With everything that he had to give, he tried to muster the strength to open his eyes. He wanted to see his face.

In his mind's eye, Jazz could see concern draped across Montre's nervous face, the same concern he always wore. He'd always been there for him when he needed him the most. He had been Jazz's strength when he was weak, the voice of reason when Jazz overreacted, and Jazz's conscience when he wanted to lash out at the cruelness of the world by being cruel himself. He was, indeed, a friend. Probably his only friend. Jazz needed to see Montre's bright brown eyes and his cherubic face now more than ever, but his heavy eyelids simply would not open.

Jazz heard the door creak open, the sound of footsteps, and someone questioning Montre. He heard Montre explaining that he was his roommate and best friend, but Jazz wanted to tell the person that he was far more than that to him. In fact, Montre was his very soul.

I have to wake up, Jazz kept repeating in his head.

"Doctor, how is he? When is he going to wake up?" Jazz felt probing hands on his arm, as if someone was checking his vital signs.

I have to wake up, he thought again forcefully.

"I wish I could be more definite, but there's no way of predicting these kinds of things. He could wake up now, tomorrow, in a month—"

"Or *never*?" Montre asked with concern.

"Or never," the doctor affirmed in an unsettling, matter-of-fact tone. "We've done just about all we can do. He went through a very brutal beating and we've repaired his injuries, but it's really up to him now. He needs to know that he is loved. Keep talking to him. I'm sure he can hear you." The door opened and the doctor disappeared into the bustling hallway.

Montre moved closer to Jazz and placed his hand on his head and rubbed it gently. "You hear that, Jazz?"

Jazz got a whiff of the awful body oil Montre often bought from the Jamaican man who sold incense on campus. That scent filled his nostrils and Jazz hoped that it would force him to cough, which would be a most welcomed sign of life, but he remained still. He could feel the warmth from Montre's breath as he rubbed his head and spoke life into the room.

"You know that you are loved. Don't you dare give up, you hear? Don't you dare give up."

His forceful words compelled Jazz to try harder to move. In his mind, he grunted, but in reality he made no audible sound.

"I need you to be strong and to fight your way back to me. You have a lot of life left so don't you even think about letting that bastard who did this to you get away with it. Come back to me."

His fiery words infused him with a sense of urgency and purpose that was stronger than any desire he had ever felt. Jazz could *feel* his words.

"I'm sure you know this already, but I love you. If I could trade places with you, I would. You have to come back to me. The doctor said you don't have any permanent damage, so now it's all up to you. Come back to me."

Jazz tried to shift his body. He wanted to sit up, to stand up, to cry out, to move, to giggle, to raise his fist in protest—anything to let the world know that he survived, but his body would not yield to his desire. Jazz had always been a fighter. He had survived the verbal assaults thrown his way like javelins by his stepfather. He had survived his fire-and-brimstone condemnations regarding his homosexuality. He had even survived on his own when, at seventeen, his stepfather cast him out of the house into the mean streets of D.C. that became his home. A few scars on his body would always be reminders of what he endured because his stepfather wasn't "Christian enough" to understand unconditional love.

Yet, Jazz was cunning enough to survive his ordeal. He learned to trade on the only commodity at his disposal: his perfect seventeen-year-old body. He learned that if he was persistent enough, he could get anything he wanted out of men who were driven by desire and lust. He soon learned he could reap the benefits of being the trophy partner of some sophisticated doctor or businessman.

Soon enough, he met a thirty-seven-year-old Italian lover with jet-black hair and smoldering eyes on Pennsylvania Avenue during D.C.'s Capital Pride event. The moment they saw each other, the fuse of their passion was lit. Jazz convinced him that he was nineteen and they soon started a passionate relationship, which resulted in Jazz moving into his downtown high-rise condo that overlooked most of D.C.'s monuments. Unfortunately, eight months into their relationship, it all ended when his lover met an untimely fate after his Mercedes S-500 collided with a drunk driver.

Before his family came and claimed everything, Jazz was able to make off with a stash of cash that his lover kept hidden in the apartment. As he watched his lover's casket being lowered into the ground, Jazz realized that he could never count on anyone to take care of him—not his family, not his stepfather, and not his lovers. In the end, they all left him alone.

Jazz became determined to finish school, go to college, and make something of himself, in spite of his circumstances. Never again would he allow his welfare to be determined by the will of someone else.

Montre's quiet sobs brought him back to reality.

I have to move. I have to, Jazz thought to himself. He recalled all of his memories and knew that if he could survive his past, he could survive anything. He wouldn't be victim to The Messiah.

Yet, in spite of all his mental efforts, his body remained still.

✝✝✝

Montre stood over him, gently stroking his hair, and holding his hand. As he gazed upon his friend, he thought about the first time he and Jazz took a road trip together. They wanted to go to a party in Philadelphia and decided to throw caution to the wind and hit the road. They packed up Montre's Dodge Neon and hit Interstate 95 North.

While on the road, India Arie's song "Brown Skin" pumped through the CD player and in an unrestrained moment, they both belted out that song, word for word. Jazz wasn't a singer, but Montre's melodious voice covered Jazz's off-key antics. That song became their official anthem for the rest of the weekend and their trip turned out to be far more fun than they envisioned.

Montre smiled at the memory and before he knew it, he started singing. His voice was wobbly with emotion at first, but as the lyrics came to him, his voice became sturdy and he felt the song. He continued to gaze at his friend, who was immobile.

"Every time you come around, something magnetic pulls me and I can't get out disoriented, I can't tell my up from down, all I know is that I wanna lay you

down," he sang with a subtle fiery passion. When he sang those words in the car that Philadelphia weekend with Jazz, he didn't realize how poignant those lyrics would come to be. He loved Jazz even though his love was unrequited. They had never spoken directly about it, but his feelings were clear. Yet, Jazz valued them being friends more.

As Montre neared the end of his tune, he felt Jazz slightly squeeze his hand. He let go suddenly, startled by the faint indication of life.

"Jazz, was that you?" he asked, not sure if the squeeze was involuntary. He grabbed Jazz's hand again. "Jazz, if you can hear me, squeeze my hand. Please, baby, squeeze. Let me know that you hear me."

He waited a few seconds. Nothing. No movement at all. He sighed audibly and was about to release his hand when he felt it again.

"Jazz, if you can hear me, squeeze my hand three times."

Jazz squeezed his hand three times in succession and Montre let out a loud scream. He let go of Jazz's hand and raced into the hallway to find a doctor or a nurse or anyone who could witness this miracle.

He returned moments later with the doctor, and grabbed Jazz's hand and asked him to repeat the motion. Jazz complied.

"This is a good sign, right?" Montre asked like an excited child.

"It's a *very* good sign. Very good."

"So, when is he gonna wake up?"

"I still can't answer that but, hopefully, very soon." The doctor patted Montre on the shoulder and exited the room.

"Jazz, I'm so proud of you. I'm going to go downstairs and call your mother since I can't use the cell phone in the hospital. I'll be right back."

Jazz heard Montre's quick footsteps followed by the sound of the closing door. Jazz could squeeze Montre's hand, but could not understand why he couldn't wake up. More than anything, he wanted to open his eyes.

He had no perception of time as he lay there. He didn't know how long he'd been asleep or how long Montre would be gone. So he waited.

Moments later, he heard the door open again and the sound of footsteps that came to a sudden stop. Then silence. Jazz felt as if he was being watched, and he listened for the sounds of movement. Then he heard the heavy footsteps move in his direction, then stop again. He felt as if some-one was toying with him, testing his reaction. He felt a presence in the room that made his spine tingle. He could feel his body involuntarily twitching in response to whatever force loomed before him.

"My son," the voice said in a soothing yet haunting tone. Instantly, Jazz panicked. His nightmare was again his reality. "I came to heal you and to bless you. My mercy and blessing will rain down on you like waters. And you will share with the world the glorious news of my return."

Now, more than ever, Jazz needed to speak. He tried with all his strength to open his eyes and open his mouth so that he could scream for help. He had to let the hospital know that this lunatic was lurking about the facility. He had to warn the world but the more he struggled, the weaker he felt.

He felt himself panicking and slipping into darkness again, but he did not want to be lost. He told himself to calm down. If The Messiah had wanted him dead, then he'd be dead by now, he told himself. He tried to steady his breathing so that he would not lose what little consciousness he had left.

Then Jazz felt the cold hands of The Messiah on his forehead. "Your faith has made you whole."

With those words, he stepped away from Jazz and moved toward the door. "Remember our covenant. Do not be weary or afraid of your task. If anyone is ashamed of me and my words in this adulterous and sinful generation, the Son of Man will be ashamed of him when he comes in his Father's glory with the holy angels."

A tear rolled down the side of Jazz's face from each eye as the door closed. Seconds later, it reopened and he stiffened again. His body could not stand any more emotional trauma.

"Hey, Jazz, I'm back. I ran into another doctor outside. He said you will be fine. Thank God," Montre said.

If only you knew, Jazz thought. *If only you knew.*

Chapter 5

Jazz rose from his coma on the third day.

It was a dark and damp Sunday morning. The menacing gray clouds rolled together in an ominous dance and the drizzle that fell to the earth covered everything with a fine layer of moisture. From the look of the clouds, it was only a matter of time before the drizzle became a deluge.

His first breath out of the coma took a lot of effort. He woke up suddenly and was overcome by the feeling of suffocating. In a frantic state, he shot straight up in bed and took a desperate and violent inhale that flooded his lungs with oxygen. However, the longer he sat upright, the easier and more relaxed his breathing became. Within minutes, his breathing normalized and the choking sensation faded.

As he looked around the room perplexedly, he felt as if he had suddenly been delivered out of a horrible nightmare. His mind was hazy and his feelings were discombobulated. It took him a few moments for his eyes to focus enough so that he could take in all of the details of his surroundings. He looked at the intravenous tube connected to his arm and all of the other machines in the small room. The memories of the nightmare he thought he had been delivered out of suddenly came rushing back to him in living color.

He relived everything.

The horror of his reality hit him with force. The images that pounded his head were so clear, so real, and so powerful that they almost knocked him back to the bed.

He remembered the encounter.

He remembered being aroused.

He remembered the smell of his stranger.

He remembered the danger.

Then he remembered the pain.

And the sound of the bottle colliding with his skull reverberated in his head.

The pain.

The degradation.

The voice of The Messiah echoed in his ears.

It was a sound that he could not escape and a sound he would never forget. The raspy coldness of The Messiah's voice sent chills up and down his spine. *Even at that moment.*

He remembered the handcuffs.

He remembered the sharp stone.

He remembered the pain.

He remembered the feeling of being cut.

He remembered praying to God.

As he recanted, he heard a voice in his head. *I have not forsaken you, my child. I am here to deliver you for I am the Father, the Son, and the Holy Spirit.*

Jazz trembled.

The hairs on the back of his neck stood on end as if danger had surreptitiously entered the stale hospital room. He panicked as he looked around the small, darkened space. He looked toward the bathroom when he heard sounds and saw a dull light emanating from underneath the old wooden door.

He listened to the sound.

Someone was praying.

Jazz's fragile heart raced.

He held his breath. He wanted to call out for help, but his voice abandoned him. He wanted to call for the nurse, but he was in the grip of a paralyzing fear. He could not move. Terror controlled him. Had The Messiah changed his mind and come back to finish off the job he started?

Maybe this psycho realized he had erred by letting Jazz live and now had come to rectify his error.

Thousands of chilling thoughts—each one more horrible than the one before it—filled Jazz's head. Tears began to fill his eyes, but he fought them back. He didn't want to make the slightest sound and feared even the falling of tears from his eyes would alert the interloper to his awakening.

The light in the bathroom went black.

Jazz listened, with heightened fear, to the sound of the turning knob and the creaking of the door—and the pounding of his heartbeat. The three disjointed sounds worked in tandem to intensify the dread that took refuge in his heart. Whoever lurked in that small room would soon be revealed. The seconds that it took for the light to dim and for the door to open wide were filled with fear and anxiety. Still, Jazz remained focused on that door.

There wasn't much else he could do. He was hooked up to all sorts of machines and he could not scream. He certainly didn't have the time to run out of the room, even if his legs were able to move. All he could do was wait. Wait to meet his fate. Wait to be sent to his maker.

The angst-filled seconds lingered far too long for Jazz.

Then Montre stepped out of the darkened room. He dropped the small black bag containing his toiletries to the floor and stared at his friend in disbelief.

Jazz let go of his fear and exhaled.

When Montre saw Jazz sitting erect in the bed and staring at him with wide eyes, he sent a silent "thank you" prayer to God for sending his friend back to him. Only moments ago when he stepped into the restroom, nothing indicated a change in Jazz. He lay there, motionless. As he had for days.

"Jazz," Montre said in an unsteady I-can't-believe-this-is-real voice. He could not contain the raw emotions that had collected over the last three days. Montre rushed over to the bed and touched Jazz's arm and felt the warmth of his skin, which put Jazz at ease. "I knew you'd make it. I knew you'd come back."

"How—ummm—" Jazz struggled to speak.

"No, don't try to talk now. Take it easy. I'll call the nurse."

Chapter 6

Gabriel spent most of the previous day in solitude, avoiding extended conversation, and opting to work out of his home instead of going into the office. He simply was not up to being around people. His run-in with Garrett had taken a lot out of him and some of the feelings that consumed him after Robert's infidelity had returned and shook his core.

He was brought out of his thoughts by the sound of the ringing telephone. He wasn't in the mood to speak to anyone, so he let it ring until the machine picked up. He listened to Garrett's message asking how he was doing. He mentioned that he was going to stop by later in the afternoon, but Gabriel wasn't ready to see him. He hadn't been able to rid himself of the thought that Garrett was seeing someone else.

Even though they were not exclusive, Gabriel couldn't help but feel a twinge of jealousy. He exhaled and as soon as the message ended, he walked over to the machine on the counter in the dining room and hit the "delete" button. He had two other messages and assumed they were from Garrett, since he hadn't taken any of his calls.

He walked into the kitchen and grabbed the half-pint of Ben & Jerry's Chunky Monkey Ice Cream from the freezer—it was his favorite comfort food. He pulled a spoon from the drawer and was ready to dig in when he looked down at the bulge underneath his white T-shirt. He sighed. *If I eat this, I'll go to the gym later today. It's about time I started using the membership I'm still paying dues for.* In his heart, he knew he wasn't going to the gym today. Or tomorrow. Or even the day after. But at least he thought about it.

On his way out of the kitchen, he hit the "play" button on the machine to listen to the other messages. He'd only heard the phone ring when Garrett called, but he guessed someone had called while he was soaking in the tub with the music blaring throughout the house. When the message started playing, he was surprised by a familiar voice that he hadn't heard in a while. It was from his friend and informant Faith Murphy who worked as a detective for the Metropolitan Police. Back when Gabriel was doing investigative reporting, Faith had supplied him with a lot of information regarding police investigations and gave him access to things he otherwise wouldn't have been able to view, including crime scenes.

"Gabriel, you need to call me back. I have some information that I *know* you want to hear. I'm at home and I'll be here all night." The message was left at 5:37 p.m. He listened to the second message, which was left at 9:13 p.m.

"Gabriel, I don't know where you are tonight, but listen to me. I think he's back—The Messiah."

Gabriel dropped his ice cream and leaned in closer to the machine so he wouldn't miss a word.

"There is a kid over at Medical Center who I think was attacked by The Messiah. His name is Jazz McKinney. Meet me there tomorrow at noon and we'll talk. And Gabriel, keep this on the low."

Gabriel suddenly wished he had answered his phone.

Listening to the tension in her voice caused Gabriel's heart to skip a beat. His breathing accelerated and a strange mix of fear and excitement gripped him. For a few seconds, he couldn't move. All he could do was stand and stare at the machine. He replayed what she'd said over in his mind. Had he heard her correctly? Did she say that The Messiah, the most notorious and vicious serial killer D.C. had ever known, had come back?

Gabriel quickly picked up the ice cream container and tossed it into the sink. His mind was racing and his thoughts were in overdrive. Could it be true that The Messiah has returned? If so, why? Why had he left? Why had he left a survivor this time? What happened?

There were so many things to consider. Gabriel leaned against the kitchen counter for a few seconds to collect his thoughts. Was this a nightmare or a dream-come-true? If he could somehow get the scoop on The Messiah it would definitely resurrect his career from the purgatory in which it lingered.

He thought about the nobility of once again having his articles featured on the front pages of local newspapers. If it was true that The Messiah had returned, there were few folks who knew more about him than Gabriel and that had to work in his favor, he figured.

Gabriel had devoted countless hours trying to get inside The Messiah's head in order to crack the case and reap the spoils of victory. He shuddered at his selfish thinking. At a time like this, how could he think about his career? A boy was in the hospital after what had to be a brutal assault and thoughts of the resurgence of his career was the most prominent thought he had. Even though he felt pangs of guilt at his thoughts, selfish motivation was usually at the heart of most good deeds. If he were to help the police catch The Messiah, surely he was entitled to some benefit.

He pulled himself out of his trance and dialed Faith's number. He got her voicemail and then tried her cell. Again no answer. He raced upstairs, taking them two at a time. He rounded the corner and darted into his bedroom to find something—anything—to put on so that he could get over to the hospital quick.

He saw a pair of old jeans on the floor and threw on an old black cotton T-shirt. In his mad dash around the room, he stubbed his toe on his bedpost and screamed out like a madman. The pain shot through his toe, raced up his leg, and brought him to his knees.

The pain was so intense that he thought he fractured his big toe, but even the thought of broken bones wasn't enough to make him forget about The Messiah. Gabriel knew that if Faith was correct, and she usually was, and he had returned, the pain he felt in his foot was miniscule compared to what was coming. The anguish this city would feel would be legendary.

As he rubbed his toe, his curiosity and nervousness delivered him past his pain. The Messiah had never left a victim alive and Gabriel knew that if this boy was in fact a victim of The Messiah and not some copycat attacker, then he had been left alive for a reason. But why? That he needed to find out. Had the boy seen the face of this killer? Or had the boy somehow escaped after a great struggle? Neither thought provided much comfort.

Chapter 7

Gabriel was in the car and driving down the slick city streets before he could even process what he would do or say once he got to the hospital. *The Messiah*. That's all he could think about. Those two little words occupied all of his thoughts. Those words rang over and over in his head and brought with it the knowledge that, if he had returned, this city was about to change. *If it's true, may God have mercy on us all*, he thought.

The rain that poured from the skies like hail pounded his windshield so hard that he suspected the next drop would crack the glass on his Ford Mustang. His wipers could not clear the water away fast enough to make the streets visible. He was traveling on a wing and a prayer. Gabriel took his hand and wiped away some of the fog that had gathered on his windshield so that he could see, but his efforts had little effect.

He peered through the streaks he left, hoping it would be enough, but the torrential rain was blinding. He wanted to pull over and give the rain time to subside, but he had to get to that hospital. He had to verify his fears. He had to know. He had to know why this boy was *chosen*.

Once he got to the hospital, he veered through the parking lot like a man possessed searching for that all-elusive parking spot that was close to the front of the hospital. He circled a few times but decided he didn't have the time to waste. He pulled into the next available spot that he saw—which was much farther than he would have liked—and threw the car in park.

He grabbed his cell phone and dialed Faith's number and hung up in frustration when her voicemail picked up again. The rain was still coming down in buckets and he didn't have an umbrella, but he couldn't wait any longer. He had to weather the storm. He opened the door and darted like an Olympic sprinter across the parking lot, leaping over puddles and pot-holes that had become small concrete lakes.

When he reached dry land, he was soaked and stood underneath the awning for a few months to collect his thoughts.

"Damn, this storm ain't no joke," a voice from behind him said. He looked over and saw a tall, thin black man with short dreadlocks dressed in a maroon smock and blue jeans looking at him.

"I left my umbrella at home. I guess it pays to check the weather," Gabriel replied.

"Looks like you could use a towel. It's cold as shit in the hospital and with that wet shirt you got on you gonna get sick."

"Well, that's just my luck."

"If you come to the fifth floor, I'll get you a towel."

"Really?" Gabriel spoke in a surprised voice. He wasn't sure what he had done to elicit such kindness from a stranger, but he wasn't about to turn it down. From his style of dress, Gabriel surmised that the man worked in the hospital and his offer sounded like music to his ears.

"Sure. I can't leave a brother hanging. I'll be up in about ten minutes. You can meet me by the nurse's station in the back." The man reached into his pocket and pulled out his cell phone. "I gotta make a quick call."

"Sounds like a plan, man."

Gabriel excused himself and walked through the automatic double doors. "Excuse me," he said once he reached the visitor's desk. "I'm here to see a patient."

"Patient's name?" the receptionist asked with a smile.

"Uh, McKinney. Jazz McKinney." Gabriel didn't want to pull out the slip of paper on which he jotted down the name after Faith left it on his machine.

She typed the name into the computer and looked up suddenly. "Are you family?"

"Yeah, I'm his brother," he lied easily.

"Well, I'm going to need to see some ID." She pressed her lips together and waited for Gabriel. He reached back but didn't feel his wallet. He then remembered that he never picked up his wallet. He could see it still sitting on the nightstand where he always kept it.

"Shit, I left it at home. I got a call that he was here, and I rushed right over in the rain."

"I can't let you into the hospital without some identification—you know, security policies."

"Please, Sheila," he said, reading her nametag. "He's my brother. I need to see him."

She looked at him skeptically. Gabriel wore a desperate expression on his face. He ran through a thousand things to tell her to get her to soften her stance. He thought about flirting with her or killing her with kindness. As he thought, she stared up into his distraught face.

"What you need to do is dry off," she said. "Take this badge and go to the restroom before you get pneumonia."

Gabriel was about to get an attitude when he looked at the visitor's pass she handed him on the sly. It had a room number on it. He smiled at her and she smiled back.

"Thank you," he whispered.

Without hesitation, Gabriel marched through the hospital. He wanted to ask someone where the elevators were located, but he didn't want to bring any undue attention to himself. Besides, elevators couldn't be too hard to find. As he walked, he caught a glimpse of himself in the glass and realized he looked a mess. The nurse was correct: he did need to dry off.

He took a quick detour into the restroom and tried to do something with his wild hair. It was wet, so he slicked it back with his hands, but the tiny curls would not stay put. As he looked at himself in the mirror, he could see the Italian traces of his father's ancestry in his face and remnants of his mother's distinctive Afro-Caribbean lineage. Gabriel always protested when people thought he was of Spanish descent, but looking in the mirror, he could understand people's confusion. His honey-colored skin and brown eyes gave him the appearance of a Brazilian model.

Once he stepped off the elevator onto the seventh floor, he became slightly queasy. It had been some time since he had been in a hospital, but it never failed that each time he stepped into the sterile environment, he had a physical reaction. He hated everything about hospitals, including the sights, sounds, and the smells.

He followed the signs to room 731, carefully avoiding eye contact with teary-eyed visitors, while walking quickly down a long corridor that eventually dead-ended into two rooms. An armed guard with bulging biceps sat in a chair against the wall reading the newspaper. Right above his head was a sign that read 731. *Damn*, he thought. His mind raced as his tried to devise a scheme to get past the gargantuan guard. He had not been brought all this way, through the pouring rain, only to be stopped at the gate. He needed to get into that room. He needed to see for himself. But the guard didn't look as if he was going to merely wave Gabriel into the room.

Gabriel didn't want to draw attention, and he wasn't ready to approach the guard because he didn't have a plan. *How could I have not been prepared for this?* he asked himself as he slowed his approach and took an unplanned turn down an aisle. Protection for the man made perfect sense. How could he not have protection? The police would have been extraordinarily derelict in their duties if they had allowed the only survivor of a serial killer to remain unguarded.

In his rush to get to the hospital, he didn't think about the obstacles that would be in his path, but the dedicated journalist in him certainly wasn't about to let a few unexpected barriers block his path. He had come too far too soon to be turned away. He had to find a way—he knew that he could.

As an investigative journalist, he was used to making a way out of no way to get a story. He'd have to call on that ingenuity now. As he bypassed the nurse's station, he feigned the kind of worried smile appropriate for a concerned relative who was visiting an ill family member on that floor. A group of nurses engaged in heavy conversation were in the middle of a shift change and barely took notice of Gabriel. The hospital floor was scattered with people with long faces and sad expressions. A group of people had gathered in the corner to comfort a grieving woman whose low sobs were turning into muted wails while two young children played carelessly nearby.

Gabriel took particular notice of a small-framed elderly man who listened intently as a doctor explained the conditions of his wife. Gabriel tried to not seem as if he was eavesdropping, but something drew him to the conversation. He studied the man's expression and demeanor in case he suddenly had to call upon his acting skills. Gabriel watched as the man brought his hand to his mouth in order to muffle his gasps. The doctor's facial expression did not change, but the old man's face was completely covered with pain.

With the hustle and bustle of the busy hospital and the comings and goings at the nurse's station, Gabriel's presence didn't raise any eyebrows. His fake smile did catch the attention of a nurse who had grabbed her purse and walked out from behind the station. She exhaled audibly and made her way toward the elevator in a hurry. Gabriel wanted to catch up to her, but didn't want to make it seem obvious. All he could think about was getting into that room to speak to Jazz McKinney, and he hoped she'd provide some information.

He needed to get into that room so that he could see for himself if the damage to this boy was the work of The Messiah, but he also wanted to know what to expect when he got into the room. Was the boy conscious? How badly beaten? The worst thing Gabriel thought he could do was walk into the room with a shocked look on his face if the boy was conscious.

He reached the elevator at the same time as the thick nurse, who pushed the button for a down elevator. She reached back and pulled a clip out of her hair and shook her blonde shoulder-length locks. She looked at him and smiled. Gabriel smirked. She looked as if she wanted to say something to him, but opted to keep her silence instead. From the look on her face, Gabriel surmised she sensed his uneasiness. Discreetly, Gabriel searched her face. As he studied it, he noticed a few subtle lines in the corners of her eyes, but overall she had a kind face and a warm energy.

When the elevator door opened, Gabriel held his head low and started shaking it back and forth.

"Are you alright?" she asked as she reached out and touched his shoulder.

"No, not really, but I'll be alright," he said between fake sobs.

"You sure? Is there something I can do for you, sweetie?" She rubbed his shoulder as a way of comforting him.

"Well, I was out of town and found out my brother was in some kind of attack. I'm not sure what kind of condition he's in and don't know what to expect when I walk into the room."

"Who's your brother?"

"His name is JP—I mean Jazz. I call him JP, but his real name is Jazz. Jazz McKinney."

"Oh," she said with concern.

"That doesn't sound good."

"No, it's not that. I'm one of the nurses on his floor and he is actually recovering nicely. I can't imagine what that poor boy went through."

"What do you mean?"

She looked at him curiously. "Has anyone told you anything?"

"No, I got a voicemail from my sister saying I needed to get over here, and now I can't find her and I don't know what to do." Gabriel was surprised because he managed to really call up some fake tears that time. Gabriel laid it on thick, and she seemed to believe every word he spoke.

"Sweetie, he's going to be fine. He's been through a lot, but the worst is behind him. He's out of the coma, and all his vital signs look good. He's actually speaking now."

"So, I won't gasp when I walk into the room? I'd hate for him to see my expression and have a relapse."

"You'll be fine. And your brother will be fine. In fact, he has a friend in the room with him now."

"A friend?"

"Yeah, I think his name is Montre. Do you know him?"

"Nah, I don't know all of my brother's friends."

"He definitely needs you now. This is a time for families to come together." She patted him on the shoulder and gave him a quick nod as the elevator door opened and she stepped out. Before completely exiting, she hit the button for the seventh floor to send Gabriel back to meet his "brother." "You can do this," she said as the door closed.

Gabriel smiled at his cunning conversation. *He still had it.* He had found out the basic information he needed to know and all he had to do was quickly devise a plan on getting past King Kong who guarded the door. And he had to be prepared for the other person in the room with Jazz.

When the elevator doors opened on the seventh floor, the hospital presented a solution for him; it was lunchtime. He looked down the hallway and saw service workers dressed in maroon vests and jeans beginning to distribute trays of food to each room. Huge gray metal food carts, which had four rows across and ten rows down, were placed at stationary points throughout the corridor.

Gabriel watched one worker grab a tray of food from a row and walk into each room, only to return empty-handed. The workers were making their way down the long hall, but it would be a few minutes before they reached Jazz's room. A light bulb went off in his head, but he'd have to act fast. He turned around to face the elevators. He had to get to the fifth floor.

Once on the fifth floor, Gabriel scoured the hallways for about ten minutes and was about to give up the search until he saw the man from outside coming out of a linen closet.

"Hey, man," Gabriel called, realizing he didn't get the man's name earlier.

"There you are. I thought you got lost."

For the first time, Gabriel noticed a strong, southern accent that elongated the man's short words. "Actually, I did," Gabriel lied.

An awkward silence filled the next few seconds as they stared at each other. Gabriel wasn't sure what was going on. He didn't get a gay vibe from the man, yet, here they were standing in the middle of the hallway, gazing at each other like schoolboys. Although Gabriel did find him attractive, now was not the time or the place for such an encounter.

"Oh, let me get that towel for you." The man turned and reached for the door of the room he had exited.

"Wait a second," Gabriel said and he instinctively reached out and grabbed the man's arm. "What's your name?"

"You can call me Teddy."

"Teddy, I'm Gabriel. Out of curiosity, why are you being so nice to me?"

Teddy gave him a perplexed look and smiled. "You D.C. folks are a trip. Can't nobody be nice to y'all up here."

"Where are you from?"

"Alabama—Huntsville."

"Ah, a Southern gentleman. I was trying to place your accent," Gabriel said with a wide and coy smile, while deciding to turn up the charm. Gabriel knew that his smile often drew people to him, and he decided to use it to his advantage. "Well, living in D.C. for any extended period of time teaches you to be cautious. I figured since you were being so nice, you *had* to want something."

"Yea, and that's sad. But I didn't say I didn't want anything *from* you," Teddy joked and entered the room. Gabriel laughed and followed him. The door closed behind them.

"Listen, Teddy, I have another favor to ask."

Teddy's eyebrows raised in curiosity.

"My little brother was admitted the other day, and I want to surprise him and make him laugh."

"Okay. Wassup?"

"This may sound strange, but I was wondering, well, if I could borrow your vest for a minute so I could deliver some food to him?"

"You want me to take off my clothes, don't you? It's okay, you can admit it." Teddy laughed, obviously amused by his comment.

Gabriel looked into his eyes and smiled. Teddy was an attractive man, but Gabriel wasn't trying to get involved in anything. He could hear Scott's voice in his head admonishing him for getting involved with a food service worker.

"Maybe later." Gabriel winked.

"If I gave you my vest, you know, I could get into trouble."

"What if I promised to give it right back to you?"

"What if I came by your place and got it from you later tonight?"

Gabriel had to admit that he liked Teddy's style, and he was flattered.

Even his Southern drawl was sexy. Gabriel smiled and took a pen from his pocket and wrote down a number—a wrong number.

"Okay, you have my number. Now, can I have what I want?" Gabriel flirtatiously asked.

✝✝✝

Once back on the seventh floor and dressed in his new uniform, Gabriel adjusted himself in the smock and approached a lunch cart casually. Luckily, the food crew had moved in the vicinity of Jazz's room so his actions wouldn't be viewed as out of place. He took a tray of food, shifted again. He still felt uncomfortable in his new garb but tried not to let it show too much.

He grabbed a small carton of apple juice and a container of strawberry gelatin to go along with the meal. Then he walked toward Jazz's room, trying to look as if he knew what he was doing. Once he approached the room, the guard near the door looked up at Gabriel, but did not say a word. He scowled a bit, but he was far more interested in his newspaper than he was about any visitor who approached. Gabriel walked past him and into the room without raising any suspicion. *So much for security*, he thought to himself.

Gabriel stood quietly in the back of the small space and observed the scene. He breathed quietly so as to not disturb the stale hospital air. He scanned the room for traces of any person since the nurse indicated that Jazz had a friend in the room. He saw a leather backpack draped across the chair in the corner, but whomever it belonged to was nowhere in sight. Slowly, he turned the knob on the door of the bathroom and opened it, but it was empty. Gabriel knew he didn't have much time, so he walked closer to the bed and placed the tray of food on the table at the foot of the bed. He approached Jazz cautiously, not wanting to alarm the frail, bandaged figure.

Gabriel stared at him as he slept and wondered how much he had endured at the hands of his attacker. Gabriel eyed his swollen face and blackened eyes and imagined the deranged fists of a maniac inflicting serious bodily harm on this young man.

What happened that night? he thought.

Gabriel eyed his battered face and tried to imagine what he had looked like before the attack. Even through the lumps and cuts on his face, Gabriel ascertained that Jazz was an attractive man. He imagined what his broken features had looked like before his unfortunate episode with The Messiah. Analyzing him deeper, Gabriel couldn't determine if there was something distinctive about his face or body that would indicate he had been let go for a reason. He appeared common enough. Maybe he had simply escaped.

Gabriel could not see the totality of his injuries because he was covered by a matted beige blanket. If he lifted the blanket, what would he see? Gabriel was suddenly overcome by a feeling of grief laced with terror at the thought that The Messiah was once again loose in the city. Who would stop him?

The weight of Gabriel's gaze caused a slight movement in Jazz and he began to stir in his hospital bed. Gabriel froze, not sure what he would say or do if Jazz suddenly regained consciousness. Part of him wanted to flee because he wasn't as prepared for this moment as he thought he was. But the consummate journalist in him had to speak with this man who lay before him.

"Who—who—are ya?" the young man asked in a groggy, almost incomprehensible voice as he opened his eyes slowly. "Whar is Montre?"

Gabriel could hear the concern in Jazz's voice and wanted to place him at ease before he became agitated. The last thing he needed in his weakened condition was agitation. "Take it easy," he said in a soothing voice. "My name is Gabriel. I don't know where Montre is, but I'll find him for you. I'm sure he only stepped out. When I came into your room, it was empty. I brought you some food." Gabriel pointed at the tray of food on the table.

The young man looked down at his hands and Gabriel realized he would need help feeding himself.

"How are you feeling?"

"Ha do ya think I feel?" he replied through painfully swollen jaws.

Gabriel watched the tremendous effort Jazz put forth to simply speak. A movement so simple in nature was a struggle for him. He spoke out of the right side of his mouth, only because the swelling on the left was too great. He turned his face away from Gabriel and looked toward the window. "Mirow?"

"Excuse me?"

"Mirow," Jazz said again.

Gabriel strained to understand his slurred words, but finally understood. He looked around the room, on the table, and in the closet in the corner of the room. Finally, he walked into the bathroom and returned with a mirror as Jazz had requested.

Gabriel held the mirror up to his face without thinking twice. He looked horrified, then closed his eyes and turned his head away from his wretched reflection.

"Sow much fo modeling," he mumbled.

"You know this will pass," Gabriel said, trying to be supportive. "These injuries, your face—all of this will pass. Before long you'll be out of this hospital reliving your life and all of this will be a distant memory." Gabriel, realizing there wasn't much else he could say to comfort him, reached out and gently stroked his arm. He felt a kindred spirit to this shattered soul, in spite of the fact that they didn't know each other and he had been in the room for less than five minutes.

Gabriel could not believe his luck. He had expected another food handler—a real one—to bring Jazz a tray. He assumed that the guard outside had informed the person that someone else had already entered with one. Thank goodness there was some disorganization happening in the hospital. That and the nature of humans to be lazy and happy to get out of any task—even one as simple as having one less tray to carry.

The young man looked at Gabriel as Gabriel looked at him with sympathetic eyes. Gabriel came to the hospital with the motive of the rebirth of his career. He *needed* this story. He imagined getting the scoop from Jazz before he had an opportunity to tell someone else exactly what happened, but the more he looked at this feeble young man, the more distant he felt from his original mission.

Instead of siphoning the details of his tragedy, he found himself in a place to offer comfort to someone who really needed it. His response to him was far more human than he had anticipated. He found himself wanting to comfort this man for no other reason than it seemed he needed it. Thoughts of glory and fame faded from his head. Gabriel reached down and took the young man's hand into his.

"Where is your family?" Gabriel asked after several moments of uneasy silence.

"No family."

Gabriel was able to discern his words without a struggle this time. He quickly adjusted to the slurred speech.

"Can I ask you a question?" Gabriel asked, staring at him. "What happened? Who did this to you?"

The young man's body stiffened and the physical response to the question told Gabriel that he was not ready to yet speak about the events of that night. "I'm sorry. I didn't mean to pry." Gabriel stood up slowly and walked over toward the window and opened the curtains so that he could view the rain. He gazed off into the dreary distance. As far as the eye could see, storm clouds covered the sky in deep, gray rolls. From the seventh-floor window, he could see people scurrying about the streets trying to find shelter from the hard rain. Gabriel wanted to say something profound to help the young man in his time of need, but only one thing came to mind.

"When I was seventeen," Gabriel began, "I took my first trip to New York City as part of a high school class trip. I don't think I was ever more excited about going anywhere in my entire life. I remember standing in the middle of Times Square and falling in love with the sights and sounds. I didn't care that the streets were overcrowded or that people were rude. Hell, I didn't even care that a Big Mac was like five dollars. All I knew was that I had arrived and the city was more wondrous than I had ever imagined.

"Later that night, after we had done all of the touristy stuff like seeing Wall Street and the Statue of Liberty, I decided that I was going to sneak out to see the *real city* while my classmates slept. All the tourist attractions we'd seen didn't give me a true sense of how the natives lived. I wanted to see the small, eclectic neighborhoods and find the really trendy places. So, I snuck out of the hotel around one in the morning and took a cab to the West Village." Gabriel looked over at the young man, searching for something in his eyes to let him know it was okay for him to finish his story. The young man stared back blankly, and Gabriel turned back to the window and continued talking.

"Anyway, I didn't know where I was going or what I was going to do when I got there. All I knew was that I wanted to go. After the cab driver let me out, I started walking. I'm sure I had a big, stupid grin on my face like most out-of-water tourists do. I must have walked for ten blocks before I finally stopped and asked this guy on the corner what was there to do in that area. I remember the look on his face. I'm sure he could smell my ignorance. He told me there was a cool bar down the alley and around the corner.

"The thought of going to a real-life New York bar gave me butterflies. I was too excited to protest when he told me to follow him down this alley. I didn't give a shit that I wasn't old enough to drink or that they might ask to see my ID when I got there. I figured that if I could find the spot, then I could charm my way in. And the strange part is that this guy had this smile on his face like he really wanted to help me.

"I remember following him down this alley and getting a weird feeling in the pit of my stomach. I started walking faster so that I could get out of the alley. Up ahead, I could see lights and a few people walking by laughing. I remember seeing this young, Asian lady walk by carrying a red purse. It's funny the things you remember. Before I knew it, he turned around and punched me in the face. I started swinging and landed a good blow to his nose, but the next thing I knew, someone from behind hit me in the back of the head and I went down—hard. They—I don't know how many—started kicking and punching me and didn't care that I was scream-ing. Nobody seemed to care. They beat me so badly that at some point I was unable to scream."

Gabriel paused for a second. The rain had started to let up, but the darkness of the day remained. "As I lay in the alley, the man who I asked for help spit on me and then pissed on me. I couldn't imagine what I had done to someone that they would beat me and then piss on me."

The shame of that night still weighed heavily upon Gabriel. He could feel his cheeks getting flushed and turning red.

"I remember lying there on the ground, moaning and feeling something warm being sprayed on me. It wasn't until after they left that I really realized what he had done to me. I wanted to die. I almost did."

It had been years since Gabriel had thought about what had happened to him. He bottled it up and rarely let the emotions out, but this time he couldn't prevent the tears from welling in his eyes. "I still have a scar above my right eye."

"That's fucked up," the young man spoke with unexpected clarity.

"I tell you that story because I survived. I want you to know that you will survive this, too." Gabriel wiped the tears from his face before he turned around. He wasn't accustomed to crying and certainly didn't want this stranger to see his tears. When he looked at the young man, it reminded him so much of what he had gone through. A few years earlier, in another city, it was him in that bed. "The police were never able to catch the attacker. I guess it really didn't matter because once I got out of the hospital, I came back to D.C. I haven't been to New York since. But I survived. And so will you."

In the moments that he had relayed his story, he felt that he had connected with the young man. As they looked at each other, they recognized a familiarity with each other. The longing for understanding that seemed to fill the young man's puffy eyes connected with a triumph that lingered within Gabriel.

"One day, when you're ready, I hope you'll talk to me about your experience. You can't keep it bottled up. I want you to know that I'm here for you." Gabriel reached onto the table and grabbed a pen. He took a napkin from the food tray and scribbled his name and number on it. He placed the paper on the table nearest the young man. "If you ever need to talk."

"Who are you?" the young man mumbled.

"I'm a friend," Gabriel replied and smiled one last time before he headed toward the door.

"Wait. I'm Jazz."

"Okay, Jazz. I'm Gabriel."

"Will you come back to see me?"

"Only if you want me to." Gabriel placed his hand on the doorknob.

"The man who attacked me—he called himself The Messiah. That's all I remember."

Gabriel shuddered. Although he had prepared himself to hear that, the words still landed hard upon his ears.

Chapter 8

On the drive home, the last words Jazz uttered continued to rattle in Gabriel's head. His biggest fear turned out to be true—the monster had returned. He wasn't sure what kind of impact it would have on the city or his career, but he knew everyone would feel the presence of fear like a black shadow lurking over their shoulders. Thunder again shook the blackened skies as rain began to pour with fury. It was as if heaven itself was sending a warning.

By the time he reached his red-brick townhouse, the rain relented a bit. He pressed the garage door opener and drove into the structure as thoughts of The Messiah flashed before him. He was so distracted that he almost drove into the wall, but slammed on his brakes in the nick of time to avoid causing any damage.

He walked slowly into his house as rough sounds of the garage door closing behind him filled his ears. He walked immediately into his bar area and took a seat on one of the red high-back barstools. He leaned back and rubbed his hands through his moist hair. He needed clarity, but it escaped him. He felt numb, as if all of the feeling suddenly was drained from him. If he allowed himself to feel the terror lurking in his heart, he would have a panic attack.

He got up and moved over to the cabinet where he kept his liquor. He grabbed a bottle of gin, a cocktail glass, and opened the refrigerator. He took the ice tray from out the freezer and twisted it until the ice cubes popped up. He grabbed two cubes—he always used two—and dropped them into the bottom of the small glass, then filled it with gin to its rim before adding a splash of orange juice. He hadn't drunk much the last few months and when the cool liquid hit his throat, it burned going down; he liked the feeling. It was far more palatable than the thought of the return of a serial killer.

He walked into his living area and plopped down on his sofa and turned on the television. He was drained. This news was far too much for him to process in one sitting. He thought about Jazz in the hospital and wondered where The Messiah was now and if he was tormenting someone else.

Gabriel was probably more familiar with The Messiah than most. During the height of the madman's last terrorization, Gabriel obsessed over the case and searched through hundreds of pages of police files and records that Faith had given him access to in order to discern a pattern or some other commonalities with this killer. The crimes were so brutal that they shocked the conscience.

As he reminisced, he realized that he needed a distraction, so he picked up his phone and called Garrett, but his voicemail picked up. As he held the phone in his hand, he realized he was smiling again. Maybe his insecurities were rooted in his past relationship with Robert. He didn't want to punish Garrett for another man's mistake, so he had decided to forgive Garrett about his airport fiasco after all.

He still couldn't believe that Garrett was cracking his defenses and breaking into his heart. After the horrible way in which they met, and after all of the attitude Gabriel had given him in the beginning, he was surprised that Garrett stayed in it with him long enough to actually reach Gabriel. Most men would have cut and run after the second date.

✝✝✝

Gabriel sat back and thought about their first real conversation and date. When he'd met him that evening at the doctor's house party, he never imagined that the same kind soul that stayed by his side while he suffered his panic attack, would one day become his lover. He was skeptical of such overt kindness initially, but after their first date on a dinner cruise that lasted well into the wee hours of the morning, he realized something about Garrett that set him apart from all of the other men he'd ever dated: Garrett was interested *in* him; not what he could get *from* him.

The television show he had tuned into broke to commercial and brought his thoughts back to the present. He sat up from the couch and tried to plan his next move. He felt compelled to check on Jazz to make sure he was okay; he couldn't explain why he felt so connected to the young man, but he wanted to help him through his experience. But he also needed to have more conversations with him so that he could get the story.

At some point, he'd have to have a detailed conversation with his editor to let him know that he was working on a story that would shock and awe, but he wasn't ready for that either. All he knew was that he was tired of covering fluff. The Messiah was big news, unlike the birthday party thrown by one of the Washington Wizards that he covered the other night.

He knew that covering the madman's horrid crimes would certainly propel him back into the spotlight, but would his editor trust his judgment and instinct? He needed to speak with Faith so that he could have access to police records and thoughts about the crime in order to present findings to his boss, who would definitely need some convincing from him. His boss had been burned once before and Gabriel was certain he wouldn't be eager to jump back in the frying pan on his behalf.

He picked up the phone to call Faith but didn't hear the standard dial tone.

"Hello?" he said into the receiver.

"Hey, handsome. How are you?"

"Garrett?"

"Yes, it's me. Did you forget about me already?"

"Of course not. In fact, I just called you but figured you were busy doing rounds."

"I was, but I wanted to break up the day's monotony by calling my baby. Please tell me that you still are."

Gabriel sighed. He was happy to hear from Garrett, but he was certainly getting tired of tracking him down.

"Yes, Garrett. I am," he said plainly.

"Well, that's good to know," Garrett said while ignoring Gabriel's emotionless tone. "Can I see you tonight?"

"I'm not sure. Something big has come up with work, so I'm not sure what my schedule is for tonight, but I'll let you know."

"You aren't still mad at me about the airport thing, are you?"

Gabriel sighed. "No, I'm not mad, but I'm…disappointed. It doesn't feel good to be forgotten like yesterday's news."

"Baby, please know that I am so sorry and it will never happen again. I assure that you were never forgotten, but when emergencies come up at the hospital they can steal my attention."

"I know you're a dedicated emergency room physician and I understand the nature of the work, but it still hurts."

"Well, I'm going to make it up to you in grand fashion, if you let me."

"Yeah, I guess."

"Is there something else wrong?"

Gabriel folded his arms and rested the phone between his head and shoulders. "To be perfectly honest, yes. When I got to your house yesterday morning, you were acting very strange and I got a weird vibe that I hadn't gotten from you before. It felt like I had caught you in the act—"

"The act of what?"

Silence.

"Gabriel, what did you think you walked in on?"

"It was early in the morning, I hadn't heard from you all night, I get to your house and your sheets are on the floor like you were hiding something—like you wanted to wash away evidence of him."

"Him? Him who?"

"I don't know. Whoever he is that you were with that made you forget to pick me up at the airport."

"Baby, I promise you. I am not seeing anyone else. It's only you."

"Look, it's okay if you are. I mean, we aren't committed, we're only dating, right?" Images of his old lover, Robert, flashed through his head: the lies, the excuses, the infidelity.

"Yeah, but that was your idea. I'd commit to you in a heartbeat, if you'd let me."

"I'm sure."

"Baby, don't be like that. I promise you, I was not with anyone else. The last two months have been wonderful for me and I really think we have a crazysexycool kinda thing going on here and I would seriously hate if this one small incident caused you to not trust me or see me differently. I never would do anything to hurt you. I couldn't live with myself."

Gabriel listened to the passion inflected in Garrett's desperate-sounding voice, whose tone was imbued with worry and anxiousness. In spite of what happened, Gabriel believed him. He wanted to let go, to run over and kiss and hug Garrett, but old demons made it hard for him to do so. *Garrett is not Robert. Garrett is not Robert.* "Look, don't sweat it—just don't let it happen again. I'd hate for you to feel my Scorpio sting," he said playfully.

"That doesn't sound so bad to me," Garrett said flirtatiously.

"You so nasty."

"I want you to know how much I'm feeling you."

"And I'm feeling you too. I don't want you to give me any reason to distrust you. And we can't commit to each other because we still have a lot of learning to do about each other."

"I realize that you're right, but I don't need a lot of time. When I'm around you or look into your eyes, I know. I know. I feel very differently about you than any of the guys I've dated over the past year or so."

Gabriel smiled. "That's good to know. And Garrett, thanks for the call."

"Let me know as soon as you can about tonight, okay?"

"Sure. Enjoy your day."

Gabriel hung up the phone and noticed that he had an erection. It wasn't his typical random hard-on, but one that was brought on by specific stimuli: Garrett. Gabriel shook his head and could not deny that he was excited by, attracted to, and aroused by Garrett. In spite of his feeling of apprehension, he smiled again.

Chapter 9

Before walking into the Fifth Precinct on New York Avenue, Gabriel took a second to catch his breath. He wanted to talk to Faith, face-to-face, before he went into the office and presented his story idea to his editor. He had called her several times, but kept getting her voicemail so he decided to go to her office and wait. This was far too important to his career and to the city to not be certain. He couldn't afford another blunder, and he had to make sure what Jazz had told him was the truth. He needed some sort of police confirmation.

He walked into the busy room nervously, as if he had committed a crime himself, and proceeded over to the counter. Through the six-inch thick glass that separated the police officers from the public, he could hear several telephones ringing all at once and watched as officers scurried about the room as if they were on serious *Missions: Impossible*. A stereotypical, out-of-shape, balding police officer sat in a chair behind a glass pane, with a black phone pressed to the side of his face. The officer continued his conversation and did not bother to look up to acknowledge his presence. Gabriel stood there patiently for five minutes before the officer hung up the phone.

"May I help you?" he asked uninterestedly as he shuffled a pile of papers from one side of the table to the other.

"I'm here to see Faith—I mean—Detective Murphy."

"Do you have an appointment?"

"No, but she's expecting me." The officer looked at Gabriel with incredulity seeping from his eyes. He paused momentarily, just enough to make Gabriel uncomfortable, before picking up the phone to dial her extension. Gabriel nervously shifted his weight from one leg to the other. He knew he should not have shown up at her job. If someone recognized him and saw him talking to Faith, they might surmise that she had been leaking information to him.

Gabriel took a few steps away from the window and looked down at the ground. Behind him, a commotion was brewing. A rather vocal woman with dirty blonde hair and a sagging pink leotard was talking to a burly-looking officer taking notes.

"That bitch came over to my house acting like she was all that. I told her to get out of my damned face, but she rolled up on me like she was the baddest bitch. So, I punched the ho and then it was on and poppin'!" she yelled proudly. Right as she finished her sentence, the door to the station opened and in walked a thick Hispanic woman with lipstick smeared all over her face accompanied by another officer.

"I'm gon' kick yo ass, bitch!" the Hispanic lady shouted before sounding off a string of what Gabriel gathered were Spanish curse words.

Faith walked through a protected door near the glass partition while Gabriel was caught up in the Jerry Springer drama of the day.

"Walk with me," she said as she passed by Gabriel, barely acknowledging his presence. It took him a few seconds to come out of his gaze and realize what was going on. He looked ahead of him and saw Faith marching through the lobby of the police station, her shapely legs complemented by the blue skirt she wore. Gabriel followed the quick tapping of her high-heel shoes as they hit the hard floor.

He followed her outside, to the side of the building, and into the parking lot. She put her key into the door of a blue Malibu and got in. Gabriel paused momentarily until she motioned for him to get into the car as well. Hurriedly, Gabriel followed her cue.

"What the hell are you doing? Trying to get me fired?" She put the car in reverse and backed out of the parking spot before hitting the streets.

"Where are we going?"

"Away from here. I can't risk having anyone see me talking to you."

"I'm sorry, but I needed to talk to you and you haven't returned any of my calls."

She took a deep breath and gripped the steering wheel tightly. Her freshly permed, shoulder-length hair swayed as she looked away from Gabriel as if she needed a moment to gather her thoughts. Her chestnut skin glowed in the light; outside of the red hue that colored her shapely lips, she wore very little makeup.

"Look, I went to the hospital and I spoke to Jazz," Gabriel began.

"Really?" her face softened, only slightly, as she turned toward him. "Did he tell you anything?"

"Yes," Gabriel said as he leaned toward her. "He told me he was attacked by someone calling himself The Messiah."

She cocked her neck back suddenly as she felt the force of his words.

"Damn. That's more than he's told us. In fact, he said he didn't know who attacked him when I interviewed him. How did you get him to talk?"

"Well, I have my ways. He didn't say much, but that much he did tell me."

"He actually said it was The Messiah? How does he know it was The Messiah?" Faith's perfectly arched eyebrow above her left eye raised in anticipation of Gabriel's response.

"He told me the guy said he was The Messiah," Gabriel said with some frustration. "I'm sure the kid is not making this up."

Faith sighed and took a random left at the next corner. Gabriel studied her face and could tell that she was deep in thought.

"What are you not telling me?" he asked her. She looked at him and shook her head. "Come on, Faith, tell me. What's going on here? I need some information so I can take this to my editor. Faith, I really need this story."

"And I really need to catch this guy. Gabriel, you know I want to help you, but there is a serial killer running around the city and that is far more important than getting a story. We are looking at the return of a killer who has been quiet for months. Where has he been? What has he been doing? Shit, who knows what he's going to do next?"

Gabriel took a deep breath. He had never seen her so bothered by a case before, yet, he knew that she held more information.

"Faith, I understand what this maniac is capable of. We have to let people know that he's back. It's a safety issue. You can't withhold this information from me."

She looked at him intensely as they waited at the red light. "We don't have much information—no witnesses, no DNA samples, nothing. The rain washed away any trace of evidence that was on the victim. Shit, we don't even have a statement from him. You know more about what happened than we do. But—"

"But, what?" Gabriel asked anxiously.

"Last month, I received this note." She reached into her pocket and pulled out a piece of paper that was protected by a plastic sheet. Gabriel looked at the crooked, almost chaotic, cutout magazine letters that were glued indelicately to a grease-stained piece of paper:

I am the Light of the world. He who follows Me will not walk in the darkness, but will have the Light of life.

"That's from John 8:12," she said. "Pay attention to the note. You've seen the other notes that he sent. With the other notes, he took time and care to make sure that the note was neat, but not this time. It's almost as if he's angry and out-of-control."

The words *out-of-control* rang inside Gabriel's head. *Wasn't he always out of control? Anyone who would brutally murder six people is definitely out of control.*

"The Messiah is back. What's to come next really scares me. I wish I had something more. All I know is we have to stop him before he harms anyone else. The department is mobilizing the special task force created months ago. We can't let this city be held hostage by him again." The concern weighed heavily in Faith's voice and caused it to wobble a bit.

Gabriel stared vacantly out of the window, not sure whether to run for the hills or to stay for the fight.

"My suggestion would be to go back to the hospital and speak to the victim again. Maybe you can get some more information out of him."

"The Messiah has never left a victim alive. Why do you think he did this time?"

"The only reason I can think of is to send a message."

"A message? To whom?"

"To us—to the world," Faith replied flatly.

Chapter 10

Before arriving at the hospital, Gabriel called his editor and left him a message indicating that he would be in the office in the afternoon and that he urgently needed to speak with him about an important story. His message, however, did not convey any real sentiment or emotion about what he had recently discovered. He knew that in order to get the story, he'd have to cut off his emotions and do his job and the sooner he became detached, the better. He couldn't afford to feel sorry for Jazz—or any other victim that would inevitably surface. He'd have to focus on the task at hand.

As he walked down the long corridor on the seventh floor, he smiled nonchalantly at the nurses and hospital staff as he passed them by. He wasn't sure what he was going to say to Jazz, but he knew that he had to convince him to trust him enough to open up about what had happened to him. He had to get the story.

When he approached the door, the armed guard—different from the one he previously encountered—immediately stood up and impeded Gabriel's progress.

"May I help you?" he called out in a booming voice before Gabriel could get too close. Gabriel abruptly stooped his forward march.

"Hi, I'm Gabriel. I'm a friend of Jazz's."

The guard's hardened face did not soften. "Is he expecting you?"

"Yes, I was here last night."

The guard picked up a clipboard and ran his fingers down the sheet. "What is your last name?"

"Kaine, but you won't find me on the list. The guard last night didn't have me sign in."

"Well, I don't know how they do it at night, but every visitor is required to show ID and to sign in," he said. Gabriel reached into his back pocket and pulled out the tattered tan wallet Robert had given him years ago. He pulled out his driver's license and handed it to the guard whose face seemed to be stuck in a permanent scowl.

The guard took the license, stared at Gabriel and then back at the identification card. "Sign here," he said as he shoved the clipboard into Gabriel's face. After he signed, the guard took the clipboard back and dropped it into his plastic chair. "Wait here," he commanded.

The guard turned and disappeared into Jazz's room. Gabriel hoped and prayed that he would be remembered by the patient. Gabriel made room for the possibility that Jazz had forgotten his visit because he was sure that the doctors were keeping him well medicated.

"You can go in," the guard said from around the door before Gabriel actually saw his body.

Gabriel smiled and walked around him, then stepped cautiously into the room. He was surprised to see Jazz sitting upright and using a remote control to flip through channels on the TV mounted to a corner wall.

"I see you're feeling better," Gabriel said.

"A little bit—what a difference a day makes." Jazz tried to force a smile but lingering pain obviously forced him to abandon the effort. "I wasn't sure you were going to come back. Thanks," he said in an appreciative tone.

Gabriel still had difficulty understanding his slurred speech, but he concentrated a bit harder. "Where is your buddy?" he asked as he moved a hat off the chair so that he could sit.

"He went to class."

"I hope I'm not interrupting anything."

"You're not. He was getting on my damned nerves, askin' how I'm feeling, am I in pain? How the fuck does he think I'm feelin'? I look like a fucking freak, I'm in this damned hospital, and if somebody else asks me what happened I'm going to fuckin' kill them!" Jazz's temper flared, but even in the heat of his words, Gabriel knew that he wasn't angry at his friend or the nurses who expressed concern. Through all his machismo and chest thumping, Gabriel knew he was simply afraid.

"They're only asking because they care."

"Fuck that." Jazz tuned into the television and flipped through the channels with rapid speed. One mindless program after another one flashed across the screen.

Gabriel sat back in the chair and wondered how he'd get him to open up. What would it take for the real story to come out? "Have the police been here today?"

"They're always here—asking me the same stupid fuckin' questions."

"What have you told them?"

"The same thing I tell everybody—I don't remember."

"Is that true?"

Jazz shot a quick look at Gabriel that said "back off," which let Gabriel know he was lying.

For fifteen minutes, no words were exchanged. The empty silence seemed to calm Jazz, who continued to flip channels. Gabriel secretly watched his face and knew that Jazz was deep in thought and not paying much attention to the images that flickered across the television screen.

"When you were attacked in New York, how did you get over it?" Jazz slowly turned his head toward Gabriel, who wasn't entirely prepared for the question.

Gabriel paused and took a deep breath as memories of the attack surfaced. "I tried to forget. I did everything I could to forget. More importantly, I tried to convince myself that it had never happened. I felt so stupid. I felt that I deserved what happened to me for putting myself in that situation. So, I bottled everything up and shut down emotionally."

"Did that work?"

"Hell no," Gabriel said emphatically. "No matter how I tried to forget, there was always something there to remind me. Sometimes, it was a pair of passing eyes of some stranger on the street. Or it was a certain sound or smell. Being hundreds of miles from New York didn't help either, because

I carried the attack with me. It wasn't until I really dealt with it that I was able to live with it. You never forget." Gabriel turned his body toward Jazz and leaned in closer. "You know, you can tell me whatever happened. You can't keep it bottled up inside. It'll kill you."

Just as Jazz was about to speak, they heard a commotion outside the door. Elevated voices carried harsh words through its crevices. The sounds filled the room and demanded attention and acknowledgment. Gabriel looked at the door, then back at Jazz, then back at the door before rising from his seat. He marched with due haste to the entrance and yanked it open.

"Who are you?" a female voice called out. Gabriel looked to his right and then to his left to be sure she was speaking to him. The guard stood between a woman and the door to Jazz's room. "You let him in there, but you would deny access to his mother? Do you hear me? That is my child lying up there in that hospital bed."

"Ma'am, all you have to do is show me your ID and sign here. You cannot enter his room without proper ID." The woman took a step back and flung her coal-black hair over her shoulder. She looked at him, almost as if in disbelief, before reaching into her gold Gucci purse. "I bet you went through a lot of training for this job, didn't you? How long did you go to rent-a-cop school?"

"You can say what you want, lady, but you still won't get into that room until I see your ID." The calmness of the guard's demeanor only infuriated the woman more, who produced her ID and tossed it to him. The guard calmly picked it up, looked at it and then at her. He handed her the clipboard and told her to sign her name, which she reluctantly did.

"May I see my child now?" she asked as she tapped her foot impatiently on the floor. Gabriel had stepped back into the room but heard the guard tell her to wait. Seconds later, the door opened.

"You have another visitor. She said she's your mother. Shall I let her in?" Jazz grunted but finally acquiesced.

"I'm going to give you some time with your mother. I need to make a phone call anyway."

"Gabriel, please come back. I can't be alone with her too long."

Gabriel smiled and exited the door as the sassy lady walked in. She brushed past Gabriel with her nose in the air and didn't acknowledge his presence when he spoke to her.

"My poor baby," the lady screeched as she brought her well-manicured hands to her chest. "What have they done to my poor baby?" Her heels clicked on the hard linoleum as she made a beeline toward her son. She dropped her purse in the chair and Jazz kept his eyes closed, not ready to acknowledge her presence. But when he felt the cold touch of her hand on his forearm, he opened his eyes.

"Hello, Jazz," she said softly while stroking his head. "How is my baby doing?"

Jazz didn't respond.

"Hello, Mother," he said plainly.

"What happened? How are you?" Jazz remained silent and tilted his head in the direction of the window. It had been almost a year since he had laid eyes on her and seven months since they had last spoke. He wasn't sure how to react to her or what she wanted, but he decided to indulge her a bit. He hoped guilt was among the many emotions she felt. "Your stepfather is worried about you. He sends his regards."

"If he's so worried, why didn't he come?" Jazz slurred again. "He probably thinks I got gay-bashed."

"Don't be silly."

"Why are you here, Mother?"

She took a step back, as if his question offended her motherly sensibilities. "Where else would I be?"

"Montre told me he called you two days ago. Where have you been?"

"As I told that little Montee—"

"Montre, Mother. His name is Montre, and you know that."

"Darling, I don't want you working yourself up over this. As I was saying...," she turned from him and started pacing the room, "I just found out. Montre left a message on our home machine, but your father and I were out of town. We had a church convention in Houston, but as soon as I got the message I rushed here. But don't worry about anything now. Mother's here."

The nurturing sound of her voice irritated Jazz. He wanted to ask her where this concern was coming from all of a sudden. He didn't remember her sounding concerned when her husband—his stepfather—cast him out of the house and onto the streets.

"Give it a rest, Mother."

"Jazz—"

"You show up here, out of the blue, and pretend to care about me? You've never cared about me."

"Now, Jazz, you know that's not true." She stepped back.

"You care more about him than you do your own child, otherwise you wouldn't have let him throw me away." Jazz sat up in the bed and looked at her. "And stop that damned pacing!"

"Watch your tone, young man. I am still your mother."

"You haven't been my mother in years."

She took a deep breath. "I admit that I have made some serious mistakes, but that was so long ago. Your stepfather has made some mistakes and you, Jazz, have made some mistakes. Nobody's perfect."

"You've made some mistakes? Is that all you have to say? Mother, I called you a few months ago and asked you for some money to help pay my tuition and you never called me back."

"I know, I know. I meant to, but—"

"But what?

"I—"

"Shut up. You care more about that man and being the first lady of that church than you do me. You let him throw me out onto the streets with no-where to go while you were sleeping on five-hundred-thread count sheets."

"We can't change the past, baby. If we could, I would have gladly traded places with you."

"Fuck you," Jazz said, his venomous words piercing the walls.

"Jazz McKinney! I can't believe you said that to me. Do you think it was easy raising you? Do you think you were a model child? I have agonized and suffered because of you."

"Nobody asked you to suffer. That was your idea. I'm sure it was your guilt."

Jazz watched his mother turn on her heels and stare at herself in the mirror that she pulled out of her purse. He wondered if she could look in her own eyes and see her own wretched soul. Part of him felt guilty for saying the things he had. After all, she *was* still his mother. But the other part of him had to free himself from the pain he had kept bottled up for so many years. Between his past grief and the shame of his current situation, he had to let something out. And, unfortunately for his mother, he was letting it out on her.

"Well, pardon me for caring," she replied as she dabbed the corners of her eyes to wipe away tears that Jazz was skeptical were real. As she reached in her purse and pulled out a handkerchief, she backed into the doctor who walked into the room. "I'm sorry. I didn't see you there, doctor. I'm Rebecca McKinney, Jazz's mother." She extended her hand to the doctor and he shook it.

"Nice to meet you, Mrs. McKinney. You must be ecstatic that your son is recovering so well. Two days ago we weren't even sure if he was going to wake. And look at him now," the doctor said, pointing to Jazz as if he were some animal on display at the zoo.

"Tell me, doctor," she began again, "are there any permanent injuries?"

"All of the tests we've run have shown no indication of that. We still want to keep him here for another twenty-four hours, but if we don't see anything, I don't see why he can't go home with you tomorrow."

The thought of having to endure her and his stepfather did not sit well with Jazz. He hadn't had time to think about where he'd go once he was released from the hospital. He wasn't sure if he would be allowed to go back into the dorm because of liability issues. And even though he had improved significantly, in his heart, he knew that he needed some care.

"Doctor," he mumbled, "can I speak to you...alone?"

His mother looked at him disappointedly, but eventually grabbed her purse and exited the room in a huff.

"I wanted to talk to you about what happened to me—you know, the circumcision." The doctor stepped closer to Jazz. "Will I be able to—"

"Don't worry about that. You'll be fine. Now, I won't kid you. You will experience varying degrees of soreness for a couple of weeks—maybe longer. And as much as you can, you should avoid getting an erection."

"How am I supposed to do that? Sometimes it just happens."

"I know, but you need to avoid all sexual stimuli because getting an erection will be painful and may cause the stitches to break."

"Oh shit," Jazz mumbled. He turned his head away from the doctor.

"Oh sorry, I didn't know you were with the doctor," Gabriel said as he stepped back into the room.

"It's okay. I was about to leave, unless you have some more questions," the doctor said to Jazz, who simply shook his head.

"Is he alright?" Gabriel asked inquisitively.

"He will be. He's a strong young man. He'll be fine." The doctor patted Jazz on the leg and made his way out of the room.

"I can leave if you need to be alone," Gabriel said.

"Why would someone do this to me?" Jazz asked suddenly.

"Some people are just sick." Gabriel's response rang hollow. He wished he would have said something more. He wished he could provide the definite answer to Jazz's question. He wished he had the insight into the nature of man to explain away all of the madness of the world. But, he didn't. All he could offer was hope. "The police will catch the asshole and put him under the jail when they find him. Rest assured."

"He came to visit me—here, in the hospital."

Gabriel froze. His blood ran cold. Jazz's words took him completely by surprise.

"Who?" Gabriel asked although he didn't need to.

"The Messiah."

"What? When?" Gabriel tried to calm the fright in his voice, but it took on a life of its own. "How did he get in here? Did he hurt you? Where was the guard?"

"He came the other day when I was in my coma." Jazz stared at him. "I know what you're thinking. You think I'm losing my mind. You think I must've been dreaming, but I wasn't."

"Jazz—"

"Look, man, I know how it sounds. I sound like a fucking lunatic, but I'm not."

Gabriel lowered himself into the chair at his bedside.

"While I was in the coma, I could hear everything that was said about me. I don't know when he came, but he did. He told me that by 'faith I am healed' and I felt his hands on my forehead."

Gabriel didn't know what to make of Jazz's confession. Could he have been correct? Could The Messiah have used chicanery to slip past the guard unnoticed, just like he had? He suddenly felt beads of sweat forming on his head.

"And," Jazz continued, in a low, weightless voice, "that night, when he was attacking me, he had black wings—you know, like a crow." Gabriel's face twisted with incredulity and he waited for the punch line. Surely, Jazz was joking. *Black wings*?

Jazz, deterred by the look he had on his face, seemed hesitant to continue his story. "Don't look at me like that," he said agitatedly. "I know how all this sounds. I'm not crazy. Never mind."

"No, don't stop. I'm listening."

Jazz remained silent.

"Your body has been through a lot of trauma. It's possible that you were seeing things that night."

"How do you explain his visit here in the hospital?"

"I can't. Are you sure he was here?"

Jazz did not verbalize a response, but from the look on his face, Gabriel could not doubt the strength of his conviction. "Okay, if you're sure, then you need to tell someone. You could still be in danger. My friend is on the police force. Let me call her for you." Gabriel pulled his cell phone from his pocket and pretended to dial Faith while he pondered what Jazz had told him. There was no way he was going to his editor with a story about a serial killer man with black, crow-like wings. No way. He even began to wonder whether or not he was wasting his time with Jazz. But one thing was for sure: something awful had happened to Jazz and someone just as awful was responsible for it. He had to find out who that was.

Chapter 11

The Messiah kneeled in a protective circle of stones in his damp and dark cell beneath the earth, his knees pressed against cold cement as he entered his third consecutive hour of prayer. Blood oozed from his knees and stained the floor as he rocked back and forth in a trance. Sweat poured down his naked frame as if he were worshipping in hell. He was lost in a meditative state, where images conjured by his deranged mind had life and were made flesh.

He saw fallen angels all around him, circling him, preying on him, tempting him. They pulled at his flesh and chanted in a scatting language that sounded like unrestrained shrieks. The longer he prayed, the more they tormented him. They attempted to pull him out of his carefully constructed circle of protective rocks. In between their harsh language, he heard melodies from heaven, which gave him strength to endure and carry on. He prayed harder because he knew that 10,000 angels sheltered him while he was confined to his mortal body.

Then he was on a mountaintop.

He was so high up that he felt as if he could view the entire world. Below him, he saw wondrous valleys and heard beautiful streams and mighty rivers. Flowers of bright oranges, iridescent blues, magnificent purples and sunshine yellows banded together to create a perfect kaleidoscope of sight. He looked all around him at the greenest grass that jetted up from the hillsides around him. The sun was brighter and more splendid than he had ever seen and the purified air smelled almost...holy. Doves and bluebirds flew about the earth as the warm breeze carried butterflies about the land.

"You are pleased?" a voice called out to him. He looked around him but did not see anyone. "I can give you all of this and more." He looked to his left and saw a bright image slowly come into view. Before him stood the most spectacular angel of them all. The angel had a divine smile, his arms outstretched in a welcoming gesture. He was dressed in a brilliant white robe that was sprinkled with diamonds and gold flakes. On his head, he wore a crown. "Does this please you?" he asked in a voice that spread out in all directions as he stepped forward. When he spoke, the grass and trees leaned in his direction as if they struggled to be nearer the source of energy and light. Each step he took sounded like thunder, but the sound did not convey fear; it conveyed power. "Look around you. Look at the majesty of this world. All of this I will give to you. I will place the world at your feet, if you so desire."

"At what price?"

"Join me and rule at my side."

The Messiah remained motionless as the angel walked toward him. The angel struggled to reach The Messiah, walking faster and more furiously, but he could not conquer the distance. He could not reach The Messiah. "Why do you do this? Let me be near you. Let me give you the world."

"You have been cast out once before. You cannot tempt me with what is already mine," The Messiah replied.

As soon as he spoke the words, the angel opened his mouth and let a shrieking screech escape that caused the flowers and trees to quake in despair. The flowers shrank back down into the earth and the trees toppled over as the streams and rivers dried instantly. The noise ravaged the land and rolled down the valleys, eradicating every living thing. Birds and bees fell out of the skies and landed with thuds against the hillside. The beautiful face of the angel was lost as he was transformed into a hellish creature that defied description.

Then everything went black.

The Messiah toppled over onto the hard rocks in his cell. He looked around him. He had survived another attack.

Now it was time to save another soul.

✝✝✝

"Let me go, you fuckin' bastard!" the young redhead screamed as trickles of blood seeped from the corners of her cracked mouth. "You son-of-a-bitch!" Her words filled the room with fear and force. He circled her, in his naked splendor, but did not let her curses affect the work he had been chosen to perform.

She would be blessed this day.

"You are a wicked, wicked woman. You have committed the sins of harlotry and succumbed to lust. You must repent your sins in order to enter the Kingdom of Heaven." His heavy words sounded rhythmically like war drums on the horizon. Her hands were bound behind her back and she was tied to a metal pole that rose from the floor.

"What are you talking about, you freak! Let me go!" Her cries fell on callous ears.

For weeks, Sabrina Dean had been caught up in a whirlwind, illicit affair with the wife of her husband's best friend. They had started out working on a church fundraiser together, but the many long hours had turned friendship into desire and co-workers into lovers. Their affair started with an impish wink, then an accidental brush of her arm against her chest, and soon their clandestine gazes evolved into a full-fledged affair, complete with deception and desperation. Their passion rose high and fueled desires within her that she hadn't known for years.

The Messiah had studied them in church for weeks. From the moment he saw them together, he sensed that all was not as it appeared. He could smell the sin on them. It stained their fancy dresses and expensive suits. Moral decay oozed from their pores like the foul stench of a sewage plant and lodged in his nostrils, prompting him to cough each time he was in their presence. He *knew* of their affair, even if no one else did.

From the way she crossed her legs and shifted when she walked by to the uneasiness in the other's eyes when they all gathered to exchange Sunday afternoon pleasantries at the end of service, the Messiah could tell. It was in their eyes and in their voices—their affair was rotting the church from the inside out and he knew that he had to cleanse them. He had watched them like a hawk, out-of-sight, but always around like a living shadow.

"What comes out of a man is what makes him unclean. For from within, out of men's hearts, come evil thoughts, sexual immorality, theft, murder, adultery, greed, malice, deceit, lewdness, envy, slander, arrogance and folly. All these evils come from inside and make a man unclean," he said, stressing the word *adultery*. "My child, I know all about your sins of the flesh. There is no shelter from your sins. There is no fig leaf large enough to cover your brazen nakedness. I know all about your adultery and your lies to your husband. You are unclean."

Her eyes threatened to bulge out of her head, apparently shocked that her affair was not the secret she thought it was.

"But, fear not," he started again. "I come to cleanse your blackened soul and make you whole again. I come to welcome you into righteousness. Will you repent your sins, my child? Come into my bosom and let me hide and protect you from the enemy."

She looked upon him and trembled. "I don't know what you're talking about, you goddamned monster!" she said in stark defiance of her current predicament.

"Do not blaspheme the Lord's name with your wicked tongue, Jezebel. You are unclean," he said matter-of-factly. "I will cleanse you." He turned away from her, disappeared into the blackness, and then returned quickly. Sabrina screamed loudly and wildly as a sudden exquisite pain engulfed her. The Messiah dropped the bucket of hot water he was holding and eyed her oddly as she cried out in pain. Then he filled the bucket with cold water and doused her again in an attempt to "alleviate" her suffering. There was something about her screams that excited him sexually. Maybe it was the fear. Or the pain. Or the sorrow. Whatever it was, it enticed him. He eyed her reddened flesh and imagined touching her before he brought himself out of his lustful state.

"I rebuke thee," he said, speaking to some unseen force. "Get out of here, black bird!" he screamed and ducked as if avoiding the beak of a bird of prey. "I rebuke thee!"

Then he stopped and stood quietly, and gazed at Sabrina as if nothing had happened. "Let us pray."

His piercing eyes contained a mixture of pure madness tempered with concern for her soul. He then began chanting and circling her again. She knew—beyond all doubt—that there was no reasoning with her kidnapper. She could tell from the way his body contorted as he circled her that he was void of rational thought. Her pain relented, replaced by a choking terror; yet, she became inexplicably transfixed by his carefully orchestrated maneuvers around her.

His body popped and twisted and bent in ways that almost defied human explanations. The sound of the cracking of his body as he twisted and turned burned in her ears. In composed moments wedged unnaturally between his antics, he jerked his body upright, directly in front of her, his smile as wide as oceans, and prayed. His eyes vibrated from side-to-side in small, rapid motions as his Biblical exaltations filled the air. Then, he lost himself again in his ritualistic ballet and began to circle her once more. He was completely given to the moment—to a higher power—and he continually asked for the strength to save her immortal soul.

"For the wages of sin is death, but if you confess with your mouth, Jesus is Lord and believe in your heart that God raised me from the dead, you will be saved!" he yelled over and over again.

"Okay, I believe! I believe! I'll do whatever you say. Please, let me go," she pleaded. Her voice was heavy with fear and desperation. She shook her head wildly before wailing uncontrollably. Her mascara ran down her tear-stained face, leaving crooked black lines down her white face. Her dirty blonde hair, now partially matted on the side of her head, was blood-stained red from the blow she had received to the back of her head during her abduction.

"Then pray, my child. Ask for our Lord God to forgive you of your sins. Give yourself freely and willingly, and you shall be made whole again."

"Please, please, God, forgive me. I am so sorry for sinning against You!" she sobbed between tears in a broken voice as she submitted to The Messiah's will. He stopped his march directly behind her.

"You are forgiven," he said calmly before slitting her throat and watching the warm blood ooze down her neck and body before forming into a pool by his feet.

He had found his peace.

Her body, bruised and battered, was found hours later in the Potomac River.

Chapter 12

Garrett woke up disoriented and naked, lying on the warm concrete surface near his swimming pool. Startled, he shot up and looked around the area. The night was still and quiet, not even the sounds of crickets could be heard. The moonlight reflected off the blue water of the pool, but the picturesque scene was shattered by the thought that he had no idea how he got there.

Instinctively, he reached for his nose. He felt dried blood.

He dashed toward the house, eager to shield himself from the world. Even though the rugged concrete hurt his feet he did not slow until he approached the sliding glass patio door. All of the lights were on and a note was taped to the glass—a note in his handwriting. When he was close enough, he read the note out loud:

Gabriel is on his way.
Food is cooking on the stove.
Take a shower.

This can't be happening. Not again. He snatched the note from the door, balled it up, and threw it into the trashcan once he entered the room. The scent of exotic spices filled the air while Garrett took rapid breaths. He paused for a few seconds and scanned the den. It was quiet. He cupped his face with his hands and tried not to panic. He didn't know how long he had been out, what day it was, or exactly when Gabriel would arrive but he knew that he didn't have a lot of time to ponder. He raced out of his den toward the kitchen.

Stuffed Cornish hens baked in the oven and asparagus simmered on the stove. An expensive bottle of wine that he had been saving for a special occasion chilled in a bucket on the kitchen island. Garrett stood in the middle of his kitchen, confused.

What is going on?

This was new. In his previous blackouts, he usually found some unfamiliar object, but nothing like this. This escalation shocked him beyond words.

Then he remembered that Gabriel was on his way. He turned the oven onto warm and removed the asparagus from the eye of the stove. He knew that he needed to clean himself up. As he darted through the house and up the stairs he realized his knees were sore and when he reached his bedroom, he looked down and saw little stone fragments embedded in his skin, but he could not recall how they got there. He started to panic. Not again, not another episode.

Once in the bathroom, he noticed that he clutched a lock of blonde hair that was stained red—blood-red. Hurriedly, he threw it into the toilet and flushed it down the pipes. He rushed over to the shower, turned the water to hot and stepped in, hoping the heat would cleanse him. Within minutes, steam clouded the room and began to relax him. He grabbed his body bar and lathered up.

He didn't want to think about what had happened. He could only focus on the fact that he had suffered two blackouts and disappearances in three days, and that unnerved him more than waking up outside—naked.

His spells had never come so close together. Until now.

As he lathered and scrubbed furiously, flashes of a tortured face assaulted him.

He could hear her screams.

He could see her pained face.

He could smell the blood.

So, he scrubbed harder hoping the images he saw were left over from a bad dream or remnants of some horror movie he had seen months ago that had seeped into his subconscious.

The more he washed, the more those images came into full view. He could see her tied to a pole. He could hear her voice pleading for her life.

Then, he saw a knife and he remembered the gurgling sounds she made when her throat was split and her blood was spilled. After that, everything was blank.

"Surely, I didn't do that," he thought out loud as he remembered the hair he flushed. "Dear God, what have I done?" He leaned against the tile of the walk-in shower and soon slid down to the floor as the warm water poured over his body. He pulled his knees into his chest and buried his face. Fear, shame and confusion clouded his head. He knew that he was not capable of such an atrocity, yet, everything within him told him that the flashes he saw weren't dreams, but memories. *His* memories.

He thought long and hard and tried to call upon what had happened after the woman was killed. He saw the knife slit her throat and her head fall, but he could not remember doing it, nor did he remember anything until he woke up naked. He struggled to bring forth the other details, but his mind was blank. He could not see who had actually killed the woman and he took comfort in the thought that it was not he who had cut her throat.

He pushed the thoughts out of his head as he realized that Gabriel was on the way. He had to focus on the evening and not let these crazy thoughts show on his face. As he stood up and turned the water off, he heard a voice in his head that wasn't his.

"I am He."

✝✝✝

As Gabriel drove through Garrett's exclusive neighborhood he could not help but be impressed by the homes; each one seemed to be more fabulous than the one before it. Even though he had been through the area several times, he never ceased to be awestruck.

Once he got to Garrett's spacious palace, he pulled slowly toward the metal gate and reached out to press the button.

Seconds later, the gate slowly opened and welcomed Gabriel into Camelot.

He drove up the winding driveway until he reached the top. Garrett's Dodge Magnum was parked next to a silver 7-Series BMW and a white Range Rover.

"Welcome, baby," Garrett said in overly dramatic fashion when Gabriel reached the door. He stepped forward and kissed Gabriel on the cheek and gave him a strong hug as if they were lovers who had been separated for years.

"Damn. Are you excited to see me?" he asked, laughing.

"What are you laughing at?"

"Oh, nothing, just you wearing that apron." Garrett did a little twirl in jest so that Gabriel could take in the full view. "You look almost good enough to eat."

"We'll save that for later. Come on in, silly."

When Gabriel stepped fully into the grand lobby of Garrett's home, he smiled wildly like it was the first time he had been there. The home was far more impressive on the inside than the outside. He looked around to take in all of the sights. Wonderful abstract paintings covered the walls and in each corner sat a Romanesque statue. Light music drifted into the foyer from the other room. Gabriel heard a heavy, yet very recognizable, voice singing words of a troubled world.

"I'm glad you got the flowers and took me up on the invitation." Garrett took Gabriel by the hand and led him into the den. "Make yourself at home."

"Is that Mahalia Jackson?" Gabriel asked curiously.

"Yeah. Sorry, I forgot to turn that off." Garrett grabbed a remote control, pointed it at the stereo, and ceased the soulful singing.

"It's not often you hear a man listening to Mahalia Jackson."

"Music is good for the soul. My grandmother used to play Mahalia all the time when I was a child. I guess she was hoping to save my soul. I wasn't the best-behaved child around," he said with a giggle.

"Were you the bad seed?"

"You have no idea. If I told you some of the things I did as a child, you'd think I was one of Bebe's kids."

"Damn, that bad, huh?" Gabriel casually strolled around Garrett's den.

Every time he came to Garrett's house, he felt out of place, as if his presence would disrupt the order of things. The white leather couch and chaise lounge looked very expensive, almost too expensive to sit on. If they had been in Gabriel's grandmother's home, the sofa and lounger would have been covered in plastic. He eyed the fireplace and all of the religious trinkets that adorned it. On the mantelpiece were ceramic figures of angels, and people on hands and knees praying. A colorful painting of The Last Supper hung about the fireplace.

"What's that smell?" Gabriel asked as he spun around on his heels to face Garrett. He needed something else to focus on.

"Well, I decided to cook for you. I left the hospital early because things were slow, and that gave me enough time to prepare something special. Now, I must warn you, this meal is not for the faint of heart. It'll put a little meat on your bones."

"Trust me, I have enough meat on these bones," Gabriel said, pulling on his shirt, then suddenly becoming self-conscious about his weight.

"Gabriel, you are absolutely gorgeous. I love every curve of your sexy body," Garrett said as he eyed Gabriel's body and licked his lips. "All these anorexic boys out there can't hold a candle to you. You are all man, and that's what I like about you." Garrett's words certainly boosted his self-esteem.

"Well, thank you. By the way, what's on the menu, maestro?" he asked, trying to shift the focus off of him. He still hadn't grown accustomed to Garrett's compliments.

"It's a surprise. Let me get you something to drink."

"And make it a double, Antandra," he said, imitating Jennifer Lewis in the movie *Jackie's Back*.

Gabriel plopped down on the sofa and noticed a magazine rack on the floor between the couch and a lamp. As he thumbed through the stack to find one he wanted to read, he noticed each magazine was religious in nature. Garrett had many magazines, but there wasn't a single *Ebony*, *Jet*, *Essence*, *Upscale* or *Clik* magazine—not a single publication that dealt with popular culture. There were no sports magazines, no cooking magazines, no music magazines, except for *The Gospel Music Chronicle*. Frustrated, he got up from the seat and strolled around the room. He walked over to the bookshelf and casually browsed the selections. Once again, each book had a religious theme. Gabriel looked at the bookshelf curiously and counted six Bibles.

Why didn't I notice this before?

He picked up one of the Bibles and opened the cover, which was stamped:

ANTIOCH BAPTIST CHURCH

"Would you like to hear some music?" Garrett called out from somewhere in the distance. Quickly, Gabriel closed the book and returned it to the shelf. "Sure. What do you have?" *If he puts on Yolanda Adams, I'm going to scream.*

"Check out the CDs over in the corner by the sliding patio door."

Gabriel walked over to the CD rack and perused the vast collection of CDs, struggling to find something subtle and sexy, but all he saw was gospel music. He took a step back and thought about the oddity. The few times he had been to Garrett's home, they usually ended up upstairs, in bed, watching television. Garrett hadn't given him the impression that he was heavily religious, but he surmised there were many other things about Garrett yet to be discovered. *A man with a soul.*

"Here's your drink," Garrett said in a voice rich in bravado and texture, slightly startling Gabriel. The sounds raced up and down Gabriel's spine as he reached over Gabriel's shoulder and handed him the glass. Gabriel felt a familiar fire from his voice.

"Thank you. I never knew a man could be so sexy in an apron," he said, eyeing Garrett.

"Well, eat your heart out, G. Garvin."

"Um, I couldn't find any music to listen to. What else do you have besides gospel?"

He walked over to the table and picked up a remote, pointed it at the wall and it made a low rumbling noise as it parted, revealing a high-tech stereo system and many more CDs. "This is my main system. I had the other music on while I was cooking. What are you in the mood for?"

"Don't ask me that," Gabriel said with a coy wink and smile. "Surprise me."

In an instance, the slow sounds of Topaz—one of Gabriel's favorite local jazz artistes—echoed throughout the immaculate home.

"Topaz! You get points for this. You know how much I love her!"

"Dance with me."

"Excuse me?"

"Dance with me," he repeated as he removed the drink from Gabriel's hand and set it on a nearby table.

"I haven't—"

"Shhhhhh," he said and placed a finger on his lips. Garrett took him by the hand and pulled him into the center of the room. Sweet melodies floated from the stereo as Garrett pulled him closer into his massive frame. He put his hands firmly but gently around Gabriel's waist. Gabriel looked into his eyes and tried to breath him all in. He suddenly felt protected and needed and loved and desired. All those other issues melted away. Their mutual embrace was full of promise, and Gabriel felt so at home in his arms. Their bodies, pressed against each other, swayed tenderly back and forth as their hips moved in time with each other's rhythm.

When Garrett's soft lips touched his neck, Gabriel almost surrendered every defense and pretense he ever had in that one moment. Every wall he had erected, every barrier, and every protective fence almost came crumbling down. *Almost*. He felt himself losing control and getting caught up in the whirlwind of emotions. This man had all the answers and all the power. Up to this point, they'd only spent a few nights in bed watching movies but had never had intercourse. Gabriel thought about sweet surrender and giving in to the moment, but backed away.

"Wow, that was some dance," he said as the song faded.

Garrett stood before him, a smile on his face, seduction in his eyes, and held onto his hands. "You don't have to run from me. I won't hurt you," he said.

"That's what they all say."

"Are you afraid of me?"

"Not at all. I'm afraid of *me*. You make me want to forget all of the heartache and pain I've been through. You make me want to *feel* again and that scares me. I've spent the better part of the last year locked inside myself, protecting myself from men who lie and cheat and hurt. I can't be hurt again. I can't allow myself to go through that. I almost didn't survive the last time."

"You know you deserve to be loved. You are spectacular and any man would be grateful to have you at his side." Garrett released his grip. "But you've got some decisions to make. You've got to decide if you can open yourself up."

"What if I can't?"

Garrett sighed. "Whatever happened in your past—with whatever man—has changed you, and we all have our personal pain. But at some point, you've got to decide to live again. I mean, how much control over your life do you want to give someone who has hurt you? Do you want to allow them so much power that they keep you from experiencing the most wonderful joy on earth? I read somewhere that great love always requires great risk."

Garrett spoke with such passion and conviction that Gabriel felt compelled to re-examine his life. Garrett was right: how much control should he give Robert over his life? The damage had already been done and by keeping love out of his heart, he was the one who was suffering. Robert had moved on a long time ago. Gabriel was beginning to feel as if it was his time to live and move on.

"How do you do that?"

"Do what?"

"How do you know exactly the right things to say?" Gabriel stepped back close to Garrett and grabbed him by the waist.

"I don't. I simply say what my heart tells me to say."

In that moment, Gabriel started to build his dreams upon the light in Garrett's eyes.

†††

After dinner, Garrett enticed Gabriel upstairs to his master bedroom.

"I meant to ask you a long time ago why does a single man need all this space?" Gabriel asked as they stood on the balcony. Below them, a huge swimming pool reflected the moonlight and the patio looked like it belonged at some expensive hotel. Gabriel looked beyond the pool to the grove of trees in the back that swayed gently in the summer breeze. In the clearing, he could see a dilapidated structure that looked out of place, given the rest of the well-maintained property.

"Hopefully, I won't be single for long," he said. Garrett wrapped his arms around Gabriel's waist and kissed the back of his neck.

"I want you to look up at the sky," Garrett said suddenly.

"What?"

"Seriously, look at the sky and how wondrous and perfect it is. It is truly one of the most amazing things."

Somewhat reluctantly, Gabriel focused on the sky adorned by perfect diamond-shaped droplets of light. He suddenly felt small and insignificant, as if his worries were petty compared to the power of the universe.

"Do you really think that perfection is happenstance?

"What if I told you that I wasn't sure?"

"Then I'd say you haven't been paying attention. Okay, now, I want you to close your eyes and open your ears."

Gabriel turned and looked at him curiously.

"Just do it."

Gabriel complied.

"If you listen closely, not only can you see evidence of God, but you can hear it. Let yourself go and listen to the night. I mean, really concentrate. Listen to the silent night. Have you ever wondered what's behind the silence?"

Gabriel took a deep breath and decided to do as he was asked. For the first time in his life, he listened to the night. The simple sounds he had taken for granted for years now came through in Dolby sound. It wasn't even the crickets or the sounds of an occasional car that struck him. It was the sound of the night itself.

"Did you hear it?" Garrett asked with glee. "The night speaks to us all—we just don't listen."

Gabriel opened his eyes and looked at Garrett. "I feel very…calm," he said slowly.

"God is a calming force. All you have to do is listen and walk in what God has spoken for you."

Chapter 13

"**I** know who you are," Jazz said as Gabriel stepped casually into the hospital room. It was a little past nine in the morning and Gabriel's coffee buzz was beginning to kick in. The morning sunlight shone majestically through the window on a perfect summer morning. He stopped, gazed oddly at Jazz, and then moved closer to his hospital bed. Jazz sat almost upright, with the bed at a ninety-degree angle, folded his arms tightly and looked directly at Gabriel, who was taken aback by the sudden glare.

"What?"

"Don't *what* me. You think you're slick, coming in here acting all concerned about me. You had me going for a while—I admit that, but I ain't that stupid."

Damn. Gabriel blew the rising steam from his cup of ginger tea and took a seat while avoiding Jazz's scornful eyes. He shook his head and took in a deep breath before he could look at Jazz again. The swelling of his face had begun to diminish and, for the first time, Gabriel was able to make out the prominent features of Jazz's once proud face.

"Listen, Jazz. It's not what you think."

"What the fuck is it then? You've been coming here for days acting as if you really gave a damn about whether or not I lived or died. Now I find out you're here 'cause you want something from me. You just like er'-body else," he said with emphasis. "And, the worst part about it is that I had to find out from my mother, of all people! She thought you looked familiar and did some checking. Apparently back in the day, you were all that. Now, look at you, slinking around hospital rooms for a story."

Gabriel rubbed his forehead with his hand and leaned back into his chair. "See, now you ain't got shit to say for yourself."

It's too damned early for this shit. "You're right, you're absolutely right." Jazz's head snapped back a bit in reaction to Gabriel's unexpected burst of truth. "When I first heard about you, I rushed right over here in the pouring rain to see what information I could get. I ain't gonna lie. I was thinking more about my career than I was about you. I mean, this is the story of a lifetime for me. It could resurrect my career but when I got here, got to know you, and saw what had happened to you, I started caring less about a story and more about you."

"Oh really?" Jazz asked with sarcasm-soaked words.

"Yes, really. There is something special about you. I mean, shit. Look at what this monster has done to you. He beat you, circumcised you—"

"Don't ever talk about that!" Jazz stated between tightly clenched lips.

"I'm sorry. I truly am sorry for what he did to you. I know that you didn't deserve it, but you've got to understand what a special man you are. You are the only person The Messiah has ever left alive. And, I'm sure you want this asshole off the street as soon as possible before he kills someone else."

"Why the fuck would I care about that? I'm alive. That's all that matters." Jazz's sharp words cut across the room like broken glass.

"Jazz, man, this lunatic has killed six other people. He'll kill again—make no mistake about that."

Jazz turned his head in a haughty manner and stared disinterestedly out of the window. "Ain't nobody ever gave a damn about me, so why should I care about them?"

Gabriel didn't know how to respond to Jazz's callous words. Instead of responding immediately, he took a few seconds and blew into his tea. The faint steam rose into the air and vanished into nothingness. He needed to get through to Jazz, but couldn't figure out how to touch the conscience of a man who apparently didn't care.

"What makes you think he won't come back after you?" Gabriel could tell his words caught Jazz's attention.

"What do you mean?"

"Well, he left you and only you alive—for a reason. Only you know what that reason is. He wants something from you and if you don't give it, I believe he'll be back for you and next time you won't be so lucky."

Gabriel could tell Jazz was pondering either a clever retort or his next move.

"Well, when I get out of this damned hospital, I'll leave the city. He won't ever find me."

"There is no place on this earth that you'll be able to hide from him. For all we know, he could work in this hospital and could be watching your every move. This killer is super smart and has been at this for some time. He has eluded the police and the FBI. Please, don't delude yourself into thinking that you're smarter than he is. You're not."

Jazz fell silent.

Gabriel noticed the change in Jazz's demeanor. The hardened exterior in which he cloaked himself began to fade away as a more even-tempered mood took its place.

"I tell you what," Jazz began with a much fresher tone. "I told you that I didn't remember much about that night, but over the last couple of days things have started getting clearer. I'll give you all of the details of what happened and you can do with it what you want. Hell, put it on the evening news for all I care, but you've got to do something for me."

Gabriel raised one eyebrow. "What's that?"

"You've got to let me stay with you for a while."

Gabriel looked at Jazz perplexedly, not sure if he had understood his words. "I beg your pardon?"

"Look, I don't have health insurance and now that I'm getting better, the hospital is kicking me outta here tomorrow. I can't go back to the dorm because I still need some care and the school doesn't want to assume responsibility for anything that happens while I'm there. And I'll be damned if I go to that woman's house."

"What woman?"

"My mother. If The Messiah didn't kill me, then going home with her and my stepfather certainly will. I'd live on the street first," Jazz stated defiantly.

Gabriel didn't know where all the bad blood had come from, but he learned a long time ago to stay out of family business, even though he wanted to delve into the source of the tension. "Is she really that bad?"

"Let me put it this way. She makes the Wicked Witch of the West look like Mother Teresa."

"Damn," Gabriel said with a faint chuckle. "Where is she now?"

"I had to tell her to get out because she was stressin' me out. I told her to 'be gone, before someone drops a house on you, too.'"

"You didn't tell your mother that, did you?"

"Yes, I did. Shoot, she was ordering nurses around and talking to doctors like she's a good mother. Fuck her. She hasn't been a part of my life in years and now—all of a sudden—she wants to act like the doting mother. I can't stand all of that fake shit. Then she started asking me questions about what happened as if I owed her some explanation.

"She asked me what I was doing out there so late at night. I looked at her and told her I agreed to meet some man that I had met off the Internet. Then she said, 'For what?' I asked her what did she think I was doing meeting a strange man at night at an abandoned church. The expression on her face was priceless. She can't take me—never could, so I don't know why she's hanging around here now. She don't give a damn about me.

"Then she wanted to know if I was going to talk to you about what happened. She's only concerned because she wants to make sure that I don't say anything that would look bad for the Good Reverend. God forbid that the world learns that the good reverend and the first lady of the church threw me out onto the street years ago and now his son was attacked by a serial killer while he was strolling the streets for sex. Lord knows that's more important than whether or not I'll be okay."

Gabriel saw that Jazz was beginning to get worked up and tears had started to form in his eyes.

"Okay," Gabriel began, sensing the need to change the subject before he got pulled into a conversation he wasn't prepared to deal with. "So if I let you come home with me, you'll give me a full interview about whatever happened to you that night?"

"I'll give you my entire life story—starting with Mommie Dearest."

"Well, we can talk about that later," Gabriel commented with a smile. "But, seriously, I'd like to get your story, but I'd also like to help you. You may not be able to tell, but you and I are cut from the same cloth and I have a feeling that we are more alike than we are different. I think I could help you through this. What do you say?"

"I guess I don't have a choice."

"You always have a choice—not a good choice—but a choice. I know you think that my main reason for helping you is to get a story, but I want you to know that that's not my only reason. I want this killer off the streets before he strikes again. I know him better than I know my friends, and I know he won't stop until he's forced to stop. In his twisted mind, he thinks he's helping the world.

"He truly believes he is some kind of messiah sent here to deliver us from all evil and, to that end, he'll stop at nothing—I mean nothing—to spread his deadly work. I'm sick of having to look over my shoulder every time I get out of my car or walk across a parking lot. I know he knows who I am. I am the one that got his message out—I broke the story. But, I keep thinking, what if he comes after me? So, I have to do what I can to help the police get him. If we don't get him, he'll get us—that, I'm sure of. So, Mr. Man, it's up to you. You, and only you, hold the key. You're the only one who has been close enough to see his face and lived to tell the story. That makes you extraordinary."

Jazz shook his head. "Why me? I mean, how did he select me? *Why* did he select me, of all people? I'm not a good person. I have nothing to offer anyone."

"You do now. Your life may depend on it."

"How the hell does he expect me to tell the world about him when he cracked my head open like a melon. I can barely remember that night, but I have had some flashes."

"Really? What do you remember now?"

Jazz paused before turning to face Gabriel. "I remember the smell of sulfur."

Chapter 14

Gabriel watched with bated breath as Jazz struggled up the winding staircase in his townhouse. Even though the stairs were carpeted, a tumble down them for Jazz could easily send him back to the hospital. Gabriel didn't want to see that happen, nor did he want any further delays on his interview. He sensed that Jazz remembered more than he was letting on to.

Jazz's firm grip on the railing caused the veins in his right hand to protrude. He held onto to the railing with all the strength he could muster as tiny balls of sweat began to form at his hairline. He stopped for a second, took a deep breath, and continued his glorious ascent. Jazz used what little strength he had to propel himself forward, bit by bit, one step at a time.

"If you're more comfortable, you can sleep down here on the couch. That way, you'll be closer to the kitchen if you need something," Gabriel called out as he held his breath.

"I'll be fine up here. I'm not helpless," Jazz retorted with annoyance.

"Jazz, you don't have to prove anything to me. I know what you've been through. Recovering takes time. Don't try to do too much so soon."

When Jazz reached the apex, he turned and looked at Gabriel. "See, I told you I could do it."

Gabriel smiled at him and realized that Jazz needed that victory, regardless of how small it might have appeared. Gabriel followed Jazz up the stairs and opened the door to the guest room. "Well, this is your room for as long as you need it. I want you to make yourself at home."

Jazz immediately hobbled over to the bed and collapsed as if he had tackled climbing Mount Everest.

"I'll grab your things in a little while." Gabriel took a seat on the bed next to Jazz, whose heavy breathing caused some concern.

"When do you think you'll be up for our interview?"

"How long will the cop sit outside?" Jazz asked, ignoring the question.

"Well, they're gonna play it by ear. Faith thinks the cop should be there for a few days, but who knows? They were careful to not let anyone at the hospital know where you had been discharged. In fact, she told me that they used a decoy address to throw people off the trail—that is, if anyone is looking."

"I can't believe this fucking shit."

"I feel ya on that one. This is crazy."

"When are they going to catch him?"

Gabriel could hear the exasperation and trepidation resonating in Jazz's voice, in spite of his feeble attempts to appear fearless. "Soon. They're gonna catch him soon."

"I hope you're right."

Gabriel patted Jazz on the leg and stood up. "I'm going downstairs. I have a few calls to make. Do you need anything?"

"Nah, I'm cool for now. If my mother calls, tell her I'm sleeping or dead—she'd like that."

Gabriel walked out of the room and made his way downstairs into his office. He exhaled as he rounded the corner as he thought about the magnitude of things to come. He walked over to the window, raised the blinds, and gave a reflective gaze into the bright summer day. However, deep in his bones he knew calamity skulked on the horizon, barely out of sight and just out of reach. Danger and death danced a few feet away, somewhere around the corner. *Something wicked this way comes.* Gabriel knew that bringing Jazz into his home put him in grave danger, too. Yet, his altruism overcame his feelings of imminent danger—or was it ambition?

He stepped away from the window and took a seat at his desk. He reached down and pulled open the bottom drawer and pushed the hanging files to the front. In the back of the drawer, he eyed his savior: a small black pistol that hadn't been touched in years. He had bought the gun after a break-in years ago; actually, he had purchased two guns; the other one was upstairs in a shoebox hidden in his closet. He prayed that he would never have to use them. But something about their presence in the house made him feel secure.

After several minutes of deep thought and stroking his small protector, he brought himself out of his trance and his mind shifted to thoughts of Garrett—something far more pleasant. He pulled his silver cell phone out of his pocket, scrolled through the phone book, and hit the talk button when his name was highlighted.

After several rings, Garrett picked up. "What?" he asked in a harsh tone.

"Garrett?"

An eerie silence settled in for a fleeting second.

"Garrett? Is that you?"

"Hey—Gabriel," he stated flatly.

"Umm, is everything okay?"

"Everything is fine."

Gabriel pulled the phone from his ear and looked at it curiously. Garrett's detached and almost irritable tone unnerved him. "You don't sound fine. You've been acting strange lately. What's going on?"

Silence.

"Can you hear me? Garrett?"

The sound of laughter rang in the phone. The laughter, although somewhat familiar, had an unsettling quality.

"Ahh, I got you. I wish I could have seen your face!"

"Ha ha, very funny." Gabriel wasn't amused. "I called because I was thinking about you two minutes ago," he said, trying to get the conversation back on course. "I...wanted to see you."

"When?"

"I guess tonight. Are you free?"

"Yes. See you at nine?"

"Sure."

"Good-bye."

What the fuck was that? Gabriel thought to himself as he closed his phone.

✝✝✝

He took a napkin and wiped the dribble of blood that leaked from his nose and tossed the soiled rag into the kitchen trashcan. It had been days since his covenant—since he had chosen his disciple to spread news of his return; yet, he had heard of nothing. He snatched up the newspaper from the counter and tore through it like a man possessed, searching for something about him—a paragraph, a sentence, a word—that would acknowledge his return, but he found nothing. Out of frustration, he ripped the newspaper into pieces and threw them into the air and watched them rain down onto the floor.

He raced into the den, knocking over and shattering a glass vase on the hard floor. He picked up the remote control, turned on the television, and flipped through the local stations hoping to catch a frantic sound bite from a nervous journalist about his return.

Nothing.

Not a word was uttered.

He felt insignificant.

He threw the remote control toward the fireplace with great force. The small control connected with several religious trinkets and they exploded instantly, sending small ceramic pieces across the room.

He huffed and puffed, not sure what to do.

Then he heard the voices. And the shrieks in his head. He fell to his knees and covered his ears with his hands, hoping the sounds would abate. He tried to drown out the sounds, but he could not prevent them from taking him to that darker place. He didn't want to go. Internally, a great battle raged. Garrett felt the duality in his soul and tried to force his unwanted persona back into the bottle. For the first time in many years, he was acutely aware of the presence of his own evil.

Then he heard a song. And he forced himself to sing.

128

"Amazing grace. How sweet the sound…"

He sang louder and louder until his own voice grew in strength and power.

"'Twas grace that taught my heart to fear, and grace my fears relieved; How precious did that grace appear; the hour I first believed!"

Garrett rose to his feet triumphantly. He took his hand and wiped the blood from his nose, but ultimately smeared it across his face. He marched without pause or hesitation to the bathroom in his bedroom and turned on the shower. As he disrobed, he shook his head. For the first time, he could remember the scattered thoughts of his alter ego. Garrett could never remember the actions or the deeds of his other personality, but during this attack, he felt powerful. He didn't retreat into the corners of his mind and let the other one take over. Instead, he fought. He fought back and he had won. Now, if only he could learn to do that more often, maybe he could remain in control and lock away his other self.

Am I strong enough?

✝✝✝

Ever since he met Garrett, Gabriel had been fighting what he was feeling for him, but had decided to throw caution to the wind. He wanted to surrender. He wanted to be held and kissed and caressed. He wanted to feel protected and loved and desired. He wanted to grab Garrett and bring him into his arms. He had been overcome with that feeling of the rapid flutter of butterflies in his stomach, of the thrill of that first kiss when fire met desire, and of the exhilaration and anticipation of their heated sexual exchanges. He imagined Garrett's naked body, his milk-chocolate skin standing in his room. He could visualize his seductive glide and easy slide across the room. He could see himself wrapped around Garrett, their bodies so intertwined that flesh became flesh and they united in ways that had become foreign to him.

That was until Garrett started acting strangely. First, it was the airport debacle. Now, his tone and mood over the phone unsettled Gabriel. Something was not right, but he was going to see his man anyway.

All he could do was hope for the best.

He picked up the phone and dialed the ten digits. He listed to the ringing of the phone until Scott picked up.

"Wassup, big boy?" Scott asked in his usual way.

Gabriel ignored his comment. "I got a lot going on here, Scott."

"Like what, you ran out of ice cream?"

"Damn it, can you shut the fuck up for one second?" The silence on the other end of the phone told Gabriel that he had shocked Scott with his words and tone. All he needed was a friend to talk to, but Scott often made a simple conversation very difficult.

"Okay, my bad. Wassup…Gabriel?" Gabriel walked over to his bedroom door and closed it so that Jazz wouldn't overhear his conversation. He then moved over to the bed and plopped down, more out of frustration than fatigue.

"I have a houseguest."

"Really? That sounds interesting."

"No, not that kind of guest. This is someone who really needed my help."

"What do you mean?"

Gabriel took a deep breath and told the Scott what he had discovered over the last few days.

"What? The Messiah is back? Oh shit! What the fuck are the cops doing about this? They need to have every unit, including the FBI, combing the streets to find this killer. Do you remember what this town was like the last time he struck?" Scott's anxiety sounded in his voice.

"Of course I remember. I wrote most of the stories about him."

"Then you, of all people, know what a freak this fool is. I can't understand why you would invite this boy into your house if you think The Messiah may come after him."

"I didn't say that."

"You didn't have to. I can hear it in your voice."

"I'm not afraid, but I'm not sure I'm doing this for the right reason."

"Why are you doing it?"

Gabriel paused. "I don't know. I mean, I want to make sure this kid is safe, but I also want to revive my career."

"Ah ha, naked ambition—there's the Gabriel I used to know."

"But, I don't want this to be strictly about me. I need to know if I'm doing the right thing."

"Baby boy, I can't tell you that. If your suspicions are true and you think The Messiah might come after this boy and ultimately you, then you have to ask yourself if your career is worth the risk. It's kind of hard having a career if you're dead," he said with a slight laugh.

"Very true."

"All I can tell you is to be careful—very careful."

"I will be. And, Scott, thanks." Gabriel hung up the phone and allowed himself to fall backward into the bed. *These are the times that try men's souls.*

Chapter 15

Later on, when Gabriel reached Garrett's home, before he could even ring the bell, Garrett flung open the door and his lust-filled eyes moved up and down Gabriel's frame, starting at his head, then hungrily traveling the entire length of his body. Unexpectedly—and without a word—Garrett grabbed Gabriel and pulled him into his strong arms and kissed him passionately and forcefully as they stood in the doorway.

Gabriel kissed him back, but then pushed him away. He looked into his eyes for a second before Garrett's lips met his again. He couldn't deny the heat between them.

Garrett's kisses were passionate and electrifying, but they felt oddly unfamiliar. It was almost as if he were kissing a stranger. *A rough and aggressive stranger.* But, the fire that burned between them was undeniable.

Garrett pulled him into the house and kicked the door closed.

Gabriel could barely catch his breath before Garrett pulled his shirt over his head and off his body.

Their heated embrace caused them both to lose balance and stumble onto the wall. Their tongues writhed and hissed around each other like agitated serpents. They rocked and rolled forcefully on the walls and eventually made their way into the den. They plopped onto the couch and Garrett ground his pelvis into Gabriel's body. Their hands slid all over each other in a hurried exploration of foreign terrain. They grabbed and pulled and poked on each other until their actions generated so much heat that their clothes soon lay on the floor.

Garrett's hands clutched and pawed at Gabriel's body as if he were a piece of meat while they made their way into the den, never losing their embrace. Gabriel placed his hand on the small of Garrett's back and they made their way into the room and eventually onto the floor.

Without losing rhythm, Garrett continued to disrobe Gabriel until he lay on the soft carpet completely naked and fully aroused. Garrett pulled away from him, stood up, and looked down on his naked prey. He smiled.

Gabriel reached for him, but he stepped away.

With a click of the remote control, music invaded the space. And then Garrett started moving his body as if he was on stage performing for an eager crowd. His seductive smile captivated Gabriel as he performed, slowly unbuttoning his shirt to reveal his chiseled chest. The glint in Garrett's eyes revealed more than his usual arousal. Gabriel was enchanted by something else. The sparkle in Garrett's dark eyes revealed something deeper and mysteriously enticing.

Gabriel's interest—and excitement—piqued. This wasn't the Garrett he knew, but he was beginning to like him.

The gritty voice of Tyrese singing *Straight Fuckin'* filled the room and filled Gabriel with lust. He watched, almost in a trance, as Garrett's body coiled in hypnotic ways. He pulled at his nipple ring right before his hands moved down his stone-like body. He slipped his right hand into the front of his pants and Gabriel watched it disappear into his forbidden zone. Garrett licked his lips and eyed Gabriel as if he was dinner and dessert. Then he started removing the pair of shorts that he wore.

Gabriel felt a surge of heat.

Slowly, the shorts came down.

First, over his hips.

Then they slid down his hardened thighs until they landed around his ankles.

Garrett wasn't wearing any underwear.

He stood above Gabriel, licking his lips and stroking himself.

Then he descended on him with heat and power.

Gabriel kissed him wildly and passionately. Garrett, surprised but delighted by the greeting, reciprocated in equal measure.

Garrett turned him over and licked him from his ears down to the small of his back. His tongue sent chills of ecstasy through Gabriel's eager body as it glided and pricked over his skin. The sheer touch caused Gabriel's body to quiver and convulse.

Garrett's tongue continued to make its way down Gabriel's body, gliding gently over his ass cheeks and his hamstrings, all the way down to his ankles. Once he reached the bottom, he worked his way back to the middle. And stopped. *Work the middle, work the middle.*

Gabriel moaned and groaned.

Garrett turned him over and sucked on his neck, which threatened to send Gabriel into convulsions. Garrett worked his way down and stopped at his nipples. He flicked his tongue with snake-like precision, and each time he struck, Gabriel shuddered.

Gabriel grabbed a handful of Garrett's back flesh and held on for dear life. Then he grabbed Garrett by the head and pulled him into his face. He had to taste him again. He had to kiss those lips again.

Their kisses sizzled.

The world spun off its axis.

Gabriel pushed Garrett away from his face a bit, enough to look into his eyes.

They spoke without words. Garrett must have read the desire and wanting on his face. He took him by the hand, pulled him up from the couch and they walked hand-in-hand, naked and aroused, up the stairs leading to Garrett's bedroom. Once there, Garrett gently pushed him onto the bed and Gabriel closed his eyes to heighten the anticipation.

He didn't notice the droplet of blood that fell from Garrett's nose onto the sheets.

Hurriedly, Garrett climbed on top of Gabriel, eager to complete their sexual escapade.

Garrett grabbed, gobbled, yanked and tugged at every part of Gabriel's body. His touch gradually became more forceful. His gentle nibbles soon turned into playful bites which morphed into nasty gnawing. Gabriel's moans shifted from pleasure to pain, but that was a thin line, and Gabriel wasn't always sure if what he felt was delight or hurt. He looked down at

Garrett's face while he licked on his abdomen, slowly moving his way up. The expression he wore wasn't sexy and didn't fill Gabriel with desire. He looked down at his lover, into his partner's eyes, and felt something he had never felt while making love. He felt fear.

Garrett started licking his nipples and Gabriel closed his eyes in order to lose himself in ecstasy. His über-sensitive nipples had always provided him with intense pleasure. He could feel the rapid motion of Garrett's tongue, followed by a gentle biting.

"Oh, baby," Gabriel moaned, trying to remain in the mood. "Shit, yeah." Garrett's nibbles became stronger. "Not so hard, baby," Gabriel said as he rubbed his hands all over Garrett's smooth back. Garrett, obviously lost in his own world of lust and desire, did not hear or heed Gabriel's admonition. "Baby, that hurts."

Frantically, Garrett chewed, his teeth digging into Gabriel's raw flesh.

"Baby, stop it." His words fell on deaf ears. Garrett continued to chew into his lover until he drew blood and Gabriel screamed and pushed him away.

"What the fuck are you doing?" Gabriel leapt from the bed and looked down at the spot where a small pool of blood had formed on his right nipple. "I'm bleeding. What the hell is wrong with you?" he asked before darting into the restroom.

†††

Garrett closed his eyes, felt his nose, and felt the familiar sensation of warm blood in his nostrils. He looked around the room. He looked at his naked body and his erect penis. He saw the light on in the bathroom and he heard movement, but he was unaware of the circumstances surrounding his observations. He didn't want to move. He didn't want to say anything to alert this person in the bathroom that he didn't remember what had just happened.

Then he heard Gabriel's voice calling out to him. He felt a sense of relief.

"I don't know what the fuck is going on with you lately. It's like you've become someone else overnight," Gabriel said in a voice peppered with anger. Garrett was unaccustomed to the sharp tone in his voice.

"Baby—"

"Don't baby me, Garrett. Something is going on with you and I can't sit around trying to figure this shit out. You bit my goddamned nipple until it bled!" The shock of Gabriel's words made Garrett's eyes widened. "Don't just sit there—say something."

"Baby—Gabriel—I'm sorry. I got so worked up—"

"You know I hate that rough shit. We've never come anywhere close to the roughness you showed tonight."

"I know. I'm sorry. I thought we'd try something new."

Gabriel squinted his eyes and shook his head. "I'm out of here." He turned his back and started toward the door to go downstairs and get his clothes, but Garrett hopped from the bed and stood in the doorway.

"Baby, I'm so sorry. I'll never be that rough again. I promise you."

Gabriel stared at him blankly.

"Let me make it up to you," Garrett said in a softer voice.

"You've been doing a lot of that lately. I swear I don't know what's gotten into you." Gabriel inhaled deeply and cut his eyes to the side, away from Garrett's pleading eyes.

"Well, let me start now." Garrett dropped to his knees, with Gabriel's naked flesh dangling inches from his hungry mouth.

Tonight, he'd worship at a different altar.

Chapter 16

The gathering storm outside arrived in spectacular fashion. The commanding sound of thunder shook the entire house, rattling the pictures on the walls and startling the sleeping Jazz. He instinctively and quickly jerked his body to an upright position, which sent streaks of pain throughout his body. His rapidly expanding lungs struggled to get enough air into his body. He cautiously looked around the darkened room in order to detect even the slightest movement, but all was quiet. Everything seemed to be in order, but something *felt* wrong. He looked at the glowing red numbers on the clock on the nightstand: it was 12:33 in the morning. Sheets of rain unrelentingly pelted the outside window like machine-gun fire.

"Gabriel?" he called out as he wiped the moisture from his forehead. Surprisingly, his breath was short and quick. "Gabriel?" he called again, his voice sounding panicky for no apparent reason beyond the chills on the back of his neck. The wind outside his window howled and wailed an ungodly sound that shot through his body as branches from the oak tree scratched and scraped the glass pane of his window. Through the thin curtain, he saw the boney branch reach out, almost as if it was trying to reach him through the glass.

"Gabriel!" he screamed this time as lightning illuminated blackened skies. When the lightning flashed outside of his window, he could have sworn that he saw a hollow face, cloaked by a hood, looking into the second-story window.

As quickly as possible, he jumped out of bed, but the sudden motion once again sent pain racing through his body like electric shock. He hit the carpeted floor and let out a loud scream. Although his body was aching, he had to get out of that room. He tried to stand, but found it was easier to slide across the carpet. Once he reached the door, he took hold of the doorknob and used it to buoy his body from the floor. He stood up, his breathing racing, and leaned against the door momentarily. He frantically flicked the light switch several times, but the room remained dark. Slowly, he turned to face the window, but whatever apparition he saw was no more.

Once safely into the hallway, he slammed the door to his room shut and propped himself against the wall, using it to propel him forward. The hallway was dark and silent and no noise emanated from Gabriel's room. Jazz suddenly felt alone and vulnerable and afraid. As he clawed his way down the hallway, he stopped abruptly when he heard the sound of breaking glass in his room. His rapidly beating heart pounded in his chest as he struggled to move toward safety. It seemed no matter how fast he moved he couldn't conquer the distance between where he stood and Gabriel's room. The space became a vast black ocean with swirling waves that threatened to pull him into an abyss. All he could think about was that The Messiah had come to finish him off and that thought propelled him faster, but he stumbled onto the floor.

"Gabriel!" he screamed as the heavy, frenzied patter of unfamiliar footsteps coming from his room sounded in his ears. He didn't want to turn to face his room, so he grabbed inches of carpet and pulled himself along. Sweat now poured from his open pores and drenched his pale-blue pajama top. He could *feel* his end coming. It was his time. The sound of his bedroom door creaking open forced him to turn around. If he was to die today, he had to see the face of his killer. He rolled onto his back, looked toward his room, and waited. Slowly, the door opened as lightning once again raced across the sky and the thunder rolled.

He waited.

It was time to meet his Maker.

Suddenly, a blackened, faceless figure stepped quickly out of the room and moved with bionic speed toward him, his body twisting in supernatural ways.

Then it stopped inches before it reached him.

Jazz looked into the hood, hoping to see a face, a pair of eyes—some feature—that would identify the character, but the only thing that greeted his eyes was thick blackness that remained undiluted by the lightning flashes. And before he knew it, the creature let out a blood-curdling sound that caused tiny needlelike pricks to sprout up all over Jazz's body. The creature stomped its heavy feet and black wings unfurled behind it. Then before he could scream, the creature was upon him.

✝✝✝

"Oh my God," Gabriel said as Jazz's unconscious body greeted him near his bedroom door. "Jazz! Jazz!" he screamed as he frantically started shaking his limp body.

"Huh, huh?" Jazz said as he slowly opened his eyes.

"What are you doing out here in the hallway?"

"What?" Jazz asked, eyeing his surroundings peculiarly.

"Why are you lying in the hallway? What happened?"

"I was looking for you." Jazz shook his head as if to shake away his confusion.

"Why were you looking for me? I told you I'd be back before midnight."

"Midnight? What time is it now?"

"I'm a little late. It's one-fifteen."

"One-fifteen? Really?"

"Yes, really. See, I shouldn't have let you talk me into leaving you alone. I knew it was too soon. I could've rescheduled with Garrett."

"I think someone was here. I mean—something."

"What? Someone was in here?" Gabriel jumped up and looked around the hallway as if the stranger lurked in some corner. "The police are still outside. How did he get in? What did he look like? Where did he go? Did he hurt you?" Gabriel rattled off.

"No, no. I'm fine. He broke my window and chased me into the hall-way," Jazz slurred.

Gabriel stepped cautiously but determinedly down the hallway until he reached the guestroom. He slowly pushed open the door with his keys splayed between his fingers in case he needed a weapon. He looked around the room. Everything looked fine to him. The window was not broken. There was no glass buried in the carpet and no signs of forced entry. The only sign of violence were the tossed covers on the bed. Then he thought back to what Jazz had said. He turned around to head into the hallway, but Jazz had made his way into the room.

"What the fuck? The room is nothing like I remembered. Where is the broken glass?" He shook his head. "Gabriel, did it rain tonight?"

"Yeah. It rained like cats and dogs earlier."

Jazz hobbled over to the bed and plopped down dejectedly.

"Jazz, as you can see, everything is in order. It sounds like you had a really bad dream."

Jazz shook his head in disbelief. "It couldn't have been a dream. It was too real."

"The mind has a way of playing tricks on you; especially when you're on a lot of medication."

"This is not about the fucking medicine. It was real—I know it!"

"Okay, calm down." Gabriel placed his hand on Jazz's shoulder and tried to comfort him. "I think I know what this is about."

Jazz shot him a quick look.

"I think you're more scared than you want me to believe."

"I ain't scared."

"Look, Jazz, we all get scared. There's nothing wrong with that. Fear is a natural human emotion and I don't care how big or strong you are, we've all felt it and that doesn't make you any less of a man. Fear is as real as love or pain or hot or cold and it's got to be dealt with, one way or the other. You've been through a horrific ordeal and if it had happened to me, I'd probably be comatose. The fact that you're here—that you survived—shows that you're strong, but you've got to deal with the fear or it'll cripple you."

Jazz didn't fight his words. He remained quiet as if he was letting them take root in his mind. "Why me?" he asked rhetorically, as he looked upward toward the heavens. "Why me?" Then he let out a heavy sob that seemed to last forever.

Gabriel didn't interfere. He knew the young man had to get it all out.

"I need you to tell my story," Jazz said solemnly between sniffles. "In case I don't make it."

"What? Jazz, I want you to listen to me. Nothing is going to happen to you. The police will catch this fool before he can do anything else. Trust me."

"When do you want to do the interview?"

"When are you up to it?"

"Now is as good a time as any. I don't remember much, but I'll tell you what I do."

"Let me run downstairs into my office and get the tape recorder, and I'll come back up."

"Nah, I'll meet you downstairs in the living room. I need a change of scenery."

"Do you need some help down the stairs?"

"Nah, I'm cool. If I'm going to be here for a while, then I've got to learn to manage on my own."

"Cool. I'll see you in a few."

†††

Once downstairs, Gabriel poured two glasses of wine. Part of him couldn't believe the whirlwind that was his life right now. Days ago, he labored and lived in quiet solitude, except for a couple of outings here and there with Scott. Now he was about to get the interview that he hoped would revive his career.

As he sat on the couch, waiting for Jazz, his mind flashed to his heated exchange with Garrett earlier in the evening. The more he thought about it, the more incensed he became at Garrett's odd behavior. He had never had a man bite him until he bled, as if pain and blood were inexorably bound to sex.

He remembered the distant look in Garrett's eyes.

The peculiar kisses.

The rough hands.

The clawing.

The pawing.

The force.

The aggression.

The heat.

The pain.

And he remembered feeling violated.

Their previous sexual encounters were sensual, hot and forceful without being aggressive. But tonight was way over the top and left Gabriel feeling discouraged and broken. He felt as if his budding relationship had reached that breaking point—that point of no return. How could he be with a man who he didn't even recognize at times? The last few days certainly had been anomalous and brought out qualities in Garrett that had remained hidden. Maybe it was the stormy weather. Maybe it was work-related. Or maybe it was something else.

His head started to spin from the whirlwind of emotions. Right now, he needed to focus on having this conversation with Jazz. He got up from the couch and moved into his office to retrieve the scrapbook he usually kept upstairs in his closet. With The Messiah's return, he had been thumbing through it and left it on his desk. When he walked back into the living room, Jazz had taken a seat in his chair and appeared to be very comfortable.

"See, I told you I could get by without you," Jazz stated with a weak smile.

"I see you can." Gabriel grinned and winked. He took a seat next to him and placed the book on the table. The weathered black leather book held a lot of stories, dating back to articles first published in high school. Instead of buying a new book, he kept adding pages to the old one until it was nearly busting at the seams.

"What's that?"

"I like to keep paper copies of my articles and stories. This book has all of the articles that I wrote about The Messiah."

Jazz took a deep breath.

Gabriel opened the book and flipped through the pages toward the back until he reached a picture of a young Asian woman.

"This is Ming Morris. She was the first victim," he said unemotionally. "At the time, we didn't know that The Messiah was targeting gays and lesbians. Ming was very much in the closet. It was only after her death that people knew she was a lesbian. She left behind a partner and a child. The Messiah has only killed gays and lesbians—or people he thought were homosexuals."

"Why? What's his deal? Did he get rejected by some man and never got over it?" Jazz asked, trying to inject a little humor into the macabre conversation.

"I wish I knew," Gabriel responded. "All we know is that gays and lesbians are in his trigger hairs and he harbors a deep resentment and hatred for them."

"So, you're telling me that I should become straight?" Jazz asked jokingly.

"If only it were that easy."

Jazz reached down and grabbed the picture of Ming. "She was really pretty," he said.

"She was crucified—upside-down."

"What?" Jazz asked horrified.

"In ancient times, crucifying people upside-down was a pretty common practice; the Romans were skillful at delivering torture."

"Shit."

"In fact, Peter was crucified upside-down."

"Look, I don't know much about the Bible," Jazz admitted.

"Truth be told, I don't either. I did a lot of research in connection to these killings," Gabriel continued. "My friend, Faith, tipped me off to the story—that's how I got involved. I knew from the moment she told me about it, that these weren't ordinary killings. The police were willing to dismiss it as a ritual killing, not a serial killing, but I knew they'd have more bodies soon enough. I felt it. So I did as much research as I could find on her. Ming was a professor at Georgetown and taught a class on religion throughout the ages. There was some controversy over the content of her courses; some folks thought the content was blasphemous and some conservative religious groups even formed protests against her."

"Blasphemous? Are you serious? Who says that anymore? That sounds like some shit out of the Dark Ages."

"Don't forget people are killing each other all over the world today in the name of their God. Religious fanaticism is alive and well in the twenty-first century. So, the police interviewed everyone in all of her classes, but didn't come up with anything. They even interviewed all of the faculty, but nothing. The case remained unsolved."

"You're beginning to freak me out."

"I'm not trying to scare you, but you need to be aware of the kind of nut we're dealing with."

"The next victim was a woman named Jessica Port. What happened to her, well, it's very difficult to say out loud."

Jazz swallowed hard.

Gabriel reached down and brought the glass of wine to his lips. He took a small sip of Cabernet and let it wash through him. "In the Bible, Jezebel was the daughter of a king, but also a sorceress. She tempted men to commit sins and all kinds of evil acts and she led men from the teachings of God. Jessica Port was a voodoo priestess who also read palms for money in a dilapidated house by the Anacostia subway station.

"One of her final entries was about a man coming to see her and offering her a chance to come unto Christ. By the words in her diary, she refused and threw the man out on his ass. When they found her—or what was left of her—there was only her skull, her feet and her hands. And check this out. We don't know what happened when this man came to see her, but she must have really offended him. This was the note The Messiah left." Gabriel turned the page of his book and pasted on the next page was a photograph of the note left behind. He brought the book closer to Jazz so that he could read it without straining his eyes:

"On the plot of ground at Jezreel, dogs will devour Jezebel's flesh. Jessica's body will be like refuse on the ground on the plot at Jezreel, so that no one will be able to say, 'This is Jessica.'"

"Uh, what the hell does that mean? What happened to the rest of Jessica's body?" Jazz asked in a shaky voice.

By the sound of his voice, Gabriel could tell that the more Jazz learned about The Messiah, the more he realized how much danger he was in. He had been forced into an unnatural and unholy covenant with a beast who killed without mercy.

"Well, that note is derived from a passage from 2 Kings 9:36 in the Old Testament and it is a passage regarding Jezebel. See how he replaced Jezebel's name with Jessica's?" Gabriel pointed out. "It was commanded by God that Jezebel's body not be buried. And it wasn't. Same with Jessica; it's hard to bury a body if there isn't one."

Jazz grabbed his glass of wine that Gabriel set next to him and poured it down his throat.

Gabriel continued. "Jezebel was thrown from a building, trampled by horses, and then her flesh was eaten by dogs. As far as we can tell, The Messiah was meticulous in his reenactment of this scene with Jessica. The remains the police found of her were clean—no blood, no flesh— just bones. She had to be identified by dental records. And her skull was crushed in several places—you guessed it, kicked in by horses."

Jazz jumped up suddenly. "What the fuck? Why haven't the police found this fool? I mean, all they have to do is scope out churches for some lunatic spouting Bible verses."

"I wish things were that simple. I wish the bad guys always wore black and were easy to pick out of a crowd, but this killer has proven to be very elusive. He wants people to know about him, as most killers do, but he's very cautious in what he does. His pattern only changed with you." Gabriel leaned back in the chair, not sure whether to continue or not. "Do you want to hear about the others? I can tell you what he did to Matthew and Mark. He even killed a guy named Luke and one named John. I can tell you what he did to them."

"No thanks," he responded quickly, holding his stomach. "I think I'm getting nauseous."

"Do you want to start our interview now? What do you remember about that night?"

Jazz took a long pause before replying. "I remember some things."

The look that shone in Jazz's eyes was one of hesitation and fear. Gabriel recognized it and realized that reliving what had to be the worst night of his life would be no easy task for Jazz, but the story had to be told.

"Okay, why don't we start from the beginning? How did you meet The Messiah?" Gabriel hit the "record" button on his tape recorder and placed it on the end of the coffee table nearest to Jazz. "You don't mind, do you?"

Jazz shook his head.

With the solitude of a funeral march, Jazz began. "We met in a chatroom. I started receiving these IM's from someone calling himself 'Prophet.' The IM's were cool and we chatted over the course of a couple of days before I gave him my number. We exchanged photos and talked on the phone a few times and decided to meet. We had a lot in common."

"Really?" Gabriel realized his tone carried judgment. "I'm sorry. What did you talk about?"

"What do you think we started talking about? It was all about sex in the beginning. Hell, it was a sex site. We talked about our fantasies and the things we had done in the past and the things we wanted to do. We talked about all sort of freaky shit like group sex, sex in public, bondage, but I've done all of those things."

Gabriel eyes widened.

"Then he told me he always wanted to have sex in a church. He described all of the things he wanted to do to me and I ain't gonna lie, it sounded hot. He suggested we meet at this abandoned church and I agreed."

"Do you still have the photograph he sent you?"

"I guess. I didn't delete it from my inbox, but I did give my account information to some cop so who knows what they've done with it."

"What else have you told the police?"

"Not much. When they came to my hospital after I woke up, they started grilling me and all I wanted was to be left alone. I wanted to forget everything and they kept at me."

"Tell me what happened next."

"I really don't remember much. I don't remember his face, but I remember his voice. It was deep and strong—at times it almost sounded like a growl."

Jazz closed his eyes as if trying to recall some of the details of that ill-fated night, and Gabriel poured himself another glass of wine. He knew it was the beginning of a very long night.

Jazz provided as much detail as he could remember. He described the fear he felt and how it felt to be in the presence of death. He described the sights and the sounds and the smell of the evening, but he could not recall the face of the man who had inflicted such horror upon him. He remembered small pieces of his face and how he had hit him above the eye with a rock, but he couldn't remember if he ever got a good look at his attacker or if he simply didn't remember.

As he spoke, Gabriel became fascinated with every syllable and every word he uttered. He listened attentively to the story as it unfolded in Jazz's own words.

"And that's when he took the rock and said some shit about us being in a covenant. That's when he circumcised me." From the pained expression on his face, Gabriel could tell that it was difficult for Jazz to tell his story. Jazz's head hung low and his eyes were glued to the floor as if he were too embarrassed or ashamed to look at Gabriel.

"I know that wasn't easy for you to say," Gabriel said. "But, I appreciate it. Did you tell the police that?"

Jazz took a few seconds before he spoke. "Nah, I didn't, but I assume the doctors did because they asked me about it. They wanted to know if I had any idea why he would do that—if he said anything to me."

"What did you tell them?"

"I didn't tell them anything."

"You didn't tell them what he said—about the covenant?"

"I just said I didn't tell them anything. Hell, I don't even know what a covenant is really."

"A covenant is like a pact between people," Gabriel began. "When people enter into a covenant it usually means that they agree to do—or not do—something specific. So, it sounds like, in this case, he wants you to tell the world about him."

"I guess that's where you come in. You have all the connections to tell the story so that this fool will leave me the hell alone."

Gabriel sighed. The word *covenant* sounded odd to him, no matter how many times they repeated it. He let Jazz know that he'd have to share this information with the police because it may help in their investigation.

"When he took that rock and cut on me, I was pretty out of it already and part of me prayed for death so the pain would stop, but I felt the raggedy end of the rock slicing away at me. Do you have any idea how it feels to have your dick cut? I have never felt anything so painful in my whole life. I didn't know it was possible to feel something like that." Jazz took a deep breath. "What the fuck did this bastard do with the skin he cut off me?"

Gabriel had no words.

Chapter 17

Gabriel arrived at the trendy Busboys and Poets on Fourteenth Street in Northwest Washington at exactly 5:30 p.m. Although it was still relatively early, the place was bustling with activity. Waiters scampered by carrying trays of food and drink while customers exchanged lively conversation. Faith had requested a meeting with him and by the tone in her somber voice, he had surmised that something weighed heavily upon her and he was sure that it had something to do with The Messiah.

When he was approached by the hostess, he requested a table away from the crowd and followed her to a small table tucked away neatly in a corner in the back. Gabriel figured that his conversation required a modicum of privacy. He checked his watch again, out of habit, and started thinking about his article when his phone rang.

"Wassup, Gabriel?" the familiar voice asked.

"Garrett. How are you?" Gabriel asked.

"I'm fine, but the question is are *you* okay?"

"What do you mean?"

"Where have you been? I've been calling you for two days. Did you get the gifts I sent you? The flowers?"

"Yes, I got everything. Thanks." Gabriel simply wasn't sure how to react. He had spent the last two days working on his story and intentionally avoiding Garrett's persistent calls. He had intended on calling him back, at some point, but he had gotten so wrapped up in writing the story, he didn't get around to it. And besides, he wasn't even sure what he was going to say when they spoke. Was he ready to call it quits with Garrett, or was he willing to work to figure things out? He didn't have a clue.

"Baby, I have been wracking my brain trying to figure out ways to make this thing better between us—to try to get you to forgive me. I had no intention of hurting you the other night and you can't imagine how bad I feel about it. I would never do anything to hurt you on purpose—never."

"Garrett—"

"No, please let me finish. The reason this hurts so bad is that I'm falling in love with you, and I'll never forgive myself for hurting you. You're the best thing that has happened to me in years and I thank God every day that he led you to me. If I've done anything to permanently lose your respect or trust then, I…I don't know how I can make it."

Gabriel listened to Garrett's gut-wrenching apology with apprehension and worry. He wasn't sure if the words coming out of his mouth would be enough to quench the rising fear in his heart. He wasn't sure, at this point, if he loved Garrett, but he knew that had things not changed over the last few days, that he *could* have loved him. Now, given all that had happened, he wasn't sure if love was enough. "Garrett, I'm sorry I haven't been in touch much the last couple of days. I'm working on a serious story that is taking all of my time. I think we do have to talk and get some things straight though."

"I know that everything that has happened has been my fault. I haven't been feeling that well and I've been under a lot pressure at the hospital. Things are crazy right now and I'm sorry that you're getting caught up in my shit." Garrett's voice was low and solemn and Gabriel sensed that his words were sincere, but still, he wasn't sure.

"Garrett," he said softly, "I can understand that and I appreciate you calling to apologize."

"I appreciate you taking my call this time."

"I wasn't trying to ignore you—well, okay, maybe a little bit. I wasn't sure what to say to you after the other night."

"I deserved your silent treatment."

"This isn't about punishment, Garrett. I wasn't trying to hurt you or anything like that."

"Well, that's great to hear. I am truly, truly sorry."

"Okay, stop apologizing. I'm not mad—anymore."

"I promise from here on out, it'll be nothing but smooth sailing."

"You can't promise that."

"Well, I can promise that I will do everything in my power to make things smooth. I don't like it when we're not talking."

"Yeah, me either. Truth be told, I haven't gotten a lot of sleep the last couple of days."

"Tell me about it. There were so many times in the middle of the night that I wanted to get up and drive to your house, but I didn't know how I'd be received. I didn't want to simply show up on you."

"Yeah, just showing up wouldn't have been a good thing," Gabriel said with a chuckle.

"Well, can we get together soon? Have dinner and work things out?"

"Yeah, we can do that, but I'm not sure when. I have a couple of deadlines at work, but I'll call you later so we can set something up. Is that cool?"

"Yeah, that's cool."

"Okay. Call me later."

As he ended the call, he caught a glimpse of Faith gliding like silk through the crowd, heading directly toward him. Even in the midst of the organized chaos of the restaurant, she managed to stand out like a swan. As she neared, he got a better view of her hair, which was drawn back in a tight bun and gave her thirty-four-year-old face a stern appearance. She smiled, took a seat on the opposite side of the small table, removed the small black-rimmed glasses from her face, folded them neatly, and placed them in the center of the table. A few errant gray strands protruded from the edges of her hair like straw in a field.

"You look like the teacher in school all the boys had a crush on," Gabriel said playfully.

"You like? I was tired of the old look. Sometimes, you gotta change up things."

"It definitely works for you. Makes you look tough."

"Tough? I'm not sure that's what I was going for, but thanks," she said with a light chuckle. Faith picked up the cocktail menu and glanced it over.

"I need a good, strong drink right about now."

"Is there something wrong?" Gabriel asked as he noticed a slight tremble in her hands. He peered at her curiously. He wasn't accustomed to seeing her shaken. She was the epitome of the strong black, independent woman—the sister who was doing it for herself. He reached across the table and touched her hands. "You're shaking. What's going on?" Gabriel stared her directly in the eyes as the waitress approached. Faith pulled her hands away and smiled at the waitress.

"Hi, I'm Kathi. I'll be your waitress. May I get you something to drink?" she asked in a too-perky voice.

"I'll have a Cosmopolitan," Faith instinctively said. Cosmos were her usual drink of choice.

"Make that two."

"Any preferred Vodka?"

"Grey Goose is fine," Gabriel said impatiently.

"Great. Two Cosmos with Grey Goose. Do you want an appetizer? I'd recommend the spinach dip or—"

"No appetizer. Just the drinks. Thanks." Gabriel shot the waitress a curt look and didn't give her time to respond. The smile she wore faded from her face as she nodded and then walked away in a huff, her ponytail bouncing in the back of her head.

"I guess you told her."

"I didn't mean to be rude but she acted as if she couldn't take a hint. I was trying to be polite."

"If that was polite, then I'd hate to see you when you're being rude."

"Anyway, back to you. What's going on?"

She looked apprehensively around the room. Slowly she leaned forward and spoke. "He's killed again." Her words slapped him across the face with the sting of a prizefighter. "A woman—this time."

"What? When? How?" Gabriel's shock prevented him from forming a complete sentence. "It's too soon. This is not his pattern."

"He doesn't have a pattern anymore. He's becoming frenzied. Yesterday, I got a report from the department's forensic psychiatrist. You remember, when The Messiah first struck, he did a detailed analysis of the killer?"

"Yeah, I remember. You let me look at the report."

"Then you remember that the report labeled the killer as meticulous, cautious, and extremely intelligent. He was thought to be a religious fanatic and someone who thought he was doing a service to the world. He was someone who seemed to kill for a reason—each one of his victims had violated some portion of religious doctrine and The Messiah seemed to act to uphold Christianity in his own demented way. Each murder was ritualistic and methodically executed. He had a pattern—one a month. But now, everything has changed. He's become frantic—almost desperate."

"How can you tell?"

"Most serial killers are extraordinarily cautious. They plan their killings down to the very last detail and that's how The Messiah *used* to be. Now his patterns are changing—he's getting bolder, almost as if he thinks he is invincible."

"What do you guys think is setting him off?"

"We have no idea at this point. If we don't figure it out, the body count is going to go sky-high. Right now this case is freaking me out. I can't eat, I can't sleep. All I do is sit around worrying about when he's going to strike next. I don't know why he's getting to me like this. I've seen brutal murders before, but he's taking it to another level. He's perverting the Bible to kill people. I don't know how anyone could do that."

People pervert the Bible for personal gain all the time, he wanted to say, but refrained. Instead of speaking, he reached out and touched her hands again.

"We're going to get him, trust me about that," she added.

"How did he kill the woman?"

"He beat her and tortured her, and then slit her throat. Her body was found in the Potomac River." Faith reached into her purse and pulled out an item. "And we received this note in the mail:

"The second angel poured out his bowl on the sea, and it turned into blood like that of a dead man, and every living thing in the sea died."

"That's from the Book of Revelation," she stated. "This woman was a wife and a mother. What did she do to deserve this?"

155

The note, sealed in a plastic bag, immediately caught Gabriel's attention.

"Wait, this note is handwritten but the other ones you received were from newspaper clippings."

"Exactly. I borrowed this from the evidence locker, because I had to show it to you. Gabriel, we're not dealing with the same killer anymore."

"What? There's another one?"

"No, that's not what I mean," she said as he leaned in closer. "All the evidence we have point to the same individual, but, like I said, he's becoming...something else. There is a certain rage in this note. Look at how sloppy he was in writing it. And usually when dealing with killers acting out of religious instinct, there is a certain lack of detail. They tend to act because they think God told them to and it can happen at any time—any moment—so most killers who have a God-complex lack the detailed planning most serial killers have."

"Well, at least you have a handwriting sample now."

"And that speaks to my point. The Messiah of a few months back would never have sent a handwritten note. It's not much, but hopefully we'll be able to tie it to something. I'm going to nail the bastard." Faith put her face in her hands and closed her eyes momentarily. "I keep thinking about that woman—what she must have gone through—her final moments. Did I mention she taught Sunday School at Antioch Baptist Church? They said she never missed a class. Everyone we've spoken to has spoken very highly of her. She had no enemies and always had a kind word for someone."

"Antioch Baptist Church?"

She looked up. "Yes, why?"

"It's nothing. The guy I'm dating goes there. I wonder if he knew her, that's all."

"What's his name?"

"Garrett Lord—Dr. Garrett Lord."

"Interesting name," she said. "How well do you know him?"

"We've been dating, but I don't think it's going to last," he added. "I hope she wasn't a good friend of his." Gabriel suddenly thought about being put in the position of having to offer emotional support and comfort to Garrett at a time when he was short on emotional support and comfort.

"We're talking to some more of the parishioners to see if they can offer some insight, but they have over seven-thousand members."

"I'm seeing Garrett tonight. I'll see what he knows. What did you say her name was?"

"Sabrina Dean."

"Okay. I'll ask him if he knew her."

Faith gave Gabriel the once-over. She eyed him carefully and fully, taking special note of the look in his eyes. "You didn't tell me you were dating anyone."

"Well, it's not that serious. I met him a couple of months ago and things had been cool up until recently."

"What do you mean?"

"He's been trippin'. Not showing up, not calling—you know how men do."

"I sure do." She laughed.

"I don't think I'm cut out for this dating shit. It's too much time and energy."

"Give it some time. You've only known him a short while."

"I guess."

"Gabriel, are you okay? What are you not telling me?"

"It's nothing. It's just that the last few days with him have been really strange. Sometimes I feel like I don't even know him."

"Hell, I say the same thing about Raymond."

"Nah, this is different. It's like when I look into his eyes—never mind." Gabriel stopped suddenly.

"What?"

"It's like looking at a stranger."

"That's kinda creepy."

The waitress returned with their drinks and placed them on the table in front of them, being especially careful to not spill a drop or make idle conversation. Her exterior was now cool and aloof. "Are you ready to order?"

"I'm actually not hungry right now, thank you," Faith said.

"I'll have the spinach dip." Gabriel wasn't particularly hungry, but felt a need to order something after being so rude to her earlier.

"I'll place your order," she said as she moved on to her next table.

"You see what you did to her by being a bitch? She acts like she's scared to say anything."

"You're trying to make me feel bad, aren't you?"

"Not at all," she said with a wink. She took a sip of her drink and winced due to the unexpectedly strong mix. "I spent half of the morning in church," she said, changing the subject and looking off in the distance. "I needed to speak to someone so I spoke with my priest. I was raised a devout Catholic and even through the scandals of the church, my faith remained unshaken. Those priests were men, fallible and flawed, like the rest of us. I never put them on a pedestal so when they fell, they didn't have far to fall before they hit the ground. But, Gabriel, something about this case freaks me out. I've started to question the will of a God who would allow His words and His faith to be so distorted that ordinary men could justify evil under the guise of religion. Something about this case is so evil...so depraved that I am losing myself."

"You can't do that, Faith. You've got to stay strong. This is a man doing all of these things. This is not a reflection on God."

"I know you're right; that's why I went to church. I'm more determined now than ever to find this killer and put an end to his reign of terror, for once and for all."

"Well, when the story runs, maybe that'll draw him out."

"So, you finally got Jazz to talk?" she asked inquisitively.

"Yeah, I feel sorry for him. He doesn't have anyone really to talk to. His friend had to go back to California to take care of his sick mother and Jazz doesn't get along with his own mother. She keeps calling, but he rarely talks to her. Usually, we let the machine pick up. He's trying so hard to be strong. He's got a lot on him and I knew from the moment I met him that he was terrified. Hell, who wouldn't be?"

Gabriel reached out and grabbed his drink, slowly taking a sip. He let the cool liquid slide down his throat before speaking again.

"And, he's been having really bad dreams. I came home the other night, and he was passed out in the hallway upstairs and couldn't remember how he had gotten there. I finally convinced him that the way to get rid of that was to clear his mind and tell me what really happened. Hey," he interjected suddenly. "He mentioned that he gave some cop the information about the chatroom he was in when he met The Messiah. And, he said there were photos in his email The Messiah sent of himself."

"We checked it out. He used some kind of program that prevented us from tracing the computer he used and the photo that he sent was some kid that went to Howard University. He went to the university's website and copied a picture. This guy is smart. He knows how to not get caught."

"I should've known it wouldn't have been that easy. I guess I was hoping that he had gotten sloppy."

"That would be nice, but I wouldn't hold my breath on that."

"I want you guys to catch him so Jazz can resume a normal life. As soon as I get this story out, I hope it takes him out of harm's way so that he can sleep a little easier. It's so sad, and I can hear him pacing in his room at all hours of the night. He'd never admit that he can't sleep because he's scared, but I hear him."

"That's one of the things I wanted to talk to you about," she said as she looked around the crowded space. "I need you to back off the story for a while." She looked at him straight on and did not mince words.

"What? Why?"

"Think about it. Jazz is the only person he left alive. There is something he wants from Jazz. The Messiah isn't unlike most serial killers—they all want fame. If you run the story, you would have given him exactly what he wants and we may lose our best opportunity to apprehend him. Now, on the other hand, if we deny him the fame and notoriety that he's looking for, he'll come after Jazz. And when he does, we can get him."

"What? After everything that boy has been through, you want to use him as bait? Gimme a break."

"These are desperate times," she said as she leaned in closer to him from across the table. "We've got to catch him, and this is our best shot. We will protect him. I can guarantee nothing will happen to him."

"I don't like the way this sounds, Faith. Jazz is kind of…fragile—on edge right now. If you approach him about this, he'll balk. Hell, he may even run."

"That's why I want you to ask him. Clearly, you have a bond with him."

"I can't ask him to put his life in jeopardy again, nor can I can hold off on this story. People have a right to know. Hell, they need to know that a serial killer is running the streets. They need to know to take precautions and watch their backs. You can't be serious about this. You will do more harm than good by burying this story. You can't put a lid on this. The people need to be warned."

"Gabriel, who do you think you're talking to? You know I love you, but you aren't doing this story for anything as noble as *the people*. You're doing this for your damned career, a career—mind you—that I helped you make. Had it not been for my little tips, you probably wouldn't have gotten half the stories you did."

Her words felt like daggers in his heart. "I can't believe you would say some shit like that to me." The truth of her statement rang in his ears like sirens. He knew that she was partially right, but that didn't mean that he was prepared to hear the words.

"Look, I'm not trying to hurt your feelings; I want you to keep this in perspective. I'm going to the favor bank here. Look at it this way. Yes, you could have a good story now, or you could have a *great* story if you help us catch this maniac. You'd be the reporter with all the exclusives; interviews with the chief and the FBI. Hell, you may even get a prime-time special out of this. You'd be a star."

"That's not what this is about." Part of him lied.

She looked at him. He stared back.

"Fine. I'll talk to him, but I can't make you any promises." Gabriel reached back and pulled his wallet from his pocket. He opened it up, yanked out a twenty-dollar bill, and tossed it onto the table as he stood up. "I'll let you know. You can take that spinach dip I ordered home with you."

Chapter 18

After leaving Faith, Gabriel sat in his car and thought about the complexity of what he was going through. He needed this story to be publicized soon and not solely because he was worried about his career. He genuinely felt a need and a responsibility to share this story with the world so that the imminent threat posed by The Messiah would be known.

As thoughts ran across his mind, he was forced to face the fact that Faith was right. Maybe this was the best way to ferret out this killer, but in doing so, he would put himself and Jazz in clear and present danger. After all, Jazz was in his house and regardless of how many assurances the police gave him that they were safe, he'd never feel completely safe while The Messiah roamed the streets freely.

Gabriel picked up his phone and dialed Jazz's cell phone.

"Hello?"

"Hey, Jazz, it's me. What's going on?"

"Nothing. I'm bored as hell. I can't stay in this house too much longer."

"Stop trippin'. You know you can't leave."

"Shit, I feel like I'm in prison. I need to get out and get some fresh air. I'm much, much better now. I can walk and move freely and most of the swelling has gone down."

"I realize you're ready to get out and about, but it's not safe."

"When will it be safe?"

"When the police catch this killer."

"And what if they don't? Am I supposed to stop living? Shrivel up in a corner and die?"

"They'll catch him. Be patient. Listen, I have to run by the office and then I'm coming home. What do you want to eat?"

"A man," he said, laughing. "You know it's been a minute."

"Hmm, I don't think I can arrange that, but I'll pick up some Popeyes."

✝✝✝

Garrett sat in the pew of the mega-church with a dumbfounded look carved painfully into his face. Spider web-like lines reached out from the corners of his eyes as he squinted. His tightly drawn lips were beginning to feel numb from the pressure he applied. He looked around the room and the gamut of facial expressions ranged from astonishment to disgust to pity. The tangible silence in the room was so thick that the letter being read from the pulpit was barely audible.

"I am a liar and I have deceived everyone. I have stood before you and heralded the name of GOD while secretly leading a life that I have struggled with all my days. My own fear, shame, and disgust at my behavior blinded me to the truth of the way and prevented me from seeking the help I desperately wanted."

The letter, authored by the church's founder and pastor, confirmed the suspicions and innuendo that had swirled for months. The rumors of the pastor's sexual transgressions became so pervasive that they had to be addressed openly. A month before his resignation, the pastor issued a tacit warning to his congregation to not allow lies and rumors of lies to sway them off the course of righteousness and to interfere with the good work in which the church had been chosen to perform. "It is a trick of the enemy," Garrett remembered the pastor bellowing out with all due righteous indignation.

Now Garrett sat—almost immobile from the shock—in a room full of equally shocked parishioners and he found the words coming from the mouth of Deacon Russell to be almost incomprehensible. Garrett could not fathom a deeper hurt. The pain of this betrayal was deeper than any hurt he had ever experienced.

Deacon Russell read from a letter authored by Pastor Albright who resigned— under the threat of being removed—as head of the church by the church board after he admitted to sexual immorality stemming from his year-long relationship with a male prostitute. The Washington Post *first broke the story of a prostitution ring that would reach through the community and would shock, but the newspaper did not reveal names at the time.*

"I know many of you will have a hard time accepting this. I have sinned and broken your trust. For that, I will never forgive myself. Some of the allegations regarding my conduct are false, but still, I must leave you and work with the Lord who will guide me through this valley and lead me back unto His path."

As the statement continued to be read in a solemn voice, Garrett felt a twitching in his neck, which caused him to jerk slightly to the left. As he stared at the stone-faced deacon, his vision darkened, almost as if he had tunnel vision. The deacon was slowly fading out of focus, as were the rest of the people around him. Garrett felt an ominous darkness inside him and feared it would swallow him whole.

"I have to resist," he mumbled under his breath. "I can fight this." He struggled to remain in control, but the feeling of losing control was growing.

"Stop fighting me," a voice whispered. Startled, Garrett quickly looked to his left and his right and behind him at the people in his immediate area. They were intensely focused on the deacon and paid him no attention.

Then he realized the voice he heard did not originate from anyone around him. It had emanated from within his own head!

He didn't speak, but he could hear his own voice echoing in his head, calling out for salvation, calling out for light in the darkness.

He felt himself fading away into an abyss.

Garrett shook his head and looked around the room again at the solemn, tear-stained faces. His breathing hastened and the palms of his hands became clammy and sweaty.

He shuddered.

"I am your redeemer. My children are lost. I have come to show you the way and the light. I will lead all my children to the Promised Land," the voice whispered again. The voice had a soft, peaceful tone.

Then his nose began to bleed and he knew he was losing it.

Garrett fled the sanctuary in a panic.

✝✝✝

"Doctor Lord? Hello, Doctor?" The nurse's voice startled Garrett and brought him out of his thoughts. He looked around the hospital room oddly as perplexed faces met his glance. "Doctor, are you okay? You look a bit…shaken." Garrett stood at the nurse's station, with a marker in his hand, near the big dry-erase board, as if he were about to update the status of a patient.

"Oh, I'm suddenly feeling very nauseous," he said, hoping his lie would sound authentic. "I think I need to go home."

"Well, take care of yourself, Doctor. I hope you feel better."

He smiled at the nurse, unsure of what to say, and realized he needed to step away as he tried to understand.

Garrett walked away feeling somewhat dazed. The flashback he experienced felt as if he were living in that moment again. He remembered the shame he felt at learning of his pastor's transgressions. His pastor was known to condemn homosexuality with his fire-and-brimstone sermons. Now it had been revealed that the man whom he had entrusted with his secrets was a liar and a deceiver.

Garrett still felt ashamed. He had often confessed his own shortcomings to this man. He'd had previous conversations with him about his own attraction to men and was told—in no uncertain terms—to change his ways or face the fires of hell. After his first conversation with Pastor Albright about his desires, his immediate thought was to change churches. But he had never been a quitter. He could run to a new church, but what would he find there? So, instead of leaving, he decided to stay and engage the pastor in a continuous dialogue.

When the note was read aloud, he'd remembered feeling foolish. He felt ashamed that he had been duped into believing that his pastor was an honorable man. He remembered being overcome with great sorrow, and a roaring rage he felt seared his soul. He remembered being in the church that day, but he still could not remember anything after he ran down the aisle.

Garrett walked out of the hospital, not even bothering to retrieve his things from the locker. A nagging voice in the back of his head spoke to him.

"You know who I am. I am your redeemer. Do not deny me."

"Stop it!" Garrett's unintentional yet perceptible command to himself caused the couple walking toward him to dart to the side. He walked briskly across the parking lot to his car, hoping to get in and seal the door before any other outbursts. Quickly, he opened the door and got inside.

"I'm not losing my mind. I'm in complete control. This is all my imagination. Just breathe."

"I am HE."

"Stop it! Leave me alone!"

"I am the redeemer. I am HE."

Garrett put the key in the ignition and immediately turned up the stereo to drown out the voice.

"I am Alpha and Omega; the first and the last; the beginning and the end."

"This is not happening. This is not happening," Garrett said frantically to himself. He put the car in reverse and backed out quickly, without looking, nearly swiping the side of his car against a cement pillar. He sped through the garage as tears began to swell in his eyes.

"I am not going crazy. I am not going crazy."

"Do not be afraid. God has come to test you, so that the fear of God will be with you."

"You are not God!"

"I am Alpha and Omega; the first and the last; the beginning and the end."

Garrett tore down the narrow D.C. streets, weaving in and out of traffic like a bat out of hell. His car skidded and careened down Pennsylvania Avenue, almost out of control. He needed to get away, so he put his foot to the pedal and fled the scene, driving fast beyond the U.S. Capitol, then the Washington Monument, and other popular sites.

The voice in his head quieted during the drive, but Garrett still worried. He couldn't explain what was going on with him, but the voice in his head was as real as they come. He had never experienced this before.

All his life he knew that something about him was different. There were many instances in which he simply lost time and couldn't explain his where-abouts or his actions. He thought they were simple blackouts and sought the treatment of a physician, as humbling as the experience was to him. He was used to being viewed as a god, saving lives and restoring faith. When he had to seek treatment, it was difficult to submit. But, finally, he got his blackouts under control. He hadn't had one in six months, but now they returned with a fierceness that caught him off guard. Strange notes and blood seemed to be the common thread when he lost control.

Then he thought about the voice in his head and its eerie words. *Could that voice have something to do with the blackouts?*

Garrett continued to tear down the city streets, paying little attention to others on the road, but somehow managing to avoid an accident.

When Gabriel walked into his house, the sound of music filled the air. The music wasn't coming from the television or the stereo, but it was live as if a Jazz concert was taking place. Sweet, shrill notes, full of hope and joy, were followed by dark, blue sounds, which reminded him of a melancholy day. The sing-song sounds, alternating between highs and lows, caused Gabriel to stop in his tracks and listen. He was mesmerized. Tears, blue notes, and pain touched his soul. The notes sailed into the room smoothly, gently, but they left their mark on his spirit. He imagined himself in a crowded, smoke-filled club, watching the trumpeter, who sat on a wooden stool in the center of a creaky wooden stage, grind out angst-filled note after note as the crowd swayed back and forth as he played their stories.

Gabriel put down the food and followed the sounds. As he rounded the stairs, he saw Jazz sitting in the sill of the bay window at the end of the hallway with a trumpet to his mouth. The fading sunlight cascaded through the window and coalesced around Jazz, giving him an almost divine glow. His eyes were closed and his frantic digits fingered the valves of the brass instrument. Gabriel did not move, but looked at Jazz in this new light. Jazz hadn't heard him approach as he reached the song's crescendo. He belted out the notes with powerful precision.

Then it was over.

Jazz opened his eyes and turned his head. He looked at Gabriel, who was left speechless.

"I didn't hear you come in," he said as he peeled himself from the window and walked solemnly into his bedroom, trumpet dangling at his side. Gabriel followed him.

"I had no idea you could play like that. Guess that's why they call you Jazz, huh?"

"Something like that," Jazz said as he pulled a white cloth from the tattered black trumpet case in the corner. He dropped onto the bed and started polishing the instrument.

"You have amazing talent. I really don't know what to say."

"I wasn't sure if I'd be able to play because my lips are still a bit sore, but I had to try. I hope you don't mind, but I called my mother and she brought it over here. This was the very first trumpet I ever played. She had it in her basement."

"No, of course I don't mind, but you've got to be careful."

"Yeah, yeah. I know. I shouldn't let anyone know where I am, blah, blah, blah."

"Seriously, The Messiah is *still* out there."

"Well, I should be fine. I gave him what he wanted. I've done my part. You have the story. All you have to do is your part."

Gabriel walked deeper into the room and leaned on the wall near the window, arms folded. He wasn't sure how to broach the subject of Jazz being bait for The Messiah. How does he ask this man—this child—to put his life on the line to save the world, a world that had not been particularly kind to him over the years? Gabriel took a deep breath and gazed out into the dusk. The amazingly beautiful sky offered a stark contrast to the ugliness of what he had to do.

"I bought chicken."

"Thanks, but I'm not hungry. I'm going crazy." Jazz placed the trumpet on the bed. "I had another dream."

"What happened this time?"

"The same thing that always happens. I die."

"Jazz, these dreams are not uncommon for someone in your position. Post-traumatic stress disorder is a serious medical condition. It can have some crazy effects on you."

"I'm telling you, these aren't dreams. They're more like premonitions."

His words chilled Gabriel. "Maybe we should get you to a neurologist so they can do another CAT scan."

"They did a couple when I was there. There's no damage."

"Then maybe you should talk to someone."

"Like a shrink? No thanks. I'll be fine. I need to get some air—to get out of this house and live a little. I'm so frustrated." Jazz jumped to his feet and started pacing the room.

"I know you're anxious, but you don't want to put yourself in harm's way or do too much too soon. You're body has been through a lot."

"Look at me," Jazz said as he suddenly ripped open his shirt, revealing his six-pack abs. "Do I look like I can't handle myself? I'm all better now."

"I'm sure you are, but you're still not safe."

Jazz closed his shirt and plopped down on the bed brokenheartedly. "I know you're right. I want all this shit to be over."

"Why don't we go downstairs and eat and watch a movie or something?"

"Sounds like a plan."

Gabriel walked out of the room with Jazz hot on his heels.

"Gabriel, listen, I can be an ass sometimes, but I really appreciate you letting me stay here. It means a lot." Jazz flashed his pearly teeth in a sweet, humbled smile.

"Don't worry about it. It's cool," Gabriel said as they made their way down the staircase. As they rounded the stairs, the house phone started ringing. "I'm going to let the machine get that. I don't feel like talking to anyone."

✝✝✝

"Hey, Gabriel, it's Garrett. I'm home now and I was hoping to see you. I left a message on your cell phone. Call me."

Gabriel turned around just in time to see Jazz hit the floor. "Jazz! Jazz!" Gabriel screamed when he saw him fall. Gabriel ran around the island and raced over to Jazz, who was shaking his head back and forth, his eyes open, but glazed.

"Are you okay? What the hell happened?"

"The voice on the machine. It was him—The Messiah."

"What are you talking about?" Gabriel asked incredulously as he helped Jazz to his feet. Gabriel hit the green play button on the machine and listened to Garrett's message—the only message on the machine.

As the message replayed, Gabriel noticed Jazz's body stiffen, as if it had locked up on cue. Fear seemed to paralyze him.

Gabriel's disbelief faded when he witnessed Jazz's Pavlovian response to Garrett's voice. He looked at Jazz's glassy eyes and reached out to touch him. Gabriel was unnerved at the cold skin. It was as if icy water ran through his veins.

"Jazz!" he yelled trying to bring him back out of his disconnected stare. "Jazz!"

"That voice—it's him."

Gabriel thought about all of Jazz's hallucinations, but dared not question him at the risk of making Jazz feel as if he were losing his mind. Instead, Gabriel took him by the arm and led him into the living room. He spoke in a very soft, calm, and patronizingly clichéd voice.

"Look, I know you think that I'm a nut and I know that I've been seeing shit, but *that* voice I will never forget. Whoever just called you is the man who tried to kill me—the fucking Messiah! How the fuck do you know him?" Jazz suddenly became erratic and angry, as if he had discovered some grave conspiracy against him. The look in his eyes contained more than fear and went far deeper than surprise; it was contempt.

"Jazz, that was Garrett, my boyfriend—I mean the man I've been dating— and I assure you he's not a serial killer—he's a doctor."

"I don't give a fuck if you're seeing the Pope. All I know is that was him. And you know him!"

"Jazz, I need you to calm down and take a seat," he said as he reached out to grab his arm. "Calm down."

"I don't know what's going on here or what you're up to, but this is so fucked up. Are you working with him? Are you a part of this?"

"A part of what? Don't be ridiculous."

Jazz stared at him in disbelief.

"If I was part of this, you'd be dead already, don't you think?" Gabriel said calmly.

Jazz shook his head and lowered himself into the lounger and rubbed his face in his hands. "I don't know what's going on."

"Look, from the description you gave me of The Messiah, I can assure you that he and Garrett are very different. Garrett is bald with no facial hair. You said you remembered The Messiah having a head full of curly hair.

"Have you ever heard of a wig—a disguise?"

Gabriel ignored the harsh tone.

"Would you like for me to invite Garrett over here so you can see that he is not The Messiah?"

"Are you out of your fucking mind? Have you told your boyfriend about me? Does he know that I'm here?"

"Damn, calm down."

Jazz had shot up from the chair and darted across the room.

"No, I haven't told anyone you're here. The only person who knows you're here is your mother."

"Well, let's keep it that way. I don't want to see him." Jazz's demeanor began to change from an excited and erratic state to a more lucid one. "When you've been through what I have, you don't forget certain things. You don't forget."

"There are a lot of people who sound alike. Garrett's voice may be similar to that of The Messiah but he is not the one. Maybe—"

"Maybe what? I might be crazy?"

"That's not what I was going to say."

"Why is this happening to me?" Jazz said. He couldn't fight the tears and they streamed down his face. "Why?"

Gabriel had no answers—only questions. He thought about Jazz's accusation and a terrifying thought settled upon him. *What if?*

†††

After Jazz finished his conversation with Gabriel, he went upstairs, feeling isolated, alone, and agitated. As close as he felt to Gabriel, he had to face the fact that Gabriel was not his kin. The familial bond that he so desired still eluded him. His mother was a phony as far as he was concerned and he tried to force himself to accept that the love he desired from her would never come, but this was one of those times he wished he had a *real* mother to confess his fears to.

Jazz looked at his phone as it lit up and played music. Ironically, it was his mother. Part of him wanted to pick up the phone and scream at her for not being there for him, but the other part wanted her to suffer. The damage left by silence could be profound. He had no words for her.

He sat back in the bed and shook his head, almost in disbelief. He had been alienated from his family, attacked by a predator, and was now living with a stranger. What else could go wrong?

Yet, as much as he hated his mother, part of him still wanted her in his life. He missed his sister. He missed being part of a family. He closed his eyes and before long, his mind drifted back to that fateful day at home. He recalled that day—Thanksgiving Day—when his brother, a recovering crack addict, had revealed his secret to the entire family at the dinner table. When they should have been saying prayers and being thankful over turkey and dressing, his brother dropped a bomb that ravaged an otherwise joyful occasion. Jazz remembered the victorious look in his brother's eyes as he told the family that he had caught Jazz and Maurice naked together in his room the day before. He knew that his brother expected him to deny his attraction to men—like he always had when confronted about it—but this time was different. Jazz, already tired of the lying and pretending, remained silent as his brother told of his discovery. When Jazz's stepfather asked him if it was true, Jazz stood up with his head held high and in an unapologetic voice he confirmed that he was, in fact, gay. He remembered the sound of his own voice exploding through the room. He remembered the disappointed look in his mother's eyes; and most painfully, he meditated on the venomous words she hurled at him after asking him to pack his bags and leave: "I'd rather you be a crackhead than gay."

Even now, her words rang loudly in Jazz's head. He could still feel their sting. He still felt their power.

The ringing of his cell phone snapped him out of his trip down memory lane. He glanced at it and was surprised to see her number flashing again. Now was not a good time for him to speak to her so he let her leave a message. Seconds later, he picked up the phone, and brought it to his ear so he could hear what she had to say.

"Jazz, baby. It's your mother. I wanted to check to see how you are doing and to let you know that I'm here for you and anytime you want to come home your room will be ready. Baby, I know we've had some bad times but I hope that after all that has happened you can find it in your heart to forgive me. I want to help you through this. Please let me. Please call me back." As soon as he heard her sniffles, he hung up the phone. He didn't want—or need—her crocodile tears.

Chapter 19

What if Jazz is right?

That question lingered in Gabriel's thoughts. As much as he tried to let it go, he couldn't. It held onto his spirit with a vice grip and forced him to count possibilities.

What if Garrett is The Messiah?

He thought back to his conversation with Faith. *Religious fanatic.* Garrett was a religious man as evidenced by his religious home décor, but a fanatic? Not even close. Gabriel thought about how strange he had felt when he first entered Garrett's home and surveyed the religious themes all around.

The photos.

The crosses.

The gospel CDs.

The religious books.

The Bibles—in every room, including the bathrooms.

If his only quirk is a love for God, then I have nothing to complain about, Gabriel remembered thinking.

Then he thought about Jazz and how assured he was that Garrett's voice was that of The Messiah. *Could it be?*

"Nah, that's just stupid," he said out loud as he drove down the busy highway at night. That night for Jazz was horrific and trauma such as that had a way of playing with one's mind. Gabriel wasn't sure if he could put much faith in Jazz's descriptions. He hadn't seen the face of his attacker but knew that he had curly hair and possibly a goatee.

"This is absurd. Jazz doesn't know what the hell he's talking about," he said to himself as he dismissed Jazz's accusations.

He turned up the radio and drove cautiously toward Garrett's home, but the nagging feeling would not dissipate. He had called Garrett earlier, and they decided they would meet and work through some things.

As he started singing to the tune from the radio, he started to feel the tingle in his feet. It felt like tiny needles pricking the bottom of both his feet. Within seconds, he realized that his breathing had become staggered as he struggled for air. His palms grew damp and sticky.

"Oh no. Not now. I can't do this," he said. He knew that he needed to pull over off the busy highway, but he wasn't sure he could make it. Cars moved past him quickly and he wasn't sure how he was going to make it to the shoulder of the road. Up ahead, he could see brake lights, but it took him a few extended seconds to realize that he needed to decelerate. Up ahead, flashing signs indicating lane closures that snarled traffic could be seen and the new traffic patterns brought it to a virtual standstill.

"Breathe. Breathe. Inhale. Exhale," he said to calm himself, but Jazz's words kept ringing in his ears and flashes of Garrett's face rushed through his head. "Garrett is not a killer. Garrett is not The Messiah." Gabriel felt his vision blurring and the incapacitating fear growing closer to him. He applied the brakes and slowed his vehicle only seconds before he collided with the truck in front of him.

"Get it together. Breathe. Breathe." Gabriel took slow, elongated breaths and tried to talk himself out of the attack. He tried not to focus on his dire situation or what would become of him if he had a full-fledged attack on the highway. Instead of focusing on the dangers, he decided to count his blessings. It must've been divine intervention that he took this highway, this route to get to Garrett's house instead of the other way. If he had had a large-scaled attack in the middle of D.C.'s raging traffic, he could have caused a major accident. It was a blessing that he had gotten on this road at this time and there was road construction.

"Yeah, that's a good thing. God is watching out for me," he said out loud. He was so focused on his blessing and his breathing that he didn't see traffic opening up until he heard a barrage of disparate car horns blaring at him. He looked ahead and maneuvered his vehicle across the lane and eventually onto the shoulder of the road and then off the highway completely. He managed to pull into a gas station parking lot and took enough time to get himself together before pulling off and heading toward Garrett's.

✝✝✝

"Hey, baby," Garrett said once he opened the door. He leaned in and gave Gabriel a quick peck on the cheek and beckoned him inside his lair. Gabriel didn't speak, but walked into the house and turned to face him. He hoped that any signs of despair or panic had been erased from his face because he didn't want to have to explain his minor attack. "You look really good. Have you been working out?" Garrett asked, providing Gabriel with the confirmation he sought.

"Garrett, we need to talk."

"Yes, I know, but before we do, I have something for you. Come on." Garrett took him by the hand before he could protest and led him into the den. As they neared, the familiar teal gift box from Tiffany & Co., which was located in the middle of the coffee table, came into view.

Gabriel eyed him, not sure what to think.

"Sit down, baby. Please." Gabriel eyed him again but complied.

"Look, Gabriel. I know I have been acting crazy the last few days, and I can't really explain my behavior more than I already have. I said I was going to make it up to you, and I'm so happy you have given me the chance to do so." Garrett grabbed the box off the table and handed it to Gabriel, who took it reluctantly.

"What is this?"

"It's a gift from my heart to you. Open it."

Carefully, Gabriel removed the bow and removed the lid from the small box.

"Oh my God, Garrett. This is beautiful." Gabriel instantly recognized the beautiful silver watch as its polished stainless steel glistened under the light.

"I can still remember how your face lit up the moment you saw it."

Gabriel thought back to a few weeks prior, when he and Garrett were shopping on Wisconsin Avenue in Chevy Chase, Maryland, and stopped to view jewelry on display in the window at Tiffany's. The watch that Gabriel held in his hand was the watch that he fell in love with on the sunny afternoon.

"Look, it's set at four-thirteen, which is the exact time you saw it."

"I can't believe you'd remember that."

"I remember everything about you. Baby, I love you."

Gabriel continued looking at the watch and tried not to fall more in love with Garrett. His words, the look in his eyes, the gift, the sentimentality, the romance, made this moment nearly perfect. Gabriel wanted to release all of his issues with Garrett, but something would not let him. He looked into Garrett's enchanting black eyes and wanted to profess his love for him, too, but he could not allow the words to escape his mouth.

"Baby, as much as I want to, I can't accept this gift. It's too extravagant," Gabriel said as he remembered the $2,500 price tag.

"No, I want you to have it. If you could see your face the way I see it when you look at it, then you'd know that the watch was meant for you."

"Garrett—"

"I won't take no for an answer. Let me show my love for you."

Gabriel didn't want to fight him on this issue. He didn't want to fight anymore, and he didn't want to question this man's love for him. Instantly, he felt ridiculous for even entertaining the notion that Garrett was The Messiah. His face reddened at his own embarrassment.

"Baby, what's wrong?" Garrett asked, obviously noticing the change in his hue.

"Oh nothing. I'm feeling a bit overwhelmed by all of this."

Garrett reached out and stroked Gabriel's face in the gentlest way. Gabriel looked closely and deeply into his eyes, and he did see love. But he wasn't ready to reciprocate the emotions Garrett was feeding him, so he decided to change the subject. "Baby, I have to ask you a question." He took Garrett by the hands and pulled him onto the couch next to him.

"Sure. What's wrong?"

"Do you know a lady by the name of Sabrina Dean?"

It was very subtle, but Gabriel noticed a twitch in Garrett's left eye. Gabriel was an expert at detecting changes in body language, regardless of how minute. Garrett's twitch unnerved Gabriel a little.

"Sabrina Dean? Hmm…doesn't sound familiar. Why?"

"She was murdered."

"What are you talking about? Murdered? Who is she? Why are you asking me?"

"I'm sorry. I should have explained. She went to Antioch—your church."

"Really? Well, we have thousands of members. It's impossible for me to know everyone. Do you have a photograph?"

"No, I don't, but I could probably get one."

"Oh wait," Garrett said in a noticeably different tone. "This must be about the story you're working on. This is why you've been so preoccupied. What's going on?"

"In part. I've recently come across some information that will shock this city, and this is part of it. I can't go into details, though."

"You can tell me. It's not like I'm some stranger on the street."

"I wish I could tell you more, but I can't," Gabriel said, trying to placate Garrett's inquisition.

"How do you know she was murdered? I haven't heard anything about this in church. No one has mentioned anything."

"I think the police are trying to keep it quiet for now."

"Are you going to tell me what happened?"

"Baby—"

Garrett folded his arms and looked at Gabriel. "I wish I had some information for you, but I didn't know her." Gabriel sensed Garrett's annoyance and he watched him shift in his seat.

"You want something to drink?" He rose before Gabriel could respond. "I'll pour you a glass of Chardonnay," he said as he made a hasty exit to the kitchen.

Gabriel watched him scurry away. He didn't know what was going on, but in his heart he knew that Garrett was lying to him. He could sense Garrett's deception and his discomfort with the whole conversation.

†††

When Garrett entered the kitchen, he immediately grabbed the roll of paper towels. His nose had started to bleed. He walked through the kitchen to the bathroom in the hallway with the towel stuffed into his nostrils.

Once inside, he stared at himself. The transformation was complete.

"I'm sick of this bloody-nose shit," he said in a harsh whisper as if he were speaking strongly to someone else. He inhaled deeply and stared at the person in the mirror. In it, deep behind his own evil eyes, he could see Garrett's reflection, but that poor coward was trapped in the mirror— locked away.

He smiled.

After a few moments, he exited the bathroom and went back into the kitchen where he promptly poured two glasses of wine. He downed one glass in a single gulp and refilled the glass.

"Garrett, what are you doing? Are you okay?"

I know this bitch ain't rushing me. I don't know how Garrett puts up with his whiny ass. "I'm on my way. I couldn't find the wine opener," he called out to Gabriel.

He picked up both glasses of wine and took a couple of steps before stopping. When he chose Jazz, he also chose Gabriel to be his scribe. He knew that Gabriel was behind this delay in getting the word out. *He's reported on me before, why not now? If he won't spread my gospel, then I'll make it impossible for them not to.* He looked toward the sink and the cabinets underneath.

Rat poison. Quickly, he moved over to the sink and set the glasses down. He heard Gabriel's voice call out again. "Baby, what are you doing?"

A few minutes later, he exited the kitchen, smile spread across his face, wine in hand. He entered the room as Gabriel closed his cell phone.

"Who were you calling?"

"Remember I told you that my cousin was in a car accident and he was staying at my house for a few days? I was calling my cousin to see if he's okay, but he didn't pick up. I guess he must've turned in early."

Cousin, my ass. I know who's at your house.

"Probably. I'm sure he still has a lot of recovering to do."

"He does, but he's improved by leaps and bounds."

"No doubt due to your wonderful care."

Gabriel leaned back and smiled.

He looked at Gabriel with a silent contempt. He wanted to backhand him across the face and rip the watch off his arm, but he restrained himself. *It's not his time.*

Instead, he took a gulp of the wine.

"So, what's with this story you're writing?" he asked again to see if he could make some headway with Gabriel. He hoped the wine would loosen his lips.

"Man, you wouldn't believe me if I told you."

"Try me."

Gabriel looked at him and smiled.

He could tell by Gabriel's expression that he wasn't going to talk about it.

"I don't want to bore you with the details. I'll tell you later, but right now, I've got to get home," Gabriel replied.

"Home? You just got here. You've barely tasted your wine. If you stay, I'll make it worth your while," he said seductively as his hand moved up Gabriel's thigh. Garrett's counterfeit smile moved across his face as Gabriel removed his hand.

"I know, but I really need to check on my cousin. I'm getting a weird feeling."

"You're being paranoid." Garrett moved closer and started kissing and licking Gabriel's neck.

"Baby, I've got to go," Gabriel said.

"Your cousin is fine. I'm sure. If he wasn't, then he would have called you."

"Maybe, but I'd rather err on the side of caution." Gabriel removed himself from Garrett's grip and stood up.

I hate this bitch. I ought to take it from him. "You do have a point. You probably should make sure he's okay."

Gabriel playfully grabbed both of Garrett's hands, and pulled him up from where he sat. He gently kissed Garrett, but Garrett pulled him into his body and forcefully, he stuck his tongue in Gabriel's mouth. Gabriel pulled away.

"What's wrong, baby?"

"Uh, nothing. I better leave before things get too heated."

"Don't be afraid of the heat."

Gabriel smiled and picked up his keys from the table. "I really better get going. And, baby, thanks again for the watch."

Gabriel walked to the door.

"I hope I can see you again soon."

"Of course." Gabriel walked out and he watched him through the peep-hole. Right before Gabriel reached his car, he stopped and turned and faced the house. Then he got into his car and drove away.

Your time will come, he thought. *Sooner than you think. He suddenly wished he had put the rat poison in Gabriel's glass.*

†††

Gabriel picked up his cell phone and started to dial Jazz, but on the third ring he hung up. *I'm not his father*, he thought to himself. As he drove down the winding street he thought back to Garrett and the kiss. Again, he felt something that didn't used to be in Garrett's kisses. He was a much more aggressive kisser than he had grown accustomed to. *Stop it, Gabriel. You are trippin'. What if I'm the one who's changed?*

It never occurred to him that maybe with all the stress he'd been under dealing with thoughts of The Messiah, caring for Jazz, and being pressured by Faith to hold off on a story that needed to be told, that something in him had been thrown off kilter. He realized that during the last couple of weeks he had been tired and a bit irritable.

Shit. Gabriel had been so focused on his strange feelings about Garrett that he never thought once about where those feelings were originating. The thought made him turn his car around and point it in the direction of Garrett's house. He wanted to go and speak to Garrett again, to see if he could get a better sense of what was going on.

When he got to the house, he drove right through the gate that Garrett evidently had left open. *Shit, I hope he's not leaving.* Gabriel sped up the drive and parked his car. When he got to the door, he lightly tapped on the door and put his hand on the knob. It was unlocked, so he stepped into the house.

"Garrett," he called out as he moved deeper into the house. He walked into the den, but it was empty. Then he walked into the kitchen.

"Garrett?" Still there was no answer. The house remained silent. Gabriel opened the refrigerator and grabbed a Coke from the door. He rinsed off the can, popped the top, and took a swig before moving upstairs.

Maybe he's in the shower, he devilishly thought.

Once upstairs, he walked into the bedroom, hoping to catch a peek of his naked flesh, but Garrett wasn't there and the bathroom was empty. Gabriel walked back into the bedroom and stood in the center of the room and wondered where Garrett had gone. He peeked over the balcony, but didn't see him in the pool either.

Slightly agitated, he moved over to Garrett's desk and picked up a pen to leave a note. The middle drawer was ajar and a colorful pamphlet caught his attention. He reached into the drawer and pulled out a brochure decorated loosely with the vivid colors of the gay pride flag. Gabriel was aghast.

"Re-Invention—Restoring Your Sexual Identity," Gabriel read out loud. "Why the hell does he have this?" Re-Invention was a part of the ex-gay movement, which were organizations designed to restore a gay person back to heterosexuality through various means such as intensive counseling, therapy, and spiritual guidance. Years ago, when the ex-gay movement started, Gabriel profiled a similar group and during his research he had become familiar with a lot of the groups that purported to eliminate same-sex desires.

Gabriel was very familiar with the Re-Invention Group and was even more puzzled when he saw the card from the group's founder, the Rev. Dr. Tony Mathiasen. During a feature story on one of the groups, Gabriel conducted a brief telephone interview with Dr. Mathiasen and quickly concluded that he was a quack and had done far more harm than good by reinforcing the notion that one could change their sexual orientation. He remembered Dr. Mathiasen describing his program as a "sexual re-orientation" plan that combines counseling and emotional work with Biblical teaching and prayer.

During his research Gabriel spoke with many mental health experts who testified that the well-documented damage inflicted by these programs on individual self-esteem often triggered depression and even suicide. Gabriel remembered feeling sick to his stomach because he had interviewed many people who had gone through these kinds of programs only to be left feeling worse or inadequate when they failed to become straight.

Gabriel flipped over the card and looked at the appointment time. Based on the information written, Garrett had seen the doctor two days ago.

"I don't get it," he said out loud. Garrett had never shown any indication that he had an issue with being gay. In fact, exactly the opposite. Gabriel stood in the middle of the room with a scowl on his face and his hands on his hips.

He heard a door slam downstairs.

Shit, he said as he quickly put the brochure and the card back into the drawer and closed it. Seconds later, he heard the fall of footsteps on the staircase. He stood up and moved toward the bedroom door as Garrett was coming in.

"Damn!" he screamed and swung wildly.

"Baby, it's me!" Gabriel said as he dodged the blow.

"Gabriel, what the fuck are you doing? I thought you left?" Garrett said as he unclenched his fist.

"I did, but I thought I left something. I came up here looking for you."

"I was in the garage," Garrett said as he moved toward Gabriel and gave him a hug. "You know sneaking up on a brotha like that will get you knocked out."

"I'm sorry. I didn't mean to startle you."

"What were you looking for?"

"Huh?" Gabriel asked, still somewhat distracted by the Re-Invention brochure.

"You said you thought you left something."

"Oh, yeah. I couldn't find my cell phone, but I have it now," he said as he waved the phone in front of Garrett's face.

"Why would your phone be up here? You never came up here," Garrett said suspiciously.

"I know. The phone was downstairs in between the sofa cushions. I came up here to find pen and paper to leave you a note." Garrett looked at him skeptically. Gabriel couldn't believe his lie was transparent. Usually, he lied flawlessly, when needed.

"Well, let me get home."

Chapter 20

I can't sit in this house another night, Jazz thought as he put the final touches on his ensemble. Even though he realized that he may have been wrong about the voice on the machine, he couldn't get it out of his head. It sounded so much like his attacker that even when he thought about it, he started to sweat. He needed to do something to get his mind off it. He needed an escape from this carefully constructed and gentle life he was leading. He needed to get out and get back in the game. After all, life was for the living and he was far from dead. He carefully viewed his face in the mirror and was ecstatic that the trauma he suffered hadn't left any permanent damage. His face had returned to its previous glory.

After Gabriel left, Jazz raided his closet for something to wear. He found a pair of loosely fitted jeans since Gabriel was larger, but since baggy was the new look, the jeans worked fine for him. He was determined to escape his prison and get into the city. His fear had almost kept him confined, but he was never one to give into fear. He wanted to go out and have a few drinks and forget all the madness that surrounded his world.

From Gabriel's bedroom window upstairs, Jazz could see the unmarked police car parked in front of the house and the silhouette of the officer inside. The only way out of the house was through the back door. He felt like James Bond making a daring escape from captivity.

Once down in the kitchen, he opened the liquor cabinet and poured a shot of tequila. The elixir burned on its way down, but Jazz loved the fire. He turned the television up in the living room and flipped on the lights to give the impression that he was in the room. He crept over to the window and peeled back the curtain enough to see the car in a better view. The officer sat in black cruiser and seemed to be distracted by something in the car. Jazz knew it was his time to flee.

He moved through the living room toward the back door. He didn't have a key to the house so he needed to make sure the door was left unlocked. He wasn't planning on being gone long.

He opened the door and stepped into the waiting darkness.

Once outside, he slipped through the backyard, hopped the neighbor's fence, and made his way down the block undetected. He was a few blocks from the nearest subway station and hurried down the street. The city was harsh and could take its toll on even the strongest man. As he walked down the street, swerving by passersby, he noticed the worn and weathered looks on their faces, evidence of their struggle in the District.

Even though the sound of zooming cars and jolting horns reminded him of exactly what he had been missing, he still felt a bit nervous. Shadows crept in from all sides and he felt as if he were being stalked by some force, even as the city-dwellers he passed moved on their way. He stepped off the curve into the street and walked directly in the path of an oncoming SUV, which swerved to avoid him. As he jumped back on the sidewalk, he was assaulted by the silhouette of the driver shooting him the middle finger from the window.

Take it easy. Everything is gonna be okay, he thought.

By the time he reached the U Street/Cardoza subway station, he felt a bit tired. It had been some time since he'd exerted such energy. As he stood on the escalator that descended into the bowels of the city, all he could think of was escaping back into his world, his reality full of fun and folly. He ached to hear thumping sounds and wild laughter. He missed watching the club kids dance and vogue and battle each other in the portion of the club that played house music. He missed the strong drinks and the cigarette smoke.

He missed his life.

He inserted his money into the machine to get a fare card, which allowed access to the subway. As he did, he heard the familiar bell of the train, indicating that the doors were closing. He wanted to run down the second escalator but even if he had, he would have still missed it. Instead, he walked leisurely down the escalator and turned around to take a seat on a bench at the far end of the platform. He couldn't help but notice how eerily quiet the station had become since all the riders seemed to have gotten on the train he missed. He looked up at the sign which let him know that the next train would service the platform in fifteen minutes. He plopped down on the bench and fiddled with his watch to kill the time.

Five minutes into his wait, he heard footsteps on the platform and looked up to see a man wearing a black Armani T-shirt and a pair of baggy jeans walking in his direction.

This could be promising.

The man walked toward him, hands in his pockets, head down.

That's right, come over here and sit down next to me, big baby.

Jazz tried not to stare but the way the stranger's shirt stood out on his chest demanded attention.

"Jazz." He thought he heard his name as the stranger passed, but Jazz did not see his lips move.

"Wassup?" he asked instinctively.

"What?" the stranger growled, examining Jazz with a scowl.

"Oh, I thought you said something to me."

"Fool, I don't even know you." His harsh tone shredded any attraction Jazz had toward him.

"My bad."

"Yeah, it's yo bad," he said as he kept moving. "Freak," he mumbled under his breath.

Jazz wanted to say something but didn't want to risk a fight with some idiot on a deserted subway platform. And since he wasn't completely back in form, he guessed that thug boy would beat the hell out of him.

Hell, that could be foreplay, he thought as he laughed out loud.

By the time he got to the club, the hour was late and the club was packed. He walked in, head held high, and greeted a few familiar faces. Without pause or delay, he made his way to the bar, placed an order for a drink and quickly guzzled half of it before he had even gotten change from the twenty-dollar bill he had *borrowed* from Gabriel.

He walked away from the bar and posted up next to the cement column at the back of the club. He removed the napkin from around his cup and used it to pat dry the tiny molecules of sweat that gathered on his brow. He felt light-headed and needed a few moments to collect himself. He started his club surveillance, scoping out the scene, trying to see who was there, looking around for a friend or foe, a conquest or a concubine. Shirtless muscle boys, glistening with sweat, were peppered throughout the room, taking in the wanton looks of other revelers who fed their insatiable egos. Young queens, full of life and laughter, pranced and danced and kicked their way to joy at the sound of hypnotic house beats.

Jazz took a slower sip of his drink as clouds of smoke poured from the ceiling, cloaking the room in a dense fog as strobe lights flashed. Music filled the room with a pulsing passion and Jazz could feel the beats even through the cement column. Wild faces, colored with laughter and delight, walked by him, cruising him, eyeing him up and down.

He could be here, Jazz suddenly thought. As he looked into the sea of faces, Jazz's thoughts fell on The Messiah. *What is The Messiah doing right now? Is he out seeking his next victim or is he alone in a room plotting his next attack? Or, is he in this club, in this room, skulking, stalking, plotting, devising and choosing. Is he hiding in plain sight? He could be anywhere and he could be anyone.*

Jazz suddenly felt fear float into the room and he could sense his breathing quickening.

I am not afraid. I am not afraid. He closed his eyes and tried to feel the music and the club.

"Sup, trumpet man?"

Jazz turned and saw a familiar face.

"Cedric, wassup, baby?"

"Nothing. I've been missing you. I ain't seen you in a minute. Where you been hiding?"

Jazz examined the beautiful specimen to his left. Each time he and Cedric were in the vicinity of each other, their temperatures were sure to rise. Cedric was built like a brick house, sturdy and solid, and knew how to work his assets. He stared at Jazz, licking and biting his lips seductively, while Jazz smiled.

"I've been laying low."

"I heard you was in some kind of accident. You don't look injured to me, but if you need me to check your body out, let me know."

Damn. Jazz could feel him. Then he felt himself starting to grow and instantly he felt a pain in his penis, which hadn't yet healed from the circumcision.

"Nah, I'm straight, baby."

"Damn, boy. You get finer every time I see you. What's your secret?"

"Good genes. I get better with age, like a fine wine."

"Fine, indeed," Cedric said as he eyed him from head to toe. "You wanna dance?"

"With you?" he asked in jest.

"Hell yeah. You ain't gonna find nobody better in here."

"I know that's right. Yeah, I'll dance with you, but let me go pee first."

"Do you need me to hold it?" Cedric asked while looking down at Jazz's crotch.

"Maybe later. Don't go anywhere, I'll be right back."

Jazz sauntered his way through the crowded room. It suddenly felt really packed and the music pumped louder through the speakers. People pushed and bumped into Jazz and the drink he had was beginning to take its toll. He felt slightly light-headed and couldn't wait to get to the bathroom to splash some cool water on his heated skin.

As he tried to make his way through the next room, he had to stop for a minute. The room spun. He began to hear whispers in his ear, but couldn't detect what they were saying or where the words were coming from. So he pressed on, wanting—needing—to get to the restroom.

As soon as he entered the bathroom, the door slammed shut behind him. He walked over to the sink and turned on the faucet. He cupped his hands and let the cool water fall into them, before splashing his face. He held onto the sink for balance.

"*Jazz*," he heard a voice say.

"Who's there?" he asked as he suddenly turned to face the empty room. "I said, who's there?"

There was no answer.

Quickly, he turned around but did not see anyone. Slowly he walked over to the stalls, his heart beating rapidly.

"*Jazz*."

"Where the fuck are you?" He kicked open the first door to reveal an empty stall. As he moved to the second stall, he paused. His hands were dripping with sweat. The voice struck deep into his heart, wrapping Jazz in a thick fear that almost paralyzed him.

I ain't afraid. I ain't afraid.

As he kicked in the door to the second stall, the lights in the room went out and Jazz turned quickly. He saw a shadow move in the blackened room, but the image was lost before he could make it out clearly.

Then he heard words that struck even deeper.

"*Covenant. Remember our covenant.*"

"Leave me the fuck alone!" he screamed out into the blackness. He could hear sounds and movement but couldn't see anything. The light switch was on the wall near the door, on the opposite side of the room. In order to get out, he'd have to make his way across the room blindly, hoping that whoever was stalking him wouldn't attack him. He wanted to move. He needed to move, but he couldn't. Instead, he stood along the wall—frozen.

He heard footsteps and balled his fists. He started swinging his arms wildly, even as he closed his eyes tightly.

"*Jazz!*"

At the call of his name, Jazz felt himself losing consciousness. In the flicker of a second before he lost consciousness, the lights came on and he saw Cedric racing toward him.

Chapter 21

When Gabriel got home, he crept into his bedroom, not bothering to check in on Jazz. He tried to get to the place where he wasn't consumed with thoughts about Jazz's safety. After all, he barely knew him. After his experience with Garrett, he yearned to be alone. He walked over to the blinds and peeked out, reassuring himself that the police cruiser was still there, watching over them like their protector.

They couldn't be under the watchful eye of the police forever, so he sent a prayer to God that the long arm of the law would soon catch this fiend. He committed himself to speaking to Jazz tomorrow about Faith's plan. The more he thought about it, the more he realized she was right. Jazz was their best hope and chance of drawing The Messiah out of his hiding place. Now Gabriel could take comfort in the fact that The Messiah could not possibly know the whereabouts of Jazz, but if he persuaded Jazz to take part in Faith's plan, that would soon change.

Then, his thoughts drifted to Garrett and the Re-Invention brochure. He could not figure out why Garrett would have been seeing this man, but he was going to figure it out. First thing in the morning, he was going to call the doctor and set up an appointment. He was going to meet this man face-to-face and find out the truth about Garrett. If Garrett had some deep-seeded psychological issue with his sexuality, then Gabriel had to know. He could not and would not, in good conscience, escalate their relationship if Garrett was troubled. He had to figure out what was going on if he was to continue seeing him.

Maybe the drama and the suspicion were creations of his overactive imagination. Again he thought that maybe the problem was him, yet all of the signs pointed to the contrary. Deep inside he sensed that something was wrong and he also knew that Garrett would never admit to anything. He'd have to find out the truth for himself. One way or another he'd have to find the answers to the question of why his man, the one he wanted to adore, had suddenly changed into something...else.

Thoughts of Jazz, The Messiah, Garrett, his career were too draining. Now, he needed sleep and the promise of a new day.

✝✝✝

Gabriel was awake and in the shower by seven in the morning. He hadn't gotten much sleep—far too anxious about what the day would bring. He slipped out of the shower, dried off, and slid into his clothing in record time. He wanted to do some more research before he went to Dr. Mathiasen's office.

He exited his room and walked down the hallway, pausing momentarily at Jazz's door. He didn't hear a sound. He looked at his watch. It was barely seven-thirty so he knew Jazz would be asleep. Instead of barging into his room, Gabriel went downstairs, opting to leave him a note if he wasn't awake by the time he left.

Quickly, Gabriel made a cup of green tea, poured two teaspoons of Splenda in his to-go cup and was out of the house and into his car before he knew it. He clicked open the garage door and backed his car out into the street, still comforted by the police cruiser. He took an immediate right and then a left and was on the highway headed toward Alexandria, Virginia, right outside of D.C.

The morning traffic, even at such an early hour, was brutal. It was stop-and-go traffic all along I-395 South as cars closely rode the bumper of the car in front of them only to be forced to slam on their brakes seconds later. On this particular morning, Gabriel was one of those tail-riders. He was anxious to get to the doctor's office, but uncertain of what he was going to do once he got there. He had no plan, but he was not going to leave until he got the information he came for.

He reached down and turned on the radio and listened to the Russ Parr Morning Show. He needed something to take his mind off the snarled traffic and his impending date with the good doctor. The Morning Show team was up to their usual hilarious bits, and the humor did his mind good. Before he knew it, he exited King Street and was making his way down the wide boulevard, which was less crowded than the highway.

He looked at the piece of paper on which he had written the address and realized he was near the building. He turned into the parking lot and found a space close to the street. He wanted to have a good view of everyone coming in and out of the building. It was a little after eight, and he wasn't sure when he was going to make his move.

He watched, with curious anticipation, as people walked into the four-story medical complex and wondered what ailed them. Gabriel's old dentist used to be located there so he was somewhat familiar with the building. From what he remembered, the building housed several medical doctors, dentists, therapists, psychologists, and a couple of physical therapists. It was a one-stop healthcare shop.

Russ Parr signed off the radio, letting him know it was ten in the morning. It was time to make his move. He'd sat in the car for over an hour contemplating his next step and now the time had arrived. He stepped out of the car, adjusted his shirt, and marched into the complex.

When he walked in, he immediately noticed the change in décor. When he used to visit his dentist, the lobby was drab, filled with earth tones, and a couple of wooden benches. Now, the lobby gleamed and sparkled with black and green marble.

"May I help you?" the security guard asked. Gabriel realized that he must've looked confused when he walked into the lobby.

"Uh, yeah. I have an appointment."

"I need to see your identification, and I need you to sign here and indicate who you are going to see," she said as she pointed to a blank space in the book that lay open on the desk. Gabriel smiled reluctantly and did as she said.

"This place sure has changed," he said.

"What do you mean?"

"I mean the lobby. The last time I was here, it was—different."

"Oh that. Yeah, management wanted to give the building a more professional look."

Gabriel put down the pen and reached for his ID.

"Who are you here to see?"

"Dr. Mathiasen."

"Oh," she said quickly. "He's on the third floor, suite three-sixteen."

Gabriel thanked her and walked away curiously, not giving any more thought to her change in tone.

When he exited the elevator, he walked down the long corridor, past the stairwell to suite 316, and opened the door. Four people were seated on the forest-green couch and chairs, their heads nonchalantly buried in magazines. An attractive African-American woman sat behind the desk, on the phone. Gabriel stepped to the counter and picked up the same brochure that he had seen in Garrett's drawer.

"Hi, welcome to Dr. Mathiasen's office. How may I help you?" she said as she hung up the phone and greeted Gabriel.

Gabriel returned the brochure to the counter. "How are you? I'm here to see Dr. Mathiasen."

"What time is your appointment?"

"Oh, I don't have an appointment."

"What is this in reference to?"

Gabriel cleared his throat and leaned in a little closer. "I have a problem. I need to talk to him about his program."

"The Re-Invention program?"

"Yes, that's the one."

"Well, Dr. Mathiasen has helped so many people. As you can imagine, he's a really popular doctor and without an appointment, I'm afraid he can't see you."

"Damn," he said out loud, his profanity startling her.

"Now, there's no need to get anxious. Let me check to see when his next availability is." She turned slightly to the left and pulled up the doctor's schedule on the computer. "Hmm, he doesn't have any time today—or this week," she added. "I'm sorry, but his first available appointment is in two months."

"Two months? Are you kidding me?" Gabriel's voice caused a couple of the people in the waiting room to look up.

"I'm afraid not," she said with an expressionless look drawn across her face.

"Is there anything that you can do to help me, Ms. BeBe?" he asked while reading her nametag.

"Not much. I can put you on the waiting list and if someone cancels we can call you, but that rarely happens. Would you like me to do that?"

"No, I don't think so," Gabriel said, frustration sounding in his voice. "I guess if someone really needs help, this is not the place to come."

"Not without an appointment," she said snidely as she answered the ringing telephone. Gabriel didn't like being dismissed but realized that getting angry with her would have served no purpose. As he walked out of the room back into the hallway, he became more determined than ever to get some information. Then it dawned on him that he didn't need to see the doctor. All he needed was access to his files.

And he'd get it.

He stood in the hallway momentarily, long enough to formulate a plan. Hurriedly, he scampered down the hallway, eyeing the walls up and down, searching for something that would give him an opportunity to get inside that office, but he found nothing. Frustrated, he leaned against the walls and brought his hands to his head.

"Where is it?" he asked himself out loud. In this day and age, he found it hard to believe that he couldn't find the fire alarm. Every time he watched a movie and someone needed to gain entry, all they ever did was pull the alarm and the folks in the building panicked and poured out of it, seeking the safety of an open space. But the one time he needed one, he couldn't find it. He walked slowly down the hall once again, examining every inch, every crack, and crevice, but he didn't see anything.

He was prepared to give up and exit the building dejectedly, but he decided to stop by the bathroom instead. He pushed the brown door open, stepped up to the urinal, unzipped his pants, and handled his business. When he finished, he zipped his pants and stepped over to the sink.

I can't give up. I just can't.

He pumped the liquid soap dispenser and injected his hands with a cool white substance. He turned on the water, waiting for it to warm, then stuck his hands underneath the faucet. As he lathered, he caught the reflection of a blinking red light in the mirror—the smoke detector. He turned quickly and saw the round device on the ceiling in the back of the room.

My saving grace.

Hurriedly, he looked around the room for something that he could use to ignite a small fire. He looked for paper towels, but instead of finding paper towels, the room was equipped with two electric hand dryers.

Shit.

Hurriedly, he rushed into a stall and was relieved to see rolls of toilet paper, but his relief turned to angst as he realized he didn't have anything to start a fire with. No matches. No lighters. No nothing. This was one of those times he regretted giving up smoking. He felt like banging his fists against the wall, but knew that would only result in pain.

Instead, he walked out of the restroom—coolly, confidently—recognizing what he had to do to get what he came for. He had no other choice. He calmly walked over to the elevator and pressed the down button.

When he got to the lobby, he stepped out as a couple walked in.

"That was a quick visit," the security guard said as he passed by her. "I guess you didn't need him after all."

"Actually, I'll be back in a few minutes. I got my appointment time mixed up, so I have about an hour to kill," he said while looking at the watch that Garrett had recently purchased for him. He walked briskly out of the lobby, across the parking lot to his car. He hopped in the car, sped off, and was back in the lobby of the building in less the fifteen minutes.

When he returned, he shot the guard a casual smile as he strolled by and proceeded toward the elevator. On his quick errand, he decided that before he put his plan into action, he needed to do a little more reconnaissance in the doctor's office. He needed to know how many people were in the office, including staff, and hoped to get a sense of where files were kept.

He pushed open the door and BeBe's smile disappeared from her face when she saw him.

"Sir, I've already told you—"

"Yes, I know. Listen, BeBe, is it?" he said as if didn't already know. "You said if there were any cancellations you could give me a call."

"Sir, I assure you there have been no cancellations in the last, what— twenty minutes?" she said as she took a glimpse of the clock that hung on the wall to her right.

Gabriel smiled politely in an effort to mask his strong distaste for her attitude. Although she wasn't being overtly rude, her condescending tone was starting to get underneath his skin.

"Well, since I came all this way, would it be a problem for you if I waited awhile, just to see what happens."

"Sir, you can wait as long as you like but your chances of seeing the doctor today are next to zero." She motioned toward the waiting room. "But, suit yourself," she said as she picked up the phone. "Thank you for calling Dr. Mathiasen's office. It's a great day for change. How may I help you?" BeBe's tone had made a paradigm shift, changing from condescension to perkiness. Gabriel walked away, shaking his head.

He took a seat on the couch next to a Hispanic-looking male, who smiled uncomfortably. Gabriel scanned the room, trying to get a feel for the office and the clientele of Dr. Mathiasen. Directly across from him sat another black man who appeared to be in his early twenties. He noticed Gabriel checking him out and quickly focused his attention back on the magazine spread across his lap. Gabriel reached down onto the table and grabbed the first magazine he could reach. Without paying much attention to the cover, he fanned through the pages and stopped at a picture of a group of men in what looked to be the wilderness, hugged up as if it were a father-son fishing trip. The caption read "Re-claim Your Manhood" and after reading the first couple of sentences, he quickly realized it was a magazine promoting the benefits of Dr. Mathiasen's program. *Propaganda*, he thought as he threw the magazine onto the table, which caused a few other magazines to slide onto the floor, directly in front of the young African-American man. The people seated in the room looked up at him, as if the noise had brought them out of their unsettled moods.

"Sorry about that," he said as he got up from his seat and moved to pick up the magazine. The young man, opting for kindness instead of attitude, reached down to help. "Thanks, man. I wasn't trying to hit you or nothing," Gabriel said jokingly.

"I know," he replied in a voice far deeper than Gabriel had expected. The young man returned to his seat and instead of returning to his, Gabriel got up and sat down next to him.

"Can I ask you something? What do you know about this doctor?" Gabriel queried, not waiting for the young man to respond to his first question. A smile lit up the young man's face as he closed the magazine.

"I know a lot about him. I've been seeing him for a few months."

"What exactly is this program that all of these articles and magazines are referring to? What exactly does he do?"

"So, this is your first time? Well, let me put it like this. He makes you feel like a man again."

"Feel like a man? I feel like a man now," Gabriel said, trying to be mindful of his tone.

"It's okay. I was defensive when I first came here, too. The doctor will put you so at ease that you won't feel like you have to defend this lifestyle."

"Lifestyle? This is my life."

The man chuckled. "I used to say the same thing. But once I got past all that jargon, the doctor was able to cure me from this disease."

Disease? What the hell are you talking about? Gabriel wanted to ask but didn't.

"You think being gay is a disease. So, you think it's contagious?"

"I think it can be transmitted to folks who are weak-minded—like I used to be."

"So, I guess the doctor taught you how to be *strong-minded?*" Gabriel asked with a puzzled look on his face.

"Exactly!" he said with unexpected excitement. "He taught me that life is full of temptation and urges and I don't have to act on every single one. I have learned…restraint."

"So, you're still attracted to men?"

He paused and took a deep breath. "I don't know. I don't really think about it anymore."

"If you've been cured, why are you here?"

"It never hurts to have a little tune-up," he said while gently nudging Gabriel with his elbow.

"Mr. Jackson, the doctor will see you now," BeBe said as she walked over and motioned for him to follow her. Gabriel looked up in time to see Dr. Mathiasen in the doorway, smiling, waiting for his next patient.

"Well, that's my cue. Remember, stop resisting the life God has chosen for you. I'll pray for you, my brother." He stood up and followed BeBe to a room behind the receptionist's desk.

"What a nut," Gabriel said out loud. He couldn't believe the words that had come out of that guy's mouth. Gabriel had never been one to feel ashamed or embarrassed or less than a man because of his sexuality. He had never felt the need to occupy space in the proverbial closet, but he wasn't necessarily marching in gay pride parades either. He had always maintained a quiet strength with his sexuality, ready to spar with those folks who were rabidly anti-gay, but not out looking for controversy. He had never been one who tried to force-feed his sexual orientation on the masses; in fact, he had never asked anyone to embrace his sexuality. All he asked for was tolerance.

He looked at his watch. It was time. He got up from his seat, grabbed a magazine, and walked past BeBe's desk.

"Should I take your name off the list?" she asked with a smirk on her face.

"Why don't you do that, Dede?"

"It's BeBe."

"Whatever," he said as he walked out and let the door slam behind him.

When he entered the hallway, magazine in hand, he was happy to see that it was empty. He walked directly to the restroom, slowly opening the door before stepping in. It, too, was empty. Quickly he went into a stall and rolled the magazine into a cone shape. He reached into his pocket and pulled out the cigarette lighter that he had purchased from the corner store earlier. Carefully, he stood on the rim of the toilet, lit the magazine, and watched the smoke billow close to the smoke detectors. The fire devoured the magazine much more quickly than he had anticipated. He watched the flames as they consumed the pages all at once, sending plumes up smoke through the room. Yet, the alarm did not sound.

What if someone comes in here? Gabriel suddenly became nervous and had to jump from the toilet onto the floor. He dropped the magazine into the commode and listened to the water extinguishing the flames. Gabriel stepped out of the stall and out of the smoke-filled room just as the alarm in the hallway sounded and the lights flashed.

Thank God.

Within seconds, a great commotion could be heard in the hallway as doors to the various suites were flung open and people began to pour out. Gabriel took cover behind a group of people and watched the door to Dr. Mathiasen's office open. He watched BeBe lead out the other patients, including the young man he had spoken with, but he didn't see Dr. Mathiasen leave. He moved slowly down the crowded hallway, trying not to get too close to the doctor's office, but he had to make sure the doctor had left. He knew he'd only get one chance at this. The people sped down the hallway and filed down the stairwell at the opposite end of the corridor. Right when Gabriel started to panic, he saw the doctor leave the office and join the exiting crowd.

Quickly, Gabriel maneuvered his way down the hallway and walked into the doctor's office. He looked around the vacant waiting room and stood still for a moment, listening for any sounds of movement within the back. He knew he had to move. He ran into the doctor's office and looked around. The room had a very sterile feel to it, with a black leather couch and stainless steel tables occupying its main area. The doctor's black-and-glass gargantuan desk was pushed back in a corner near the window, providing him with an excellent view of the outside world.

In the corner across from the desk were two huge filing cabinets. Gabriel rushed over to them to look inside. Each cabinet was divided by certain letters of the alphabet and Gabriel looked down until he saw the drawer labeled "H-L," then pulled on the handle. It was locked.

Damn.

Frantically, he looked around the office for anything that would help him pry open the drawer. Something told him that if Garrett was indeed under the care of this quack, then his information would be contained in that drawer.

He had to get in.

He rushed over to the desk and tore open the drawers, looking for a screwdriver, a hammer—some tool—that would help him break the lock, but the drawers only contained papers. Gabriel grabbed the silver letter opener out of a tray on the desk and went back to the cabinet. He stuck the instrument in between the handle and tried to gain some leverage on the drawer. He pulled, but when he did, the letter opener bent.

Fuck.

He looked around the room and saw a door in the corner on the opposite wall. He ran over and opened the closet door. At the top, was a red, metal box that he grabbed without thinking. The heavy metal toolbox fell onto the floor and metal tools clinked and clanked against each other as they hit the floor. Gabriel panicked. He stepped back into the waiting room to make sure no one had heard the commotion.

When he was satisfied that his mistake went unnoticed, he went back into the office and grabbed a screwdriver and a hammer. Back at the cabinet, he forcefully pounded the screwdriver into a small wedge and pried open the door. He dropped the tools and thumbed through the folders. When he got to folder labeled "Lord, Garrett," he stopped.

"This is it," he said out loud. He opened the folder to verify that it was, indeed, Garrett's folder. As he started reading, the fire alarm stopped. Quickly, he closed the cabinet and rushed over to the window. He saw people beginning to file back into the building. He ran over to the closet and kicked and shoved the tools onto the floor. He didn't want the doctor walking in and immediately seeing tools scattered about. He took the folder and ran out of the office. Mission accomplished.

Chapter 22

"Scott, what the fuck am I going to do? My man is a nut!" Gabriel screeched, head hung low at Scott's dining room table. He had driven around for hours trying take his mind off the information he had discovered in the file.

"Are you shittin' me?" Scott asked with a puzzled look. "Let me get this straight. You started a fire in an office building full of people so that you could break into the office of a Dr. Mathiasen to steal a file on Garrett—a file you weren't sure even existed, mind you. So, you get the file, read it, and find out that Garrett has been a part of some ex-gay movement to try to convert him to heterosexuality while he's been having sex with you?"

"Yeah, that about sums it up."

"Shit, you tryna go to jail, huh? You looking for some rough prison trade?" Scott joked.

"Hell no. Are you even listening to me?"

"Okay, okay. So, Garrett has been in treatment a couple of years, but clearly it hasn't worked. You must got the ill na-na," he said with a laugh as he poured a glass of water for Gabriel and handed him two aspirin.

"Whatever. The fucked-up part about this is that he has shown no signs—not a single one—of having any issues with being gay. I mean, if you're struggling with this I would think the last thing you'd be doing is dating someone and confessing your love to another man."

Scott took a seat next to him and grabbed his hand. "What you gon' do, bitch?" he said in his playful ghetto voice.

"What can I do? I gotta break up with him—tonight. I can't get any more emotionally involved with this freak. Dr. Mathiasen described him as being *pathologically conflicted* over his homosexuality."

"Damn. How does someone cover that kind of psychosis up?"

"I wish I knew. Hell, he just gave me this watch," Gabriel stated as he held out his wrist. Scott leaned in a little closer.

"Well, at least he's got good taste."

"This doesn't make any kind of sense." Gabriel tried not to focus on the forensic psychiatrist's report on The Messiah, but he thought back to his conversation with Faith in which the killer was thought to be a *repressed homosexual.* Suddenly, everything started to make sense.

"Gabriel—Gabriel!" Scott yelled.

"Huh?"

Scott paused and looked at Gabriel. "Okay. I know you. Something else is going on."

"What do you mean?"

"Negro, don't try to play a playa. I know when something is wrong with you, and it's more than you're telling me now. So, spit it out."

"It's nothing."

"Gabriel, don't make me act a fool up in here. I know this is my house, but if you don't tell me what's going on there's gonna be some furniture moving all up and through here."

"You so hard," Gabriel said with a chuckle. He rubbed his face in his hands while he thought of words to verbalize what he was feeling. "The police have always thought The Messiah could possibly be a gay man who is so conflicted over his sexual orientation that he targets other gays as a way of feeling better about himself."

"I remember you telling me that; sounds a little sketchy to me."

"Me too. I never bought that theory—until now."

"What do you mean?" Gabriel got up and walked into Scott's kitchen. He reached into the wine chiller and grabbed a bottle. He reached into the drawer, pulled out the wine opener, and pulled out the cork.

"Shit, help yourself, why don't you?"

Gabriel ignored his comment and grabbed a glass from the cabinet and poured himself a drink. He downed it with one shot and poured another.

"Damn, what the fuck is wrong with you?" Scott asked as he took the bottle of wine out of his hands.

"Garrett called the other day and left a message on my machine."

"So?"

"So? So Jazz heard the message and he freaked-the-fuck out. He was so convinced that the voice was that of The Messiah."

"Don't listen to that child. He was probably high."

"No, he wasn't. Scott, if you could have seen his reaction. He started shaking and sweating and got really scared at the sound of Garrett's voice. I have never seen a reaction like that."

Scott reached into the cabinet and grabbed a glass for himself. Without speaking, he poured a glass of wine, then took a sip of it.

"Okay, I know you ain't saying what I think you're saying."

Gabriel didn't respond or even blink. Instead, he locked eyes with Scott and the stare conveyed both of their fears and concerns.

"Just, what if?"

Scott blinked. "You think your man is a serial killer."

"No—yes—maybe," Gabriel said. The words suddenly sounded very silly to him. How could his man—the incredibly attractive doctor—be a killer? "I don't know what I'm saying, but listen to this. Garrett saw Dr. Mathiasen the day after the attack on Jazz. The day before, the files said he went to church and apparently something happened that really, really pissed Garrett off. The doctor wasn't sure what it was, but he noted that the event had triggered a change in Garrett. In his notes in Garrett's file he asked a question. He asked, *'Who is this man?'"*

"'Who is this man?' What the hell does that mean?"

"I don't know. It's almost as if he were asking himself a question. And to be perfectly honest, there have been a few times in the last week or so that I've been in Garrett's presence and I've asked myself the same thing. At times, it felt like I was talking to and kissing a stranger."

"Why didn't you tell me any of this shit before?"

"Because it sounded stupid as hell. I mean, what would you have said if I called you and told you that Garrett was making me nervous because he didn't seem like himself?"

"I would have told you to stop trying to sabotage the best thing that has happened to you in years."

"Exactly!"

"Okay, you made your point."

"Dr. Mathiasen also wrote something that stood out on the page. He wrote the words *possibly dangerous*."

"Okay, now I'm really freaked out."

"What? Not you? Mr. I-Wanna-Be-Hard."

"Shut the fuck up," Scott said. "You need to call somebody. You dating a fucking killer!" Scott slammed his glass onto the granite countertop, sending droplets of the red liquid onto the floor. He raced to the other side of the kitchen and picked up the phone. "You need to call the fucking cops and get this bastard arrested."

"Scott, put the phone down," Gabriel said as he moved slowly forward, afraid that a sudden movement would result in Scott dialing 9-1-1.

"Why? You know who The Messiah is—you've got to do something!"

"I don't know who The Messiah is—yet. And, if Garrett is The Messiah, we don't have any proof and sending the cops over to his house would ruin the entire investigation. Do you want him released on a technicality or because there wasn't enough evidence? Believe me, I have learned my lesson about jumping the gun," Gabriel said passionately while making a thinly veiled reference to his overzealousness. "Now, put the phone down."

Reluctantly, Scott complied.

"What are you going to do?"

"I'm going to call my police source and share this information. I'm going to let the cops do the investigating." Gabriel took a long swig from his glass. He had never seen Scott so flustered, so afraid, in his life. Finally Scott's usual bravado faded and gave way to his real self.

Secretly, Gabriel shared his alarm. He thought about all of the circumstantial evidence that pointed toward Garrett, but he did not want to believe. Could it be that The Messiah—the most notorious serial killer this city had seen—had been right under his nose this entire time? Gabriel's professional pride would not let him succumb to those thoughts, but he weighed the evidence.

The church meeting.

The attack on Jazz.

Forgetting to pick Gabriel up from the airport.

The strange behavior the morning after.

The strange kisses.

The rough sex.

The feeling of unfamiliarity.

Visits to Dr. Mathiasen.

The warning in his heart.

Gabriel didn't want to let on, but he was worried. "I'm sure my hunch this time is wrong," he said in a less-than-convincing tone.

The sound of his phone ringing brought him out of his trance. He grabbed his cell phone and looked at the caller ID. Ironically, it was Garrett. Part of Gabriel wanted to pick up the phone and yell at Garrett, demanding answers to all the evidence he would lay on the line. The other part wanted Garrett to convince him that the mounting evidence was, in fact, false; yet, he knew if he picked up the phone, he'd have no words to say. *What do you say to a man you wanted to love who you suspected had committed unspeakable acts? How do you ask a loved one if he's a killer?*

"If you're not going to answer that then at least stop it from ringing," Scott said in an annoyed voice. Gabriel grabbed his phone and touched the side to turn off the ringer.

"It's Garrett."

"I guess we spoke him into existence."

Gabriel looked at the clock on the microwave. It was almost seven in the evening, and he realized that he hadn't checked on Jazz all day. He had been far too preoccupied with the drama in his life to even think about him.

"I need to get home and call Faith and check on Jazz."

"Hey," Scott said. "Are you going to be okay?"

Gabriel sighed.

"You know me, like the air, I rise."

✝✝✝

Scott tried to push thoughts of Garrett and The Messiah out of his head, but found it very difficult. The more he thought about his wild reaction to Gabriel's suspicion, the more he wanted to laugh, but fear would not let him. The conversation he had just had with Gabriel sounded silly in his head and his reaction even more out of place. The odds that Gabriel was dating The Messiah were next to nil. The Messiah, he surmised, had long vacated the city for fear of getting caught and being thrown into jail for the rest of his life. Even a maniac like that had to realize there were consequences for his actions.

He remembered Gabriel's timely newspaper column and television appearances when The Messiah first started lashing out at the gay and lesbian population. He remembered feeling a sense of panic and dread that permeated the usually upbeat city. People weren't as outgoing as they had been, nor did they attend parties or clubs to the degree that they had in the past. The clubs frequented by the gay community became more vigilant in protecting their clientele with security guards and a crackdown on identification, although not a single Messiah-related crime had been committed in a club. He remembered walking into The Bachelor's Mill one Saturday night at the height of the hysteria and the place was a ghost town; usually, it was packed on Saturdays.

Scott poured himself another glass of wine and walked downstairs into his home theater. He wanted to watch *The Devil Wears Prada*, but wouldn't dare do so in front of his friends. He chuckled at the thought. As he walked toward his basement, behind him in the den, he thought he saw a shadow move. He paused to detect sounds before moving into the room.

When he walked in, all was quiet.

"I'm going to kick Gabriel's ass for freaking me out," he said as he turned and exited the room. He walked immediately toward his basement and set his glass of wine on the table. He grabbed the video from Blockbuster, put it in the DVD player, and took a seat on the plush sofa. He sipped on his wine as he waited for the movie to load.

Then he heard a static-like sound and felt a fire in his neck that sent him collapsing to the floor. The glass of red wine he held in his hand fell to the floor and stained his mauve carpet. His body shook and shivered from the electric shock he felt. He could not move but was aware of the presence of evil.

"Amazing Grace, how sweet the sound."

Scott felt a kick to his ribs that forced him to roll over onto his back. When he looked up, he tried to make out a face but his eyes were too blurry. He wanted to kick, scream, and fight, but he had been immobilized. He glanced at the small device held in the hand of his attacker—much closer to him so he could recognize it.

"I have come to save your soul," he said in a delightful voice right before he leaned down and gave Scott another blast of electricity from the taser, which sent his body into shock. Foam gathered in the corners of Scott's mouth as the blast rocked his body.

Scott blacked out, more from fear than pain.

When he awoke, he was alone—as far as he could tell—in his basement, hog-tied with a rag jammed into his throat and silver duct tape across his mouth. The room was dark and he had no idea what time it was or how long he had been out.

He tried to scream, but his sounds were muffled.

He struggled to break free of his restraints but the rope started to burn into his flesh.

He tried to scoot around the room to get away—to hide—but there was no hiding place and he realized that, in his present condition, there was no way he could make it up the stairs. His body felt loose, almost as if his muscle control had been retarded.

His eyes darted around the room with the hope that he could find something that would help him. He kept a loaded gun in a corner on the top shelf of the closet near the exit door, but his bondage denied him access.

When he realized that he was completely helpless, terror set in. He screamed again, but his voice was lost.

"Amazing grace, how sweet the sound, that saved a wretch like me," he heard a voice sing from behind him. He tried to turn, but his body would not move in the direction of the voice or the thump of heavy footsteps. The figure moved over to the fireplace and suddenly the room was flooded with the moody light of the flames. Scott's vision was blurred in the darkened room, but it was clear to him that the figure did not ignite the flames by any normal means.

Terror struck deep in his heart.

"My son, today I offer you the chance to join your Lord in heaven," he said as he stuck the metal fireplace poker into the roaring flames. "You have been chosen."

Scott tried to say something, but his muzzle did not allow for conversation. He walked over, bent down over Scott, smiled, then yanked the thick tape off his mouth. Scott screamed but the rag in his throat muffled the sound. Slowly, The Messiah pulled the dirty towel out of his mouth and walked back to the flames.

"Garrett, what the fuck are you doing?" he screamed out.

"Garrett is no more. I am HE."

"He? What the fuck are you talking about?"

"I am HE," he said in a voice that rang like thunder.

Scott's eyes almost bulged out of his head.

"Fear not, my child. Fear not."

But all Scott could do was fear. "What do you want from me?"

"I want to save your soul and welcome you into the kingdom of heaven with the Father."

"What are you talking about?" Scott yelled.

"Do you believe in God?"

"What?"

"Do you believe in God?" The Messiah took the heated poker from the fireplace and pressed it into the bottom of Scott's left foot. The sound of sizzling flesh and Scott's cries rose to the heavens.

"Oh my God! Please stop! Please stop!" Scott cried.

The Messiah stood above him and simply watched him writhe in pain.

"What do you want from me? Money? I'll give you anything—everything I have—just please stop!" he cried out.

"Do not tempt the Lord, thy God. Repent, for the kingdom of heaven is near," he commanded.

"I'm sorry. I repent. Please, forgive me!"

The Messiah walked back over to the fireplace and stuck the poker in between the glowing logs.

"Garrett, man, please stop. Whatever you're thinking about doing, please don't. If you let me go, I won't tell anyone. I promise."

The Messiah fell to his knees in front of the fireplace and started chanting. He extended his arms out from his sides, palms facing the ceiling. His body swayed back and forth and his eyes rolled toward his skull. Scott could not decipher the sounds pouring from his mouth like thick, blackening smoke, but the sounds stoked the horror in his soul. He watched as The Messiah lost himself in some kind of trance. Scott dreaded what would happen at the end of his demonic daze.

Is he going to kill me? Torture me? Scott asked himself, but did not dare answer. He had to free himself, no matter what. He had to break loose his bonds. He twisted, wiggled, and rubbed his hands together at superhuman speeds. He could feel the rope loosening, but he wasn't sure if there would be time.

Frenetically, he wiggled his wrists, even as the rope burned and ripped the skin off his arms.

I am not going to die like this.

More than anything, that thought motivated him and moved him. No longer did he pay attention to the searing sensation on the bottom of his foot. All he could think about was holding on to life, no matter how dire his circumstances or how much the rope burned into his wrists as he churned and turned.

As he wrestled with the ropes, The Messiah stood and began to disrobe, calmly and coolly. Scott watched him take care to open his shirt, one button at a time. He neatly folded the shirt and placed it on the table. Then he reached down and snapped open his belt and yanked it off his jeans. Carefully, he rolled it around his hands and stepped over to Scott.

"Please, Garrett. Please don't do this."

"Garrett is no more. There is only me; the Alpha and Omega; the beginning and the end. I come to claim you, my son; bone of my bones; flesh of my flesh."

"Stop it!" Scott's desperation had reached new heights. He suddenly started thinking about the end; the end of his life; the end of all things, as he felt the fire of the belt whip at angles across his bound flesh. The Messiah swung wildly with power and force as the leather sash whipped across his body. Scott yelled out from pain but continued to struggle with his constraints. The sound of leather cracking across black skin ricocheted off the walls.

"Your death will usher in a new era," he said as he stopped suddenly with sweat dripping from his brow. "Your death will announce to the world the Second Coming," he bellowed as he turned and walked suddenly toward the fireplace.

Then Scott popped the ropes and with the speed of a cheetah, he grabbed a ballpoint pen he saw underneath the couch and leapt toward The Messiah, all while his feet were still bound. Fueled by adrenaline, fear, and a strong sense of self-preservation, he became airborne, and right as The Messiah turned, Scott brought the pointed end of the pen down on The Messiah's right foot.

"Agggggggggggghhhhhhhhhhhh!" he screamed in pain.

"Fuck you, you crazy son-of-a-bitch!" Scott hollered. He reached down and started to untie his feet, but The Messiah swung his mighty fist, which connected with the side of Scott's face. Dizzied and dazed, another fist connected with Scott's face. His head slammed against the brick fireplace.

The Messiah pulled the pen from his foot and nudged Scott with his other foot. Scott did not move.

He was dead.

Chapter 23

As Gabriel drove down the road toward the setting sun, all he could think about was Garrett. He stopped at traffic lights, signaled when he needed to turn, obeyed the speed limits, but his mind was more focused on bigger issues.

How could it be?

Granted, the evidence he had accumulated was circumstantial and flimsy at best, but Gabriel had learned to trust his instincts above all else. He knew, without a shadow of a doubt, that something was *odd* about Garrett. His recent behavior and personality had changed so radically that it left Gabriel's head spinning. As much as he tried to overlook or ignore it, he could not because Garrett would then do something else to bring his unusual behavior to the forefront.

And beyond all of that, Gabriel *felt* everything wasn't as it appeared. He knew something was wrong. *Tragically wrong.*

He picked up his cell phone and dialed Faith's number. It rang five times before the voicemail picked up. Exasperated, Gabriel had half a mind to not leave a message, but he did so anyway.

"Faith, this is Gabriel," he said, the alarm sounding in his voice. "I found out something…crazy…about Garrett, and it could possibly relate to The Messiah case. I'm on my way home right now, so please, please call me or stop by. I'll be home the rest of the night. I really have to talk to you soon."

As he drove down the narrow city streets, he realized that he had yet to speak to Jazz about Faith's plan. So many things had happened that it slipped his mind. If Faith came over that night, it would be a good opportunity for him to broach the subject again and to get Faith to explain in detail how her plan would work. He was particularly interested in the details of the security if it became public knowledge that Jazz was staying with him.

More than anything else right now, he had to know the identity of The Messiah; he needed to know for his own sanity. He would not be able to rest. In his heart of hearts, he wanted to find some piece of evidence, no matter how infinitesimal, that he could use to exonerate Garrett and remove the cloud of suspicion that hovered above his head.

He picked up the phone again, hit redial, and let it ring. "Faith, it's me again. I gotta talk to you about Jazz and your idea. I'm sure I can get him to agree, but we need to talk. Please call me as soon as you get this message."

✝✝✝

"Jazz, I'm home. Where are you?" Gabriel called out as he walked into the kitchen from the garage. He put down his bag of groceries on the counter and started emptying the contents. It was going to be a Hamburger Helper evening for sure. "Jazz, what are you doing?" he called out again.

Gabriel stood still and listened for any sound, but the house was quiet. He couldn't detect any noise, not even the faint murmur of a distant television set. Gabriel guessed that Jazz was upstairs either sleeping or listening to some slick jazz melody at full blast on his iPod while stretched across the bed.

After Gabriel put away all of the groceries, including his ice cream, he decided that he needed some music himself to alleviate the pressures of the day. When he rounded the corner from the kitchen to his dining room, he stopped suddenly. The dinner table had been set, with place settings for three.

Did Jazz invite someone for dinner? he asked himself. He shrugged it off, then walked into the living room and over to the stereo. He pulled open the doors to the entertainment center and eyeballed his collection of music. He wasn't sure what he was in the mood to hear, but he knew he wanted something calming and smooth.

He grabbed an old Mariah Carey CD, removed it from the case, inserted it into the disc player and skipped to track number four. He wanted to hear something simple and, as he walked away, the sounds of the song "Music Box" filled the air.

Now, he was ready to make dinner, but before he started cooking he needed to check on Jazz. He had left the house that morning without so much of a word and hadn't had a chance to check on him all day. He flipped on the light switch as he ascended the staircase. When he got to the top, he walked over to Jazz's door and tapped on it.

"Jazz, you in there?" he asked through the closed door. He didn't want to bust in on him, so he slowly opened the door, cracking it barely enough to see Jazz lying across the bed, sleeping. Then Gabriel closed the door and headed downstairs to cook. Right as he entered the kitchen, he caught a glimpse of someone standing there.

He froze, not wanting to move an inch. He could see his cell phone on the kitchen counter from where he stood. A million thoughts raced through his head about what to do, but he remained still.

Then, a disheveled Garrett limped out of the shadows.

Gabriel let go of the breath he was holding in. "Oh my God, Garrett. You almost gave me a heart attack. What are you doing here? How did you get in?" he asked. Suddenly, he could feel the hairs on the back of his neck stand on end. Garrett looked at him with cold, black eyes and did not respond. "Baby, are you okay?" he asked as he took a cautious step backward. "Garrett?" Gabriel stopped as he eyed Garrett's blood-stained shoe. "Are you okay?"

Garrett had no response.

Gabriel thought about the police cruiser outside. He distinctly remembered seeing it parked outside the house when he drove up. *How did he get in here?* Gabriel looked down at Garrett's sanguine hands and panicked, but did not want to show fear.

Garrett tugged ever-so-slightly on his jeans while facing Gabriel. Then he tilted his head to the side and stared at Gabriel as if Gabriel were a puzzle he needed to solve.

This isn't Garrett.

Sensing the danger, a million thoughts raced through Gabriel's head of what he could do to evade peril. Then, he felt the tingling in his feet.

Not now. Please, not now. I can't do this now. He closed his eyes for a second to gather his thoughts. He thought about the sounds of Topaz singing his favorite song. He thought about her melodious voice and the lyrics which lauded love. *Breathe. Breathe.*

"Well, you're right on time," Gabriel spoke casually, trying to hide the fear in his voice and to take his mind off the imminent panic attack. Surprisingly, the more he spoke, the calmer he felt, in spite of Garrett's ominous presence. "I was getting ready to cook dinner, but I think I want to change music. Give me a second," he said as he turned casually toward the living room. If he could reach the door, then he could alert the officer.

"Gabriel," Garrett spoke in a sweet voice. "Come here, please."

Gabriel stopped and turned to face Garrett. He smiled. "Baby, let me change the music and I'll be right back."

"Gabriel," he said in a stronger tone.

The sheer sound of his voice sent chills up Gabriel's spine and he knew, without doubt, that he was in the presence of danger.

"Amazing Grace, how sweet the sound, that saved a wretch like me," Garrett's angelic voice covered the sweet sounds of the soft music.

When Gabriel heard the song escape from his mouth, he turned and raced toward the front door as if his life depended on it. In some way, he was sure it did. He darted across the room only to be sent reeling to the floor in a crash. Two wires shot into the skin on the back of his neck, sending shocks throughout his body and immobilizing him.

"I am HE. My name is like fire shut up in your bones," he proclaimed. He calmly stepped over to Gabriel and towered over him, curiously looking over his prey.

Gabriel's body jerked from the electric currents still running through him. Gabriel felt fear like he had never known before. He watched Garrett hover over him, staring down at him oddly, as if he were contemplating his next move. Garrett's eyes weren't wild or crazed, but reflected a curious calmness. His deep-set dark eyes almost looked peaceful, but Gabriel new it was the calm before the storm. He wanted to move, to stand, to holler, to fight, to kick, to scratch, to bite, but he could not move. He felt the tingling in his toes shoot up through his entire body, but couldn't determine if it was due to an attack or the taser which stung him again. He needed to yell, to put up his fists, to grunt, to punch, to growl, but all his power had been taken by this man—his lover. Gabriel watched Garrett loom over him, and Gabriel instinctively closed his eyes. Then Garrett hit him with another blast and the darkness came.

Gabriel couldn't remember when it happened, but he had obviously passed out. When he awoke, he was tied to a chair in his dining room. As his view came into focus, he saw Jazz bound and gagged to his left. Jazz's eyes were wide, as if he had been awake for a while. As Gabriel looked closer, he could see that fear had overtaken Jazz. Groggily, he looked around, slowly taking notice of the room. The table was set and a basket of bread occupied the centerpiece. Wine chilled in a silver metal bucket. Gabriel watched as small streams of moisture ran down its side. Candles provided a lazy glow, which added more tension to an already morbid scene.

Gabriel realized this was *the* Last Supper reenacted—and hopefully, not his *own* last supper. The gravity of the thought hit him like a ton of bricks. Suddenly, he panicked, but still did not have complete control over his body. He looked down at the thick ropes wrapped around his wrists. He could barely move his fingers let alone muster enough strength to rip through the restraints.

He looked at Jazz.

Jazz looked at him.

Their gaze conveyed their fear. Gabriel did not want to give up. When he thought about his death, he never imagined it would be like this. He imagined dying of natural causes in his bed as an old man. He imagined his children and grandchildren gathered around his bedside. Never—not once—did he think his demise would come at the hands of a maniac. Never—not once—did he imagine that he would die at the hands of someone like Garrett.

As he reflected on his life, he found it difficult to stomach the thought that his instincts had failed him for so long when, in the past, they had served him so well. Now, he learned that he had been in the presence of The Messiah for months and his internal alarm did not sound. They had dined together, laughed together, played together, sexed together, fought together and made up together, but prior to the last few days, Gabriel thought he had found the perfect lover—tall, dark, handsome, educated, sophisticated, rich and sexy. His failure came crashing down around him like a house of cards.

He wished he could offer Jazz some solace. He wished he could find the words to tell him to be strong. If Garrett—or this self-proclaimed Messiah—had any decency, he'd make their deaths quick, but that seemed to contradict his style.

Out of the darkness of the other room, a blinding light flashed suddenly and through the glow, they saw someone walking toward them. Gabriel cut through the light with his eyes to get a better view of the figure strolling toward them. As he came into view, Gabriel wanted to gasp at what he saw. The Messiah sauntered into the room, head adorned with curls, mustache and goatee intact, wearing a long flowing white robe with oversized sleeves trimmed in gold lace. On his feet, he wore brown sandals with straps that laced up his calves. His face was solemn and severe, as if something dreadful was to come.

Without pause or hesitation, he stepped over to Gabriel and ripped the tape from his mouth. Gabriel's wretched scream filled the room, but the pain of the hairs being ripped from his mustache also gave him a jolt of energy.

"Garrett," he said in an almost whisper, not sure whether or not the sound of his voice would elicit rage or a psychotic incident within Garrett. Instead of responding, Garrett took his place at the head of the table and extended his arms outward as he looked toward the heavens. He prayed silently.

"Garrett," Gabriel said again as he took in the full view of his lover. The sight of Garrett dressed in such a manner chilled him to the bone.

"Garrett is not here," The Messiah replied dryly. He eyes shot from Gabriel to Jazz and from Jazz back to Gabriel, as if he wasn't sure whom he wanted to address.

"Who are you?" Gabriel asked, but he already knew the answer.

"I am that I am."

"What?"

"I am The Messiah—your redeemer. I come to claim all of God's children."

"You're no messiah. You're a fucking psycho!" The fire of Gabriel's words smoldered across the room, leaving a trail of seared air. Gabriel's voice surprised Garrett, whose expression changed from calm to anger, and Gabriel shuddered at the thought of Garrett's response.

"I am Alpha and Omega; the first and the last; the beginning and the end," he roared in a thunderous voice. "I am He. I am the one."

Gabriel looked at Garrett as he seemed to go into a trance. His eyes glossed over and Gabriel could not ascertain if the gleam was a tear or a reflection of the candlelight.

"For God so loved the world that He gave His only begotten Son, that whoever believes in Him shall not perish, but have eternal life. Gabriel, do you believe?"

"Why don't you make a believer out of me? If you are *the* messiah, then why don't you walk on water or part a sea or something?" Gabriel's defiance was in stark contrast to the fear in his heart, yet he pressed on with his challenging words. Gabriel wasn't sure where his boldness gathered its strength, but if he was to perish, he would not go out whimpering. He'd make a thunderous noise.

"The other one tried to tempt me, too. And he incurred the wrath of the Lord, thy God."

"What other one?" Gabriel swallowed hard, not sure he wanted to hear the story of yet another victim.

"The one you call Scott. He was a wicked man, and he could not be redeemed." Garrett's voice was cold and plain, speaking of Scott's death as casually as he would read a street sign.

"What? You killed Scott?" Gabriel's words were muffled by the pain he felt from Garrett's sharp words.

"I sent him to his place where he will spend eternity." Gabriel wanted to cry, but his tears would not fall. They were not tears of sorrow, but of anger.

"Why are you doing this? What is wrong with you?" he asked between heavy breaths. Jazz tried to scream as well, but the thick tape stifled his sounds. Garrett quickly looked at Jazz as if to quiet him and Jazz understood.

"I have come back to claim my people. The world is lost to wickedness, and it is time for the righteous to come home to glory. This is my second coming and I chose you two to be the messengers of my holy word, but you have failed me. You have failed!" he screamed with unexpected force that chilled them to the bone. His eyes danced wildly in his skull and Gabriel could actually feel his rage from across the table. It was a tangible presence that spread out in all directions across the room. Gabriel feared the worst.

"Your sickness has spread throughout the land and has corrupted my church. It is a growing cancer that infects men, women, old and young. It has consumed the sinners and tempted the righteous. Some of my most devout disciples have fallen. Oh, how the mighty have fallen! That is why I have returned. I have come to save all my children and those who repent and believe in me shall not perish, but have everlasting life." He stepped over to Jazz and ripped the duct tape from his mouth. Hairs from his mustache littered the tape and, when it was yanked off, Jazz could only scream.

"Please, please, stop this. Please. I'm sorry. I'll do whatever you want me to do," Jazz pleaded.

"You had your chance. You were warned. You have broken our covenant and, for that, there is no forgiveness for I am a vengeful god and vengeance is mine!" He reached around and backhanded Jazz across the face with so much force that Jazz fell over onto the floor. "You have failed me!" Garrett cried out in anger. "You have failed and now you must die!"

"Leave him alone, you sick freak! It's me that you want."

The Messiah quickly jerked his head toward Gabriel. "Your time will come, my child." He stepped over Jazz as he lay on the floor, crying desperate tears.

"Why are you doing this to us?" he asked between sobs.

"You two were to be my greatest disciples. Gabriel, even your name is heavenly. You were to be my messenger and announce my return. You, too, have failed!" Garrett took a deep breath and shook his head. "Do you think it was happenstance that I met you at that party? It was not—it was ordained! You were chosen by me. You were the one, but you would not yield. You would not renounce your selfish and sick ways!"

"What sick ways are you talking about?" Gabriel lashed out in anger.

"You know of your filthy ways," he said calmly.

"*My* filthy ways? Garrett, what about yours? That filth you're talking about *we* did together!"

The Messiah paused. "Garrett is no more. He was merely a vessel—a hollow shell."

"Whatever. So, you don't remember all the times you and I had sex? What do you say about that? If Jazz and I go to hell, then you'll be at our side!"

Garrett stopped. He turned slowly and eyed Gabriel from head to toe. "Garrett is no more. We are the Father, the Son, and the Holy Spirit. Garrett is no more."

"Oh really? How convenient," Gabriel said with disgust. "You are so worried about us being gay that you forgot about yourself. I can't even count how many times I've been naked with you, laying on top of you, feeling your body pressed into mine. What does that make you?"

"Garrett is no more! There is only me—alpha and omega—"

"Beginning and the end—yeah, yeah, I get it."

Garrett's eyes bulged in his head. "Do not mock me, my child. Do not mock me."

"Why are you doing this?" Jazz asked from the floor. "Why me? Why me?"

"I chose you, my child, because I wanted to save you from the fires of hell. I wanted to spare you eternal damnation. I wanted you to be the greatest disciple of all! You were to carry news of my return to the four corners of the world, but you failed me. You failed the Lord, thy God."

Gabriel listened as Jazz's sobs became moans. He wished that he would have done the story sooner. He wished that he could find a way to spare Jazz whatever fate might befall him at the hands of Garrett. He decided, in that moment of desperation, that if he had to sacrifice himself to save Jazz, then he'd do it. Hopefully, they both wouldn't be placed on the sacrificial altar.

Gabriel studied Garrett's face carefully. He looked at his eyes as they shifted rapidly in his head. He watched his demeanor and his long gait as he moved across the room almost effortless.

"Why now? Why are you doing this now?"

Garrett paused momentarily before walking to the head of the table. He stood there and stared at Gabriel before speaking. "No one knows about that day or hour, not even the angels in heaven, nor the Son, but only the Father. As it was in the days of Noah, so it will be at the coming of the Son of Man. Before my return you had heard of wars and rumors of wars, but see to it that you are not alarmed. Such things must happen, but the end is still to come. Nation will rise against nation, and kingdom against kingdom. There will be famines and earthquakes in various places. All these are the beginning of birth pains."

"What are you talking about?" Gabriel asked out of exasperation. "Answer the question—that's the least you can do!"

"Satan is always busy. The great corrupter has taken too many of my children. He has weaved his wicked into the hearts of many, even my most faithful prophets. He has corrupted prominent ministers from Colorado to Oklahoma to Washington, D.C., and all across this vast land. America has fallen and become a land of wickedness where the evil that lives in the hearts of men goes unchecked. I have said before that many will turn away from the faith and will betray and hate each other, and many false prophets will appear and deceive many people. Because of the increase of wickedness, the love of most will grow cold, but he who stands firm to the end will be saved. And this gospel of the kingdom will be preached in the whole world as a testimony to all nations, and then the end will come."

"You are out of your mind!" Jazz screamed from the floor.

Garrett marched over to him and stomped his chest, causing him to scream in pain. Gabriel heard the cracking of his ribs.

"You will not speak again." Garrett's dull voice was heavy and dry, but conveyed a sense of authority that Gabriel felt compelled to resist, in spite of his predicament. He hoped that by confronting Garrett, Jazz would remain quiet. Gabriel hoped that the longer he engaged Garrett, the greater the chances of someone discovering them.

Suddenly, the room was filled with Gabriel's boisterous laughter. He threw his head back and opened his mouth widely so that his mirth would be unrestrained. "You are such a fucking joke," he stated.

Garrett immediately turned his attention toward Gabriel who continued in his hilarity. In two fell swoops, Garrett was upon him and slapped him across the face with an open hand. The sound of the slapping against flesh rang louder than the laughter and the sting from the blow set Gabriel's face on fire, but he was determined not to yield to this maniac's will.

"Is that all you got?" he said as he spit out a wad of blood that had gathered in his throat.

Garrett looked at him, smiled, and shook his head. "For then there will be great distress, unequaled from the beginning of the world until now—and never to be equaled again."

Internally, Gabriel quaked at Garrett's words, but he would not convey that fear. He watched as Garrett moved over to Jazz and lifted the chair from the floor so that Jazz stood upright. Gabriel looked deep into Jazz's eyes, and the fear he felt washed over his face like waves.

"Your blood—your sacrifice—shall seal your place in heaven." Garrett looked directly at Jazz when he spoke, then disappeared into the kitchen. As soon as he left, Gabriel struggled to free himself. With all the force he could muster he tried to loosen his bonds, but they did not yield. Beads of sweat formed on his forehead as he struggled—he would not give up the fight. He twisted, turned, rotated, rubbed, pulled, and yanked his wrists in the futile hope that the ropes would loosen, but they did not. Instead, the rope dug deep into his flesh and burned his wrists. Gabriel could hear Garrett humming the tune to "Amazing Grace" from the kitchen.

"Jazz—Jazz," Gabriel said in a forceful whisper.

"It's over—we're gonna die," Jazz replied as he sobbed.

Gabriel watched his face and he could tell that Jazz had accepted his fate. His hope had faded and now he waited for The Messiah to return to deliver him.

"No, we're not going to die. We are going to live, but I need you to get it together."

"We're gonna die, don't you see? He has returned for us."

Jazz's words shocked Gabriel. Surely, he had not fallen under Garrett's spell. "Jazz, snap out of it. You're not going to die."

Right then, Garrett stepped back into the room carrying a large butcher's knife.

"I shall offer you as a burnt offering to the Father. I shall spill your blood on the mountains and make you whole again."

"Mountains? This is D.C. Ain't no mountains around here, you stupid fool!" As the words punched their way out of Gabriel's mouth, Garrett took the knife and sliced Jazz's right cheek.

"Shallow cuts, shallow cuts," he said in an emotionless voice.

"Just kill me! Kill me now!" Jazz hollered.

"Garrett, leave him alone. Sacrifice me instead."

"You are not worthy of sacrifice, but you, too, shall pay dearly for your sins."

"Garrett, please, listen to me. We can get you help. You're sick. No court in the world will convict you."

"Why do you insist on calling me Garrett? There is no Garrett!" he yelled as he sliced at Jazz's left cheek. Blood ran down his face from the slits on each side of his face. This time, he didn't scream when the steel blade met his flesh.

"Okay, I'm sorry, please put down the knife. No one has to get hurt here."

Garrett looked at him oddly, almost as if the words that left Gabriel's mouth had offended him.

"You have hurt the Father because of your wickedness. Your apologies are worthless. The sacrifice must be paid in blood and it must be now."

Gabriel watched as Garrett started to disrobe. He wanted to ask what he was doing, but decided he needed to focus on an escape plan. Gabriel searched his mind for something that would bring Garrett back, but now he wasn't sure if Garrett had ever existed. There was only *He*—the alpha and omega; the beginning and the end.

As he pondered his next move, he caught a glimpse of hope in his right eye. Out of his periphery, he saw a figure slowly creeping toward them. Was he dreaming or was this real? He slowly turned his head and received a most welcomed confirmation. Faith was moving toward them, gun pointed at Garrett, as he pulled the robe off his body, revealing the loin cloth that covered his private parts. As the robe hit the floor, Faith emerged from the shadows.

"Drop the knife and put your hands up!"

Gabriel held his breath as she aimed her pistol at Garrett's chest. Garrett did not flinch. He stood, with outstretched arms, and a look of utter defiance draped across his face.

"No weapon formed against me shall prosper."

"I got a bullet that says otherwise. Now drop the knife and step slowly away."

Garrett did not comply.

"Sir, I will not tell you again. Drop the knife. Don't make me shoot you."

"You cannot stop the apocalypse. The time of the Lord is now."

"Put the knife down."

"Garrett, please put the knife down. We can get you help." With Gabriel's words, the fire in Garrett's eyes shone bright and he lunged at Jazz, knife in hand.

The sound of a single gunshot rang out.

Garrett stopped and looked at the hole in his chest. He stood there, eyeing it, as if in disbelief. Blood ran out of the hole and trailed down his abdomen. He threw his head back and let out a laugh; an ungodly one.

"You think you have won? You think you have stopped The Messiah. You have only incurred his wrath, foolish woman." He stretched out his arms again while still holding the knife. He stumbled a bit and struggled to remain upright.

"Stay where you are and put the knife down."

"You have won nothing!" he yelled as he let out a hellish shriek that pounded its way through the tense atmosphere. His startling sounds didn't resonate as human, but sounded like a wounded jackal caught in a steel trap. His body began to contort and jerk in jagged violent intervals. Gabriel watched this body—his lover's body—twist and turn in odd ways. He could hear the loud cracking of his bones as his body coiled and popped. His eyes rolled to the back of his head and his body behaved as if he was having a seizure. Knotted foam gathered in the corners of his mouth.

"Drop the knife!" Faith commanded again. As he struggled to remain standing, he gritted his teeth. Suddenly, all of the strange movement ceased and he lunged once last time.

Another gunshot rang out in the night. Again, the bullet entered his chest and sent him reeling back. He dropped the knife and stumbled around the room, clutching onto the table for balance.

"My God, My God, why hast Thou forsaken me?" he cried out before he fell backward into the window. The force of his weight caused the glass to break and he fell out of the window. Faith slowly moved toward the window and peered over the sill, then let out an exasperated sigh. She turned back toward Gabriel and the look in her eyes confirmed what he knew, but still needed confirmation about: his lover, Garrett, The Messiah, had met his own crucifixion.

EPILOGUE
AND SO IT WAS WRITTEN...

Gabriel hit the "send" button on his e-mail, with his story of The Messiah's return—and demise—attached, to his editor. Gabriel discovered the killer's trigger—he was called back into action upon hearing the news that Garrett's pastor resigned from the church due to homosexual conduct. Garrett—or The Messiah—felt the need to cleanse the church, as he had many times before.

Upon further investigation, Gabriel found that Garrett had been under the care of a therapist for the six months in which the killings stopped and The Messiah vanished. Evidently, Garrett had gained some control over his alter ego, but the news of his pastor's indiscretions dismantled the shield Garrett had erected to cage in his deranged other half.

This story was to run on the front page of the paper, with a byline giving credit to Jazz for his part in the construction of the article. The story would surely propel Gabriel back into the spotlight, but his hunger for the fame and glory had been replaced by a more subdued feeling of accomplishment and satisfaction. He had almost lost his life at the hands of a mass murderer and that tempered his ambition, although he and Jazz had spoken about co-authoring their story in a novel. As he thought about what his life would be like after the story and potential book, he remembered what it felt like to be in the spotlight:

The exploding light of camera flashes.

Tape recorders constantly shoved in his face for a quote.

Questions hurled in his direction at ninety miles per hour.

Interview requests for every news talk show.

Back then, he wasn't fully prepared for the whirlwind that had ensued in the immediate days following the breaking of his story. Once the paper hit the stands, it catapulted Gabriel into the limelight and he was praised and lauded for his investigative work.

That was then, this is now.

He sat back in the chair in his office, his arms folded behind his head. He thought about Jazz and his life and his relationships with his family that had been forever altered because of hatred. He thought about how Jazz was forced to use his *cunning* to survive on the streets when he was unceremoniously evicted from his home. He thought about how those experiences shaped Jazz into the man that he was now. Gabriel then smiled when he thought about how far Jazz had come in his life. Even though he was far from perfect, Jazz had accomplished a lot. He had finished high school, gotten into college and was poised to graduate without any assistance from family. He didn't have a lot of friends or many folks that he could turn to for support. Gabriel applauded Jazz's steely resolve.

He smiled again. He was proud to know Jazz and to know that, in spite of all he had been through, Jazz would still graduate on time, with a little extra effort. He was, indeed, a survivor and a friend. They both were. Gabriel knew that Jazz would soar to new heights and be more than he ever thought he could.

Now, more than ever, Gabriel realized what was important in life. He felt compelled to reconnect to his life and his passions. So much had happened to alter his way of thinking. For the first time in a long time, he wasn't preoccupied with his career. He no longer felt a burning need to be on the front page. Instead, he rested in solid gratitude that he had survived and that The Messiah's reign of terror had come to an end.

He felt sorry for Garrett, though, and through it all, he accepted the fact that part of him did love Garrett. And, Gabriel had to re-learn to love himself. He didn't need any man or any church to tell him that he was a child of God. After his story ran, he hoped that people would learn to think for themselves and question religious authority and doctrine. He hoped people would reject churches that spread hate instead of love because the damage that is done is immeasurable. How many more deaths would be triggered by misguided religious teachings?

Gabriel learned that Garrett, who in many ways personified homophobia and self-hate, had been raised and punished in a strict religious household and thus had created an alternate ego to deal with his innate feelings. He had never learned to love himself and instead had secretly struggled with his attraction to men for years. As he was taught, he couldn't be a part of God because of something he couldn't control, so he had to *become* a god to create his own rules. He had allowed the opinions of the self-righteous to deny him a relationship with the *real* God.

Gabriel would not live like that.

Instead, he would live in love.

ABOUT THE AUTHOR

Lee Hayes is a graduate of The Bernard M. Baruch College, City University of New York, where he received his Master of Public Administration degree in 2005. He is the author of *Passion Marks* and *A Deeper Blue: Passion Marks II*. He currently lives in Washington, D.C. Visit the author at www.leehayes.info